TEMPTING
THE EARL

TEMPTING
THE EARL

●

Wendy May Andrews

AVALON BOOKS
NEW YORK

0Z Z310

F
And

Published by Thomas Bouregy & Co., Inc.
160 Madison Avenue, New York, NY 10016

Library of Congress Cataloging-in-Publication Data

Andrews, Wendy May.
   Tempting the earl / Wendy May Andrews.
        p. cm.
   ISBN 978-0-8034-7756-8 (hardcover : acid-free paper)
1. Nobility—England—Fiction.   2. Mistaken identity—
Fiction.   I. Title.
   PS3601.N5528T46 2010
   813'.6—dc22

                                        2009045270

PRINTED IN THE UNITED STATES OF AMERICA
ON ACID-FREE PAPER
BY HADDON CRAFTSMEN, BLOOMSBURG, PENNSYLVANIA

To Andrew for being my everything.
To Mum and Dad for always believing in me.
To Aunt Marlene for the fabulous critique.
To Chelsea for giving me a chance.

arm and assisted her in climbing out with as much dignity as she could muster.

George's sensitive feelings were further abraded by the state of her attire, and he exclaimed in dismay over her dishevelment.

"I have had a very trying day, sir. Pray control yourself," Emily said with quiet dignity as she gathered her scattered wits before raising her eyes to look around. The sight of the large but welcoming manor house spread out grandly before her was surprisingly soothing to her. She had no idea where she had arrived, and she was struggling to come up with a plan of action. This was an effort, since she was still rather inexperienced in life, not to mention exhausted. She was wondering how much of her circumstances to reveal and decided that silence would be her best option at the moment. She was just arriving at that conclusion when her gaze was caught and held by the haughty stare of the most elegantly handsome man she had ever encountered.

Lord Philip, the eighth Earl of Yorkleigh, had paused in the act of entering his grand home and was watching the interchange curiously as his valet tried valiantly to deal with this strange development. Lord Philip's usually cynically bored eyes widened slightly in surprise as he took in the spectacle of a shabby urchin being assisted from the boot of his carriage. The girl stood shivering slightly from the late-night chill as she gazed about. Philip's nostrils flared at the sight of her dirty, tattered clothes, but he could see beyond that that she was a beautiful young woman. With a good scrubbing she would have gorgeous blond curls accompanied by a pale ivory complexion, and despite her slightly emaciated state he could see that she still had some pleasing curves hidden under the rags she was wearing. Since he had reached his majority, he had grown somewhat accustomed to beautiful women showing up in the unlikeliest places trying to catch his attention, but those females always managed to be dressed in their best. Until now he had yet to find a dirty and ragged one climbing out of his carriage. His curiosity was piqued.

"What's going on here, George?" he called out in slightly accented French as he approached.

Emily was fluent in the foreign tongue but felt unsure how to proceed. *Have I gone all the way to France?* her confused mind questioned. That hardly seemed possible. Would it reveal too much to acknowledge her understanding? She waited nervously to see what would develop as the young lord approached the rear of the carriage. Up until very recently Emily had led quite a sheltered life, and she felt unprepared to deal with a handsome nobleman in her current state.

No amount of dirt could hide the refinement in Emily's face and bearing. Philip wondered dispassionately what this beautiful but bedraggled creature was doing huddled in his carriage. His left eyebrow rose in a questioning look as Emily burst into speech.

"Thank you kindly for the ride, monsieur. I truly appreciate your hospitality. Now I must be off. *Adieu,*" she stated with dignity. She had decided to speak in English, since she was almost certain they were still on British soil.

With that Emily attempted to sweep past the astonished valet and earl, but Philip caught her arm as she swept by him. He hesitated to get involved in what was obviously going to be a troublesome situation, but he was not going to be responsible for allowing this chit to wander off into the night.

He had just decided earlier that week that the deep well of boredom he was experiencing of late was getting on his nerves, and he had been wondering what to do about it. This strange development might alleviate his ennui somewhat, so he decided to bestir himself.

Up close he could see that she really was quite young, and although he rarely troubled himself with the mundane details of other people's lives, he felt an uninvited urge to help this one, despite her obvious reluctance to admit her need for such.

"Not so fast, my girl. Where are you going to go? It's nearly dawn, and the village is a couple of miles away. You look like you will blow away in the wind or fall asleep in the nearest ditch. I cannot permit you to be traipsing around the countryside in this state. I demand to know who you are and what you were doing in my carriage. Have you run away from your employer? What is his name? I don't recognize this uniform. Speak up, girl," he demanded when she didn't respond to his inquiries. He was accustomed to having people jump to attention when he spoke and was vaguely irritated by her silence.

He shook his head in disgust, wondering why he was bothering to get involved, but he could not back down once he had committed himself to assisting the chit. Still, he was already regretting the impulse that had prompted his involvement.

"Well, you need a place to stay at least for tonight. I

cannot send you off like this. Come, I will let the house-keeper look after you for tonight, and we shall see what is to be done with you in the morning. George, take her to Mrs. Simms and see that she has something to eat and somewhere to sleep." Then Philip swept off into the house, leaving behind a wide-eyed Emily and a concerned George to deal with the situation.

Mrs. Simms was only slightly less bewildered than the valet had been as she took the bedraggled young woman off to the servants' quarters to be cleaned up, fed, and put to bed. She had known the earl his entire life and was some-what more used to his fits and starts than poor George was. She was appalled at the state the poor girl was in. Her clothing was tattered and filthy, emitting a slight but un-pleasant odor, and her shoes were nearly in pieces. When these were removed, it was obvious that her feet would need some attention; they were raw from rubbing on the poorly fitted fabric. Mrs. Simms had some powerful oint-ment she knew would do the trick quite nicely. The young woman would feel right as rain by morning.

"What's his lordship up to now—taking in more strays again, is he? He usually contains himself to animals." She was burning to ask Emily ever so many questions, but she wisely bit her tongue, as she could see that the girl was practically fainting with exhaustion. "I guess all our ques-tions will keep until the morning, eh?" she asked rhetori-cally as she tucked Emily into the clean linens. "But there certainly seems to be some mystery behind you, isn't there, my dear?"

Emily merely sighed as she sank into the soft pillow and fully entered the sleep she had already been drifting in and out of while the housekeeper fed her, then helped her to clean up and change into a spare nightgown. She had barely even noticed when Mrs. Simms anointed her aching feet with a pungent-smelling ointment.

Mrs. Simms shook her head in wonder as she quietly left the room, questioning what tomorrow would hold for this newest, no doubt temporary, member of the household.

Moorfields, Bethlem Royal Hospital (otherwise known as Bedlam)

Tonight was the night that was going to make or break her entire future. Morbid fear held her firmly in its grip. Emily's heart was racing as she crept down the damp and dingy hallway, trying to close her mind to the sights, smells, and sounds of captivity as she attempted to make her escape.

"If I do not make it out of here tonight, I really shall belong here. This place would make the sanest person go mad." Emily clamped her teeth over her lips, unsure if she was thinking the words or saying them aloud, terrified she would speak and give herself up for capture.

She felt faint. Her knees wobbled with each step as she forced them to propel her forward. Anxiety gripped her every nerve. As she inched past the gruesome cells of sedated inmates, she struggled with a keen sense of guilt. She would be free, and all these poor souls would remain in their miserable bondage. Her mind and heart cringed as she heard the ceaseless chanting of some unfortunate individuals trapped in their own insane world.

Emily steeled herself, tamping down raw emotions as

she grasped her courage and made a dash toward the last door between captivity and freedom. *Oh, no! Are those footsteps approaching?* She squeezed herself into a shadowy corner to see what would transpire, too weak to make it to the door in time. Struggling with her feelings and mental sluggishness, she held her breath in order to avoid the stench permeating the small space she was crouched in. She then realized that her fear was getting the upper hand. She had only imagined the sounds of pursuit. With a grunt of disgust at her own stupidity she crept to the door and saw that her prayers were answered—it was not locked.

With a sense of exultation, she stepped out into the midnight darkness surrounding the stone edifice that had been her prison for an untold number of weeks. Despite her efforts to keep count, she had accidentally lost track of time somewhere along the way. She paused in her steps, lost in thought, trying to figure out how long she had been there. *This is no time to be thinking about that!* She scolded herself for her lack of concentration as she squared her shoulders, took a deep breath, and ran as fast as she could.

She looked around frantically as she scurried through the eerie shadows surrounding the imposing granite building. *I have got to make it. Tonight is my only chance,* Emily thought urgently over and over as she stumbled, regained her footing, and ran on toward the open gate and freedom.

Poor Colette's ill-fated escape effort means the gatekeeper is joining in, celebrating her capture. There's a chance no one will notice me gone. They think I'm still asleep from that awful mixture everyone gets at night to "keep us tranquil."

Emily cringed in suppressed horror as she crept past the immense statues of muted gray marble above the gate, *Madness* and *Melancholia,* grinning down grotesquely at any who passed through their portals. *Just looking at that pair would make you crazed,* thought Emily wryly as she continued on her way. Her mind drifted for a moment as she contemplated what sort of artist would lend his skilled hands and craft to molding such gruesome parodies. Again she recalled herself to her senses, forcing the thoughts out with an extreme effort of will as she gave her head a quick shake and scuttled off to the shadows of the lane, urging herself to safety.

She ran as fast as her feet could carry her through the bushes alongside the lane, ignoring the weakness of her body. Her worn and tattered "uniform" provided little protection from the elements as a light drizzle began to fall, adding to the misery of an already unbearable situation. But nothing could deter her. Her feet grew heavy in their shabby shoes, but as she imagined the gargoyles of Bedlam bearing down on her, she was able to force them to a faster pace. Her legs burned from the exertion, being so unused to movement over the past weeks, and she quite suspected that her feet might be bleeding. Emily found herself welcoming the pain, since it helped her concentrate as she fought the effects of the sedative. She fled on toward freedom in a state of semiconsciousness, not truly believing she would make it to safety, not even knowing where safety could be found, not even really caring as long as it was anywhere but back in the asylum.

Trudging alongside the mud-slicked road, Emily had no idea how much time had passed. She finally came to a small country inn and pub. Emily paused to catch her breath behind a small bush. She felt a ray of hope burst upon her troubled mind as she found the courtyard momentarily empty of stable hands. There were one or two conveyances left unattended in the courtyard, and Emily took a chance on the closest one. She scampered over eagerly and climbed into the boot of the carriage. She shoved aside the various bags and blankets of the unknown strangers she would be sharing the carriage with. Making a little nest for herself in the cramped space, Emily was wryly amused to find a reason to be thankful that she had lost so much flesh during her captivity.

"I'm free! I do not care where this carriage is going; anywhere is better than that asylum Edwin had me thrown into! Why couldn't I have just given him what he was really after? I wouldn't have cared; I just could not marry that horrid Max he is so fond of. Well, I'm free of Edwin now too. I hope this carriage is leaving soon. How long will it be before they notice I am missing and the guards start searching for me? Are they already looking for me? It would be perfectly dreadful to be caught now. I truly would belong there then; I would go completely mad if I was caught and sent back." Emily realized with disgust that she was actually giving voice to the thoughts in her head and clamped a thin hand over her mouth to stem the flow of words. Her mind whirred with conflicting thoughts—delight to have escaped the asylum and fear of discovery warring for supremacy.

Just as Emily started to seriously consider climbing out

of the carriage trunk to continue her escape on foot, she heard the crunch of footsteps approaching. She tried desperately to remain silent as squeaks of fright threatened to burst from deep inside her. She was afraid to even breathe for fear some slight sound would betray her presence. Emily was unsure if it was a pursuer or the rightful owner of the carriage and wasn't sure which possibility scared her more; either way she profoundly did not want to be caught. *Please don't look in the boot,* she thought desperately.

Suddenly she heard voices commanding that the carriage be brought around, then the scurrying of feet as it jerked into motion and the horses were harnessed up and shifted restlessly. She clutched the blankets of her nest to her face to ensure no sound escaped her lips as she struggled with her composure. There was a swaying motion as the occupants climbed into the main carriage.

Emily heaved a heartfelt sigh of relief that no one had had anything to deposit in the trunk as the carriage picked up speed. Finally she was on the way. Freedom at last!

Chapter Two

Emily awoke with a start, relieved to realize she had been reliving events in her dreams, not reality. She was initially bewildered as she gazed around the unfamiliar room. It was clean and smelled good but was sparsely furnished with only a narrow bed, a serviceable chair, and a small bureau. There were no wall coverings, and the window treatment was very plain. She concluded with a small smile that this was a servant's bedroom. The quiet struck her as the greater change of circumstances; at the asylum there was never silence, not even in the wee hours of the night. She was unsure how she felt about being in servants' quarters, but it was a vast improvement on where she had been.

As all the happenings of the previous day dawned on her, Emily contemplated what could possibly happen next. She was still lost in thought as Mrs. Simms knocked on the door gently before she entered. She bustled in once she discovered that Emily was awake.

"Lawks, girl, we thought you would sleep the whole day away. It's good to see you have survived the night. Some in the kitchens were placing bets to see if you would make it or not. Such a sight you were last night, eh? So what's your name? I am Mrs. Simms, in case you don't remember from last night."

Emily smiled again as she took in the plump figure of the earl's housekeeper. Mrs. Simms had a pleasant, round, open face with slightly rosy cheeks. Her countenance put Emily at ease and made her feel she could confide in the older woman, but she steadfastly ignored that feeling. Past experience had firmly convinced her she could not trust anyone.

"I remember," she answered shyly. "I am Emily. Thank you so much for feeding me last night and finding me something to wear and somewhere to sleep. I feel like a new person today."

"You are very welcome, dearie. And you look like a new person too. Such a bedraggled mess you were last night. The master wants to see you once you're up and about, so you had best be getting up and at 'em. Here's a spare uniform you can wear—looks like it should fit you, but either way it's a sight better than what you had on when you arrived. You can come and have a wee bite to eat in the kitchen as soon as you're up and dressed. Then I will take you to see his lordship." Mrs. Simms never missed a beat as she bustled around the room, pulling back the blankets and hustling Emily out of bed and into the borrowed frock.

"Thank you, Mrs. Simms," answered Emily meekly as

she followed the housekeeper out the door and down to the kitchens. She was grateful for the kindness of the servants as she was given a cup of warm milk and some toast. She eagerly ate what was provided and listened somewhat wistfully to the teasing banter among the kitchen staff. It was not too long before Emily and Mrs. Simms were standing in the hallway outside his lordship's library and Mrs. Simms was knocking on the door.

Emily was once again struck with trepidation, wondering what the earl would decide to do with her. From the snatches of information she had gleaned thus far from Mrs. Simms and the other servants, it seemed everyone thought quite highly of the earl, despite his outward impression of being much too high in the instep, but Emily felt she would reserve judgment until she had seen for herself. From her own experience of the high nobility, she was not expecting a paragon of virtue, as the servants would have had her believe. Of course, the servants usually knew the most. Well, she would see for herself soon enough.

She stiffened her spine and bolstered her courage with the thought that she had survived thus far. He could not possibly do anything worse to her than she had already experienced, no matter how good or bad he was. With that thought she walked in with her head high when the earl called for them to enter.

"Thank you, Simms, that will be all." Philip dismissed the housekeeper distractedly as he eyed the young woman Mrs. Simms had delivered to his library. Philip was again struck by her innocent beauty; she had an aspect of untouchability about her as she stood before him. He was unsure of how to go about handling the situation with this young female. It had never been his responsibility to interview potential domestic staff, nor had he much experience in interrogating people. And her ethereal appearance was highly distracting, he concluded as he gathered his thoughts before he proceeded to question her.

He began by trying to get her to explain her situation. "Well, Emily, is it? I can see you have been well taken care of by my staff. Now maybe you can tell me what you were doing stealing a ride in my carriage last night."

He tried to look stern as he questioned her but marveled at the look of proud defiance he saw her trying to control as she gazed at him without a word. Despite his ennui of late, Philip had a deeply abiding tendency to root for the underdog, and this girl was obviously trying to deal with some sort of burdensome problem. The earl was intrigued. Despite his haughty consideration for his own consequence, he sincerely wanted to assist the girl. He admired the courage that was obviously a part of her character; the fact that she would hide in his carriage was a testament to it. Of course he would not mind seeing her beauty about the estate either, he thought with a small smile, fascinated to see the play of emotions dance across her face as she tried to answer his questions.

Emily realized that this manor would be an excellent place to hide from Edwin. Being a servant would provide a perfect disguise while she tried to figure out her future. She was terribly afraid of her guardian's catching up with her and what he would do with her if he did. She had no one to trust; even this handsome young lord could be a threat, if he knew what was at stake. The need to be skilled at subterfuge had never before arisen in Emily's life, and she didn't know how good she was going to be at lying, so she kept her story as simple as possible.

"Yes, my lord, I am Emily," she replied with a dignified lilt. "I truly did not mean to steal from you. I just needed to get away. I was serving as lady's maid in a grand house, but I could no longer stay there. I saw your carriage and hopped aboard, as I did not see the harm. I am without a post now and hadn't the fare for the stage, you see," she continued somewhat cajolingly. "Thank you so much, my lord, for the meal and the place to stay last night. Your generosity is deeply appreciated. Perhaps you need a maid? I would be most happy for a position, sir," Emily concluded hopefully, then lowered her eyes as she waited to see what the earl would do.

"Who was the lady you were serving?"

"I would rather not say, my lord. I ran away and will not be going back. They were cruel," Emily replied fiercely and with a note of finality.

Philip wondered at the dignified and refined speech and recognized a real thread of fear in her voice despite the defiant tilt of her head. He knew there was much she was leaving out; however, there was sincerity in her voice as she expressed the cruelty she had experienced. Looking at her beauty, he thought that the lord might have made improper advances. Perhaps she had not actually run away but had been thrown out by the lady. Maybe she was even in a "delicate situation," he surmised. But good-naturedly he decided, *we will cross that bridge when we have to. I cannot turn my back on her; she is obviously in some sort of trouble.*

As she had answered his questions, he had observed the play of emotions across her face; she had vacillated between defiance and fear. Fear seemed to be winning out, and he hesitated to press her. *In the meantime, Mrs. Simms says we could use another housemaid. She doesn't look too sturdy. I wonder if she will hold up to much work,* he thought before speaking aloud to her.

"Well, Emily, what were your duties for the 'grand lady' you were working for before?"

"I assisted her with keeping up the library and with her correspondence. I also worked with the gardeners a couple of afternoons each week when milady went out visiting, besides looking after milady's wardrobe and toilette," she improvised.

"Sounds as if you were kept quite busy. Did you enjoy your work, Emily?"

"Oh, yes, particularly in the library and in the garden," Emily exclaimed with enthusiasm as she thought, *and that at least is true. I loved the library and the garden.*

"My secretary, Mr. Dale, is the one in charge of the library. You can assist him with his duties there, and perhaps Henri can use an extra pair of hands in the gardens. Mrs. Simms will tell you what duties she has for you as well. We shall see how this works out for the time being."

"Thank you, my lord," Emily murmured with as much deference as she could muster, trying not to reveal the elation bubbling up inside her at the prospect of being safe and reasonably comfortable for the first time in months. Having enjoyable work to do would be the icing on the cake.

"You may familiarize yourself with the library for now,

and when Mr. Dale is available, he can advise you on what assistance he might require."

"Thank you, my lord. I will try not to disturb you while you work."

With that Emily turned and started gazing about her for the first time since she entered the vast room. She gasped with pleasure at the splendor of the collection. Massive bookshelves ran from floor to ceiling, crammed full of priceless editions. Some, she could see, were quite old and rare, and the variety was endless. This was obviously not just for show but a true collection by a real book lover, one she would take great pleasure in exploring.

She approached the nearest shelves and reverentially reached out a hesitant hand to touch a heavy volume. "Sophocles," she whispered to herself as she delicately fingered the next volume and took a deep breath of the unique scent of the books.

The earl was watching her with a mixture of curiosity and appreciation. *What an odd little baggage she is. What serving wench knows anything about Greek philosophy? Who is this girl so lovingly handling my books?* He watched her classic profile as she bent over the next volume she was examining. Her skin was slightly flushed, and her eyes were sparkling as she absently glanced up at him. She was startled to catch him watching her, and her gaze turned wary.

She hesitated, then said politely and formally, "You have a wonderful library, my lord. It will be a great pleasure to work with your books in whatever capacity your secretary sees fit. Thank you for this opportunity."

"You are quite welcome, Emily. I have never seen anyone

take such pleasure in my library. You obviously have been educated." He said this last bit with a questioning lilt in his voice, again assailed by curiosity about this mysterious young woman.

With that, Emily's face closed up and lost its animation. "Yes, my lord," she replied, and she turned her back on him in what some might consider a rude manner coming from a servant. But the earl realized she was desperately guarding her secrets, whatever they might be, and did not take offense at what was obviously an instinctive effort at self-preservation. His curiosity, always ready to surface, was fighting to get the better of him. He wanted to press her for answers to all the questions burning in his brain but was unable to think of a way to get her to tell him what he wanted to know.

He turned back to his papers and tried to ignore her presence in his sanctum. As time passed, he could almost do it, but he would hear her sigh over some tome she was examining, and he could not help himself. He would gaze admiringly at her youthful beauty as she peered into his books. The night's rest had obviously served her well, and she had apparently been scrubbed to within an inch of her life, he thought with a smile as he noticed her pink skin and the obstinate curls that were trying to defy the severe hairstyle she had tried to force upon it. Her allure was distracting, and he was increasingly frustrated with the maid's innocent presence in his library. Despite his experience with women, he knew she was not in any way trying to attract him, and that somehow added to the effect and his frustration.

He was never so happy to see James enter the room as

he was that day. "Where have you been?" he demanded crossly.

James was startled at the uncharacteristic snarl in his master's voice. "It is the usual time for me to arrive, milord. Is aught amiss?" James questioned concernedly.

"No, no, James, I'm sorry. It has been a strange morning. Come in, sit down, and let's get to work. Oh, you should meet your new assistant," he said with a rueful chuckle. "Emily, come over here and meet Mr. Dale. James, this is Emily. She will be helping you with the library and whatever other jobs you see fit to give her. She is quite taken with the books. Maybe you have some assignments for her there?"

Philip watched in amusement as his normally unflappable secretary had trouble keeping his jaw properly shut as he took in the young woman being introduced to him. James' cheeks reddened. Although able to converse intelligently upon many subjects with the aristocratic crowd the earl associated with, the young secretary occasionally became painfully shy when attempting conversation with women, particularly attractive ones, and the sight of this one clearly tied poor James into knots.

Always gracious, Emily tried to put him at ease. She dropped a brief curtsy and said, "I am pleased to make your acquaintance, sir, and shall endeavor to do all the tasks you may assign me as diligently as I am able. Perhaps you have something in mind I could start on," she suggested gently, recognizing his shyness but oblivious to its source.

James gathered his composure and pondered for a moment, refusing to look at her. He shoved his lanky dark hair off his forehead absently while he gazed at the earl in perplexity. "Well, the books desperately need to be cata-logued and an inventory taken of which ones need to re-ceive some maintenance. Is that within your realm of experience?" he questioned hesitantly.

"Oh, that is most excellent. I could start on that right away. Thank you, sir. Excuse me, my lord." And she bowed herself gracefully away to start her work, happy to have something constructive to do, taking her mind off her wor-ries.

James' wide-eyed stare turned to Lord Yorkleigh. Philip just shrugged helplessly, at a loss for an explanation, so they started in on the paperwork that was always piling up for the landlord of vast estates.

A few hours later the two men decided to call it quits for the day, and the earl offered his secretary a glass of liquor. As he got up to ring for the butler, his eyes caught on the shapely ankles of his new maid.

"Emily!" he almost yelped as he looked up at her on the ladder. "Whatever are you doing up there? Get down at once. You will trip over your skirts and fall and break your neck. What were you thinking?" he demanded crossly. He knew he was being unreasonable—that was what the lad-der was for, after all—but he just could not help being concerned for the girl's safety.

"I am so sorry, my lord. I was just trying to reach that last volume of Josephus. I thought it would be best to shelve them all together. I did not wish to disturb you at your work, my lord. I'm sorry for upsetting you," Emily explained in a rush as she bobbed him a deferential curtsy, hoping desperately he would not ban her from the library.

She had had the best day in ever so long. She had greatly enjoyed listening to the informative dialogue between the master and his secretary. She was amazed at how involved the earl was with all the infinite details of running his estates. It impressed her that he knew about the lives of his tenants. Most in his position did not even know their names, she was sure. He was very proud, but her estimation of him had grown, and she wished to learn more of the management details of being a landlord. It would be very useful information to have if she could ever get her own affairs straightened out.

Philip raked a hand through his dark, wavy hair, trying to contain his tumultuous feelings, realizing he was being strangely irrational with regard to the young woman standing with calm dignity before him. After heaving a frustrated sigh, he dismissed her for the day. "That will be all for today, Emily. Go see Mrs. Simms and get a new assignment from her. We will not be requiring your services here for the rest of the day. You can work out a schedule with Mr. Dale tomorrow."

Emily bobbed another quick curtsy and left the room with relief. The earl had not banned her from his home or his library, and she knew she would be safe there for a while. She went off in search of the housekeeper, determined to be an efficient servant in payment for the guardianship the earl was unaware of providing for her.

Chapter Three

The next day Mrs. Simms directed Emily toward Henri, the head gardener, having informed the startled older man that the young miss was going to be assisting him. His slightly disheveled look increased in disarray as he tugged on his wiry gray locks, ranting over this seeming slight to his botanical genius.

"Never had a she-person helping out in the garden before. Don't know what's going on with his lordship, that I don't! Of what use is a she-person going to be to me, that's what I'd like to know . . ." He continued grumbling as he paced in front of her.

Emily was a bit taken aback. Realizing how the gardener felt about her dubious help made her uneasy, but she put on a brave face, cleared her throat loudly, and announced, "I'm here, sir, ready to be of assistance."

"Well, let me have a look at you. I don't think you'll be

of much use—you're much too scrawny. What I need are some strapping young men. What's his lordship thinking, that's what I want to know." He drifted off into his grumbling again.

Emily's eyes were wide with indecision, but she set her shoulders and said firmly, "I may be small, sir, but I am a good worker, and I have experience working in a similar style of garden in the past. If you will give me a chance, I would like very much to be of assistance to you in the earl's gardens."

Henri shrugged in a decidedly foreign manner and waved a hand toward a distant garden. "Go see what you can do with the flowers. The heads need removing, and so do the weeds. I'll check on you later and see what you're capable of."

"Thank you, sir. I will see you later, then." With that Emily made her way happily to begin her tasks, determined to prove her abilities and worth to the grumpy older man.

Lord Yorkleigh stood at a distance, debating the wisdom of interrupting the slight figure bent over her work. He had been wondering if he had taken a blow to the head that he couldn't remember, so distracted was he by thoughts of this young woman. He had been unable to settle down to work that morning, disturbed by wondering what she was up to. He had been disgusted with himself but had once again succumbed to his curiosity and gone off in search of her, leaving James to deal with details in the library. Henri had made it quite clear what his opinion was on the matter of a woman's dubious assistance; it had been a highly amusing exchange.

So there Philip stood, admiring Emily as she tugged vigorously at the stubborn weeds Henri was testing her on. As he had left the house, an impulse had caused him to pick up an old hat and pair of gloves left in a cupboard by his mother. Thinking of Emily's pale, delicate-looking skin, he had thought she could use them, before he realized that none of his servants displayed much vanity. He was starting to feel awkward just standing there looking at her, so he strode forward briskly to interrupt her.

Emily was just then wishing she had a broad-brimmed hat and some gloves and supposing that she would have to get over her vanities now that she was a maidservant, when a well-manicured hand appeared before her eyes holding out just those things. She looked up in amazement, a delighted smile gracing her face.

"My lord, how did you know that was just what I was wishing for?"

"I figured you would burn that fair skin of yours in the sun out here all day. I don't think that's a sight Mr. Dale is prepared to face when you are helping him in the library," Philip prevaricated as he took in the information that she really hadn't a clue about the way things usually worked. It had been an impulsive gesture, bringing the hat and gloves as an excuse for seeking her out. He had not actually expected her to accept the articles so readily. It was members of the ton who concerned themselves about maintaining their creamy complexions.

He grew ever more intrigued with his secretive little maid. What kind of servant was she, this beautiful young woman with a closetful of secrets? He was powerfully attracted and yet frustratingly disturbed by her. She was heartbreakingly beautiful, but he could not forget the bedraggled mess that had climbed out of his carriage boot just days before. And he was repulsed by his own attraction to someone from the servants' quarters.

He was drawn to her in a way he had never felt before. He argued with himself that it was merely compassion for an obviously troubled young woman, completely ignoring the fact that others in his employ had trouble in their background and he had never felt the intense need to observe and protect them that he did with this Emily.

He shook his head and left her to her work after seeing that she was getting along well in the gardens. He observed that Henri hadn't dismissed her yet. *Even that surly old coot isn't immune to her charms,* Philip thought with a chuckle as he wondered if everyone on the estate would fall at her feet.

After the earl left, Emily had the vague sensation that the sun had gone behind a cloud, but when she stood to stretch out her sore muscles and glance around the now immaculate patch of garden, she could see that the sun was still blazing in the spring sky.

The gardens and the woods beyond gave her a comforting sense of security; she was safe in her anonymity as one of Yorkleigh's many maids on the vast estate. No one would bother her here, and she could find contentment. She was determined not to give in to defeat.

It was wonderful to breathe fresh air, and she could not seem to get enough of the sweet smells as she continued to work. Emily wondered absently if she would ever be able to forget the horrendous stench of the asylum. She could not stop herself from taking deep, gulping breaths of the air, so clean in contrast to the pungent odors she had had to deal with for so many weeks.

She was delighted to be in a garden again after so long, but she had quite forgotten how much work it could be and was feeling the consequences. Spending so much time in a tiny cell had weakened her, she realized as she felt the strain of bending and pulling. She struggled to continue, not wanting to be labeled as lazy, trying to please the cranky Henri.

The work felt progressively harder, and Emily was beginning to suspect she was not going to make it, when her nemesis showed up to survey her accomplishments. His wizened old face gave away little of what he was feeling, and Emily held her breath to see what he would say. He grunted his approval at the amount of work a tiny female had been able to get done and told her to report back to him early the next morning. Emily gratefully slipped away to the kitchen to beg a snack from the cook's helper before searching out Mrs. Simms to see what she was to do next. It was a very exhausted young maid who slipped gratefully into her bed early that evening, and a deep, dreamless sleep claimed her as soon as her head settled onto her pallet.

Emily's mind and body soon adjusted to the routine of gardening with Henri in the mornings and working in the library under the direction of Mr. Dale in the afternoons. Her cheeks were soon blooming with a healthy color reminiscent of the roses she tended under Henri's gimlet eye. Emily discovered that the cranky old gardener had a soft spot under all that crust, and they came to an understanding of each other. He soon forgot she was one of the hated she-people he so distrusted and accepted her into his circle of friends. Emily, in turn, was delighted by his gruff sense of humor and basked in the joy and camaraderie she found among the staff at Yorkleigh. No one asked too many questions—it seemed many had secrets of their own—but they were a close-knit group nonetheless, and Emily found that the bruises on her heart were slowly healing. As her body adjusted to the heavy workload, her mind recovered from the ordeal and turmoil she had been through.

Her previous *joie de vivre* returned, and it was an open, happily smiling face that confronted Philip as he entered his library upon his return to his estate after an absence of some days.

Chapter Four

Lord Philip was in the nearest thing to a rage he had ever experienced before, preoccupied with the unexpected emotion as he entered his previously male sanctum. He had been in London for a week—and bored. This was becoming a problem. In his entire life he had never before experienced such an overwhelming sense of ennui, and it seemed to be worsening. He had always been content, aware of his blessed lot in life and all that it entitled him to. He had been comfortable with his position in the upper ranks of society that his wealth and title granted him, as well as the way lesser mortals toadied to him because of that position. He had enjoyed the freedom of having every exalted door opened to him, most men envying him and most women being available for his entertainment. But it was all beginning to pall, and he was finding the experience unnerving. His regular associates were becoming bores, the endless round of social engagements, sporting events, balls, routs, and parties bordering on deadly dull, and he was angry that his previously excellent existence was no longer quite so excellent.

The only thing that interested him of late was being on his estate looking after all the varied business connected with the earldom, which he had previously left in the hands of the solicitors. Now he found himself wanting to take more control. *I am becoming staid,* he thought with disgust. Next he would be wanting to set up his nursery and bounce babies on his knee! The thought made him shudder in revulsion, then set off an interesting reverie about just such a situation. *Of course,* he reasoned, *he* did *have to secure his succession someday. Maybe he* should *set up his nursery.* Thus was his disheveled state of mind as he entered his library, only to come upon the cherubic face of his charming maid.

Emily's mind was elsewhere, and she yelped in surprise when his lordship walked into the room. His face was a study in contradicting emotions, and she was surprised to see him actually displaying feelings, since her previous impressions of him were of coldness and pride, despite the kind gestures he had shown her. The last thing she would have expected was to see him looking so angry and yet somehow sheepish. *What a contradiction the man is,* she sighed to herself as she straightened from the obligatory curtsy she had executed upon his entrance.

What can he possibly have to be so grumpy about? She wondered as she waited expectantly for the earl to say something. The two stared at each other, nonplussed, for a moment that felt like an age to Emily. She grew uncomfortable with the silence and had to break it. "Welcome home, my lord. Was your journey successful?" she inquired politely.

"No, it wasn't," he barked. Philip felt foolish for snapping at his maid but couldn't seem to stop himself from taking out his bad humor on her. He had never experienced feeling unsure of himself in all his twenty-nine years, and the experience was one he would quite happily do without. Not wanting to prolong his exposure to the unsettling maid while in his current state of mind, he attempted to rid himself of at least one irritant.

"What are you doing in my library, might I ask?" he questioned haughtily.

Not appearing at all put out by his attitude, Emily replied, "I am working on the catalogue of your library for Mr. Dale and attempting to figure out an acceptable order for your volumes of poetry. I'm debating between writer and subject classification. What do you think, my lord?"

Taken aback at being questioned about literature by a servant, Philip mumbled incoherently in reply while wondering how to get rid of the unwanted distraction. He rolled his eyes at himself in disgust at his own wishy-washy behavior.

I am the earl in this house; I make the rules! I can just tell her to leave, he reminded himself before he suited thought to words.

Emily was surprised at the pique she felt at being told to leave the room and found herself bristling in response, but she managed to restrain her lips from uttering any of the thoughts bouncing through her head. She contented herself with "As you wish, my lord," as she curtsied and let herself quietly out of the room.

Philip was disappointed not to be more pleased to have the library himself. He realized he was acting irrationally but had no idea what to do about it. He concluded he needed a drink. *That ought to solve everything,* he thought self-derisively as he settled into his chair by the grate and filled his glass. He rolled his eyes once again at his own foolishness as he tossed the first one back, realizing it was going to be futile.

Several weeks went by, and Emily grew more confident. She had many discussions with Philip's secretary, Mr. James Dale, as she reported to him regularly on her progress in the library. They sometimes discussed various works of literature or the research she had come across recently, and James soon forgot to be uncomfortable in the surprisingly knowledgeable young woman's presence.

Lord Yorkleigh was surprised to see his normally reserved secretary engaged in animated discussion with the maid when he walked into his library. His entry must have been silent, as neither noticed his presence. Philip stood quietly enjoying the spectacle before him. James had removed his spectacles and was gesturing emphatically with them, while Emily's flushed countenance and gleaming eyes showed her enjoyment of the debate.

Philip had again been absent from the estate for a couple of days and had missed the routine he was growing to enjoy so much as he took up more of the workings of the earldom. And, he regretted to admit, he also missed the disturbing presence of the beautiful young thing now in heated debate with Mr. Dale. It was obvious that the two had grown quite used to each other and were enjoying the mental stimulation they each caused the other. Philip was fascinated by what he was hearing.

"But surely, Miss Emily, you cannot really think Sophocles is better than Shakespeare!" Mr. Dale demanded incredulously while raking a hand carelessly through his ever-unruly hair.

"I can, and I do!" Emily declared emphatically. "Actually, if you think about it, Mr. Dale, they are really quite similar. Both wrote for the common people. And while Mr. Shakespeare managed to suit his plays to multiple levels of society, when you read Sophocles in his original language, you can see that his turn of phrase is really quite superior to that of Mr. Shakespeare." Emily had not given any thought to how much she might be revealing about her education and was startled when Philip spoke from where he was standing near the door.

"You read Greek, Emily?" he asked in obvious amazement, instantly regretting interrupting the tirade he had been so enjoying.

Emily jumped in surprise, then let out a squeak as she whirled around to face him and hastily executed her curtsy.

"Just a little, my lord," she answered shyly while searching for a way to extricate herself from the latest mess she had gotten into. "I suppose your lordship will need some privacy to speak with Mr. Dale. Good day, my lord, sir." And she curtsied herself from the room in a rush.

Mr. Dale and the earl looked at each other and burst out laughing. "What a strange girl she is! How many of the servants even know who Sophocles was, do you think, James, let alone have an opinion as to his scholarly abilities?" asked the earl.

"I doubt if any of them would, my lord," admitted James. "I wonder why she contents herself with digging in your gardens and dusting your shelves when she could be a teacher or governess somewhere. I find I am dashed curious about her background."

"As am I, James. However, only time will tell if the evasive Emily will ever admit her secrets. But she is certainly right about one thing: We have much to do. Let us get on with the work for the day."

"Good day, my lord," Emily called out with a smile as she teetered on a rickety old chair in the attic one day later that week. "Whatever are you doing up here in the attic, my lord? You are going to get yourself dirty!" she admonished just before sneezing at the cloud of dust she had disturbed.

"Emily, get down from there this instant! Why, pray tell, am I forever finding you in some death-defying position? To answer your query, I happen to own the place. I might ask whatever *you* are doing up here?" Philip was merely teasing, but he was delighted to watch a blush steal into Emily's cheeks as she struggled to pull a crate down off the high shelf she was reaching for.

"My lord, I assure you, I am supposed to be up here," she began earnestly before she caught the glint of amusement in the earl's eye. "But I'm sure you knew that, didn't you?" she continued with a bit more spirit as she stuck her tongue out at him cheekily. "I was told by a reliable source that there is a whole trunk filled with interesting things that should be in the library. I had just about gotten it before I was so rudely interrupted."

Philip smiled in good cheer at her pluck. "Well, if you must break your neck, be sure to do it on your own time. I wouldn't want the maids to have to clean up after you."

Emily gasped in mock outrage and threw her rag at him as they both broke into laughter. While Emily was still giggling, Philip reached up and grabbed her about the waist to help her down. As his hands closed warmly around her, the laughter died in her throat, and her mouth went dry as unfamiliar feelings coursed through her. A long moment ticked by as they both felt they were falling into the depths of the other's eyes. He held her in midair as though frozen before gently setting her on the floor. Emily felt a tingling, shivery sensation rush through her as her entire body broke out in gooseflesh. She gazed in wonder at the earl, filled with new and amazing feelings she could not put a name to. For an unguarded moment Philip felt such a powerful attraction to the young woman that he could barely take a breath. As used as he was to such things, he was surprised at the intensity of his feelings and could only stand there gazing in wonder at her. Emily cleared her throat uneasily and stepped back. Philip dropped his hands as though burned.

"Yes, well, thank you for your concern, my lord," Emily began awkwardly. "I will just continue with my search for that trunk." And she turned her back on him.

After a moment of stunned disbelief, Philip commanded her harshly to get the help of one of the footmen before he turned on his heel and stalked from the room.

Philip got back to his library in a distracted state. He was at a loss to know why he was so drawn to the strange young woman. She was such a contradiction, he mused. She was distractingly beautiful, and he had to struggle to keep his thoughts about her under control. And then there was her obvious intelligence; he could see that she had been educated. It came through whenever she spoke, both in her refined speech and her extensive knowledge. *The chit knows Greek philosophy!* he thought in amazement. *But what was she doing in the carriage boot, dressed in rags, and now dusting his shelves?* he wondered. He had never taken up with any of his servants, and he was surely not going to start now. Still, it disturbed him to be so drawn to her.

A few days later, despite his best intentions, Philip found himself once again roaming about, looking for his beautiful maid. This time he was searching the extensive gardens. He finally came upon her in a back corner of the rose garden wearing the gloves and hat he had brought her weeks ago, singing a beautiful French melody in perfect pitch and accent. His French was not by any means perfect, but to his ears hers sounded as if it was. He again marveled at the perplexing package that was his new servant while he took a moment to enjoy the scene she made and her melodious singing. When she came to the end of the song, he began clapping, which startled Emily into whirling around in apparent fright. Despite her newly found comfort on the estate, she still had nightmares and often started at sudden noises.

"Oh, you scared me, my lord!" she pronounced as she

began to blush, realizing he had been witness to her warbling. "Were you standing there for long?" she asked shyly, hoping he had not.

"Are you embarrassed, Emily? You have no need to be, let me assure you. You have a most beautiful voice."

Emily was delighted with the compliment but unsure how to respond, since she had no way of verifying its accuracy.

Before the silence became uncomfortable, Philip continued. "Where did you learn such perfect French?" he asked, trying to find out more about her.

"Oh, here and there," she responded vaguely as she turned back to her weeding.

Frustrated, refusing to be dismissed by a maid, Philip decided to question her further. "Why do you never admit any information about yourself? What are you hiding? Why all the mystery, Emily? Where do you come from, and why are you a servant when you have so obviously been well educated? You could easily hold a much higher, more comfortable position."

Emily had stiffened noticeably. "I am perfectly comfortable just as I am, my lord. Thank you for your concern," she responded in an icy tone.

She was quite obviously not going to reveal anything about herself, and Philip was annoyed, unaccustomed to being denied.

Despite his annoyance, though, he could not ignore his steadily growing attraction to her. It was a constant source of dismay and confusion. He had never been attracted to one of the lower classes nor taken advantage of anyone in his employ, as so many of his counterparts were prone to do. Maybe all this country air was addling his brain, he thought in wry amusement as he walked away.

As the days passed, Philip found himself wandering the house, keeping an eye out for Emily, "bumping into" her wherever her various assignments took her in the vast manor. He would engage her in conversation and delight to see her face light up animatedly as she enthused over whatever subject they were discussing. He would puzzle over why her face suddenly lost its glow and she would excuse herself politely as she returned to her work.

One such example was the day Emily had been assigned by Mrs. Simms to polish the furniture in one of the bedrooms in the guest wing. Due to her work in the gardens and the library, Mrs. Simms used Emily only for extra projects, rather than her having a regular assignment each day. Because of this, if Philip was interested in checking on her, he was required to either ask the housekeeper or wander until he found her himself. His pride rarely allowed him to ask Mrs. Simms, so it often took him a while to find Emily. He reasoned that this was an excellent way to keep informed of the goings-on in his house, to remain aware of the state of all his chambers.

On this particular day it had taken an inordinate amount of time to nonchalantly find the beautiful young woman. Of course, she had no idea he was searching for her as she vigorously rubbed the ornate old furniture with the special concoction Mrs. Simms had provided for her use.

As Philip approached the room Emily was working in, he could hear her singing an old nursery ditty. He chuckled at the memories the melody conjured up. When he reached the open door, he joined in with Emily's singing. She jumped in surprise at his deep baritone but quickly recovered and finished the song with a flourish.

Clapping with gleeful abandon, Emily grinned at the earl enchantingly, completely forgetting the obvious difference in their stations. "Well done, my lord. How do you know the song? My nurse assured me it was a special song just for me," she complained teasingly.

The earl quirked an eyebrow at Emily's reference to her nurse, a luxury only indulged by the higher stations, but for the sake of their camaraderie he chose to ignore her involuntary revelation. "My nurse must have been friends with your nurse, since she told me the same thing when she sang it to me," he said drolly, enjoying the sparkle in Emily's eyes.

While they were talking, Philip had stepped into the room and sat upon the bed as Emily continued polishing the fireplace mantel on the other side of the room. She had grown more accustomed to his visits, and as she rubbed the waxy concoction into the fine wood, they chatted about other songs and stories they remembered from childhood.

As always Emily was oblivious to the effect she was having upon Lord Yorkleigh. Had she realized, she would, no doubt, have been quite uncomfortable, but as it was she was blissfully unaffected. Philip, on the other hand, was becoming increasingly uncomfortable as he watched her working and laughing and talking so naturally. His attraction to the beautiful young maidservant was getting out of hand, and despite his enjoyment of her company, he found it angered him to be affected so.

Philip decided to try to find out more about her. "What was your nurse's name? Mine was Mrs. Brady," he said casually.

Emily must have realized she had revealed too much in her relaxed conversation and tried to disengage. "Oh, my lord, I really should get this room finished. Mrs. Simms shall have apoplexy if I am not finished soon. And I have to meet with Mr. Dale very shortly. It has been ever so nice reminiscing with you," she said in not-so-subtle dismissal.

Philip was keenly disappointed and grew haughty as a result. "Very well, Emily, I shan't keep you. Do continue. And don't forget the sideboard," he commanded imperiously before he stalked from the room.

Emily regretted the need for distance with the earl. She truly enjoyed the conversation they occasionally enjoyed but realized it could go nowhere. Lord Philip was an earl, and she was his maidservant. Nothing aboveboard could come of it, she concluded with a sigh once he was gone.

As Philip realized how important these little interludes with Emily were becoming to him, he was appalled. He began studiously avoiding her. It would certainly not do to develop a *tendre* for the maid, no matter how attractive she might be.

Emily sensed his confusion and was saddened by his withdrawal. She was the happiest she had been in ever so long and owed it in large measure to the earl. But she knew it was for the best to keep a distance between them; she dared not trust anyone to help her solve her problems.

Chapter Five

The manor was all aflutter. "Her ladyship arrives to-day!" The excitement was on everyone's lips. Emily was intrigued by the sense of devotion everyone obviously felt for the countess, the earl's widowed mother. She had found herself caught up in the excitement as the entire household was dusted, aired, polished, and shined until the large house practically glowed. The entire staff was feeling quite proud of themselves as they assembled in the grand entry dressed in their best pressed uniforms, waiting to welcome the mistress to her old home. Emily had been catching snippets about the grand lady in the week of preparation. She had learned about the deep love the earl's parents had felt for each other and the great kindness the countess showed to everyone she came across.

Everyone had a theory on why the countess had chosen

to make her home on one of the lesser estates after the death of her dear husband. "Too many memories," some claimed sagely, while others were firmly convinced she was making the way clear for the current earl to bring home his own countess. "Doesn't want to sit around and be the dowager in her own home. Best to start fresh elsewhere in her own time," was the understanding Mrs. Simms had of the matter. Emily figured the housekeeper would probably know best, but she waited with an air of anxious anticipation along with the rest of the household as the time of the arrival drew near.

Nearly everyone in the household had a story to share with Emily as an example of the countess' kindness. Meg told of the time she had been sent to visit her family for a week when her mother had taken ill, while Ann described the time the countess herself had visited her bedside when she had caught some illness. Mrs. Simms had many such stories of things the countess had done for various tenants, from financial assistance to visiting after a new birth. Emily found it difficult to believe that anyone was such a paragon of sweetness and light. But once again she resolved to wait and see as she joined the rest of the Yorkleigh staff in the foyer of the grand manor, waiting for the countess to arrive.

The earl could barely repress a chuckle as he realized that nearly his entire staff was assembled in the front rooms of his home, all dressed in their best, chattering excitedly, admiring their own work, and wondering aloud when milady would arrive. Even scruffy old Henri was combed and polished and trying to look busy in the hedges surrounding the front drive. Philip caught himself looking for Emily to see if she would enjoy the joke, since their sense of humor usually so closely coincided. But how could she? he asked himself impatiently. She was one of them. He saw her standing in a corner, gnawing nervously on her lip. He felt a deep longing to go to her and soothe away whatever anxieties were bothering her, as well as a baser desire to run his thumb over the tender lip she had been absentmindedly chewing. Philip was shaken with irritation at his own missishness. He was turning into a green lad over a chambermaid!

Emily was taken aback as she glanced toward Philip and caught him scowling fiercely in her direction before he strode abruptly into his library, slamming the door behind him. The occupants of the hall jumped and flushed somewhat guiltily, and there was a moment of stunned silence before the excited chatter resumed, slightly more subdued than before the earl's interruption. Finally everyone breathed a sigh of relief when the stable lad who had been sent to watch the lane came dashing in the side door. "The coach is coming!" he exclaimed breathlessly. Everyone scrambled into proper position as the shiny black coach with the earl's family coat of arms swirled to a well-sprung stop in front of the low front steps. The groom solemnly opened the door and let down the stairs with a flourish, bowing low before assisting the countess from the coach.

"Thank you, Jimmy," acknowledged Lady Clara as the young groom flushed with pleasure that his lady had remembered his name. The elegantly aging countess made slow, graceful progress into the house, greeting the more senior staff while the rest bustled about, getting her bags and leading the cooling team of horses away, along with the coach, to be rubbed down and rested from the journey.

Emily had never witnessed such a scene; the mistress of the house was obviously adored by the staff. She hung back with the other newcomers to the household, unsure what her role was when others were so obviously eager to be of service and receive acknowledgment from the Lady Clara. Philip emerged from his library and strode into the melee, and a path opened for him among the milling crowd. There was open affection between the countess and her son as the earl greeted his mother warmly, then drew her forward to be introduced to her newest maids when she informed him that her personal maid had been detained due to illness.

"Mother, we have added to the household since you were last here. These three young ladies will be happy to assist you in any way, I'm sure. This is Susie, Megan, and Emily. Emily has some experience as a lady's maid, so she will attend you while you await the arrival of Smitty. How fortunate that she is with us, since your own personal maid was detained," he pronounced coolly while barely glancing at the maid in question.

Lady Clara greeted the girls and then followed Mrs. Simms up to her rooms, having no clue about the trepidation inside her new "lady's maid."

Emily was appalled. She never should have said she was a lady's maid. She had made it up, figuring she would never be caught in the lie, since this was essentially a bachelor's establishment. Because of her great trepidation that day she had first arrived, she could not even remember exactly what she had told Lord Yorkleigh about what she knew how to do.

She had been so pleased to be assigned to the library and gardens, along with doing various chores for Mrs. Simms. Dusting was easy to master. She had simply asked the maid who had shown her to the room she was supposed to start in that first day if they had a special technique she was supposed to follow in this household. Molly had looked at her strangely and said, "No, you just do it the normal way, like this," demonstrating how to use the damp cloth followed by the dry one. Emily nodded knowingly and said, "Of course."

But now there was no one to ask. She was sure Lady Clara would expect her to know what to do, and she hadn't a clue. She had barely paid attention when others had worked around her in the past. Why hadn't she taken notice of these types of things? she berated herself silently as she followed in the wake of Lady Clara and Mrs. Simms, noting glumly the warmth between the two women as Mrs. Simms updated the countess on news of the household.

Neither woman noticed the turmoil the young maid was in as they progressed towards the countess' rooms. Emily was frantically wracking her brain, trying to come up with a sequence of logical duties a lady's maid would accomplish. *First, I guess we would need to unpack. Maybe other maids will help with that, and I shall need to oversee and ensure that everything is in order and nothing needs pressing or mending. I'm not too sure how to press the clothes, though. Maybe they can be sent to the laundry! That could work out well. All right, what else? Helping milady to dress and prepare for the day and for meals and so on. Oh, no! Her hair! I shall have to dress her hair!*

Emily nearly shrieked as she realized how far out of her depth she was. *This will teach me never to take anyone for granted again, won't it? Think! The worst that can happen is that she will expose me to Lord Yorkleigh as a fraud, and I will be sent away. I can deal with that. I have survived worse. I can survive this. Besides, since I have survived worse, I should be able to work out how to be a fine lady's maid. I am reasonably bright—it shouldn't be* that *hard.* And on that heartening thought, they arrived at the countess' chamber, where Emily's new role was to begin. Emily took a deep, fortifying breath and entered the suite.

Emily had never known such tiredness existed, not even that first day working with Henri. *The amount of work that goes into the toilette of one highborn lady boggles the mind,* she thought groggily as she sank wearily into her comforting bed. Lady Clara had wanted to catch up with her son, and they had sat up together rather late. Emily was certain it was her obligation to wait for her new mistress in order to help her prepare for bed and put away milady's dress and things. She had been right. Lady Clara had not been at all surprised to see her and had politely informed her which nightgown she wanted. By then Emily was familiar with the countess' wardrobe and where everything was, so she hadn't yet disgraced herself. *But there's always tomorrow,* she thought with a wry smile as she drifted off to the comfort of her dreams.

Her duties arrived much too soon the next morning as

one of the other maids shook her urgently awake. "Hurry, you'll be late. You have to get your dusting done afore you take the countess her morning chocolate. She likes it to be prompt and hot when you wake her up at nine o'clock," urged Tess, one of the more experienced maids. She was Mrs. Simms' niece, so Emily trusted her judgment but lamented her timing, as it seemed she had just laid her head down two minutes ago, and now it was time to rise again.

Emily was shocked to see that the sun was already up and she was the last of the female staff to get up. She hurried through her own morning routine, then ran down to the kitchen to swallow a bite to eat before rushing through her dusting duties and dashing back to the kitchen to grab the mistress' chocolate.

She was feeling rather breathless as she stood outside the countess' chamber just before the clock struck the ninth hour. She took a second to collect her breath before she knocked. There was no response, so she let herself in softly. She wasn't too sure of the correct method for waking the grand lady. She rather doubted Tess' method would be the acceptable way, as she wryly remembered the vigorous shaking she had received a few hours previous. She found herself thinking longingly of the services her dear Mary used to perform but caught her self-pity midstride. That was a different life, she reminded herself sternly. It was best to get on with the job at hand. With that she took her courage in both hands and approached the big bed.

"My lady," she whispered, "it is time to get up." There was no response. Emily hesitated before drawing closer and reaching out tentatively. She let out a squeak just before her hand reached the sleeping figure. Lady Clara was blinking at her as her hand wobbled, and she caught the tray with the chocolate before it could spill.

"I am so sorry, my lady," Emily gasped. "I thought you were still asleep."

"I didn't mean to startle you, Emily. Your whisper and the smell of my chocolate were enough to wake me," Lady Clara answered kindly as she began to rise. "No one can make my chocolate quite as well as the cook here at Yorkleigh. It is one of the things I miss most about living here," she continued almost wistfully. "But I am here now for a while, so I will enjoy it wholeheartedly for the present," she went on briskly as she propped herself up against the headboard with an abundance of pillows and then accepted the steaming cup from Emily's now steady hand. "So, my dear, what shall I wear today, do you suppose? Which of my frocks were you able to get the wrinkles out of so far?"

Emily turned surprise-widened eyes on the countess. "I thought I was supposed to prepare all of them, my lady. I had the assistance of some of the other girls, and we fixed up everything. There were a couple of pieces that we had to send to Sue in the laundry, but you can pretty much take your pick."

Lady Clara was impressed. "Well, aren't you an industrious one? My regular maid must be showing her age." Clara laughed kindly. "Excellent! Well, I will be visiting the house with Mrs. Simms, checking on supplies, so get me something serviceable and not too fussy. If I need to change later in the day, I shall ring for you."

As Emily helped her mistress dress and prepare for her morning with the housekeeper, she was gratefully reminded of all the times she and the other girls had done one another's hair while she was at school. Not that she could give the countess a schoolgirl's hairstyle, but at least she didn't disgrace herself. She kept it simple, and things seemed to work out. She heaved a sigh of relief as the countess left the room after reminding her what time she would need her services to prepare for supper. Emily quickly tidied up the chamber before rushing off to the library to fulfill her obligations to the lord's secretary.

The earl was slightly taken aback to see her. He thought he had solved the irksome problem of always running into this attractive little maid when he had assigned her to his mother. He was disappointed that his plan was not as effective as he had thought it would be and disgusted with himself that it was even necessary. He abruptly demanded to know what she was doing in his library and why she wasn't with the countess.

"My lord, she will not need me until late this afternoon to prepare for supper. I can accomplish much here in the library in the meantime. My other duties for Mrs. Simms are finished as well," she replied with quiet dignity and a sense of pride. "I shall try diligently not to disturb you, my lord. The shelves I am currently working on are way at the far end of this chamber—you shan't even know I am here." She curtsied politely as she turned to commence her work.

Philip shook his head in frustration. None of his other servants would consider talking back to him, nor would they ever give thought to asking for extra work. But he could not help noticing the obvious pleasure the young maid took in her efforts in the library. *You shan't even know I am here,* he quoted derisively to himself as he watched her start upon her task. She obviously had a studious bent, as she seemed familiar with most of the books she came across.

Annoyed with himself, he turned to his desk and decided that maybe today would be a good day to ride out and visit his tenants. Maybe his mother would like to accompany him. Emily barely noticed him leaving as she pored over another musty old volume, lost deep in thought in the realm of literature, blissfully unaware of the turmoil she was continuously causing for the usually levelheaded earl.

Chapter Six

"**Y**ou are awfully quiet, my son. Do you wish to share what is on your mind?" questioned Lady Clara gently as they whisked along briskly in the buggy on their rounds of the tenant farmers.

"Just minding the team, Mother. These horses haven't been out for a while," he prevaricated.

Lady Clara merely raised her eyebrows. "Wherever did you find that young maid, Emily? Her diction is so refined. She certainly does not sound as if she is from around here."

The countess was surprised as he answered her question, telling the story of Emily's arrival on the estate. She listened carefully, amazed not only at the scant details of the young woman's story, but also at the tone her son was using. He seemed strangely invested in the telling, as well as highly conflicted, and she wondered why. She was vastly curious about the young woman, wondering why the maid was so secretive about her past. Maybe she was uncomfortable confiding in her son. Philip, she knew, could sometimes be cold and haughty if he thought someone was trying to take advantage of him. She would try to get the young woman to confide in her. It sounded as if she was in some kind of trouble. Clara loved to be needed; she would help this Emily if she could.

"The fact that they had foreknowledge does not mean they caused it to happen!" Emily declared vehemently.

Philip was taken aback to hear Emily's raised voice. He had just opened the door to his library and was surprised to see his secretary deep in debate with the young maid. The earl marveled at her heightened beauty, her face flushed and her eyes sparkling in defiance. He listened for a few minutes to the intelligent debate being waged. So engrossed were the two in their subject, they hadn't noticed him enter the room. They were debating the Greek playwright, Sophocles, again. He felt his admiration grow for the young woman as she regained control of her strong emotions and continued the debate in her refined, dignified speech.

As he felt his heart growing warm toward her, he abruptly cleared his throat to make his presence known. Mr. Dale started in surprise, and they both flushed guiltily as they turned to Lord Yorkleigh with widened eyes and bated breath.

"Sophocles will have to wait, Mr. Dale. I need you to draft some copies for me. Emily, I believe the countess will be requiring your services shortly. You are excused," he dismissed her gruffly as he turned his back on them and poured himself a stiff drink.

"So, Emily, how long have you been with us here at Yorkleigh?" The countess was watching Emily in the mirror as the girl concentrated studiously on the design she was trying to create with her mistress' hair.

"Almost six weeks, my lady," Emily replied steadily.

"Mrs. Simms speaks highly of you."

Emily blushed with obvious pleasure. "Thank you for saying so, my lady. Mrs. Simms is one of the best women I have ever known. I think his lordship is quite fortunate to have her in his employ," Emily replied loyally.

"Yes, Yorkleigh is fortunate to have her. She has been here most of her life. She is familiar with all the goings-on of this household—and of the surrounding country-side," the countess mentioned pointedly. She continued questioningly, watching the play of emotions that crossed Emily's face, "You never mentioned where you came from before arriving at Yorkleigh."

"No, my lady, I suppose not," replied Emily flatly, hurrying to complete the hairstyle—so she could put an end to the intimacy of the moment and thus the questioning? Lady Clara wondered. Just a couple more pins and she would be done. The countess was wondering if she should press for answers. So far she had not asked much of anything, yet she could tell that Emily was already getting the fidgets. She decided on another tactic.

"You express yourself very well. You must have been well tutored."

"Yes, my lady, I was. There, you are all set," she said

with obvious relief. "I do hope it meets with your approval. Will it do?" Emily asked a bit nervously.

Lady Clara took pity on her. "As usual, Emily, you have worked wonders. Now, what shall I wear to charm the local gentry?" she asked with a laugh.

The earl had invited some of the local families for a small soiree for the countess to greet all the neighbors at once. Emily helped the countess select a gown and the various accessories needed for the evening.

Lady Clara was again impressed with Emily's eye for colors and fabrics. "You've been well trained, Emily. Your last mistress must have had a flair for fashion." She saw Emily flush, but the girl said nothing. The countess continued, "You are a gem. It was very fortunate for me that you were here. I am going to miss your services when Smitty finally arrives. She doesn't quite have your knack for things."

Emily simply smiled and wished the countess a good evening.

"You need not wait up for me tonight, Emily. It could be late. Just leave out my nightclothes, and you can deal with my gown in the morning."

"Thank you, my lady," Emily replied as the countess swept from the room.

A few days later the countess had just received news that her personal maid would be arriving the next day, having recovered from her indisposition, when Emily came to help her prepare for dinner.

"Tell me, Emily, what else do you know how to do? Your good education must have prepared you for more than this. There isn't even a lady for you to attend to here at Yorkleigh most of the time."

"That is true, my lady, but his lordship has assigned me to assist his secretary, Mr. Dale, and I also work with Henri, the gardener, whenever Mrs. Simms does not need me for something," replied Emily with quiet satisfaction.

"You seem remarkably contented but somewhat out of place here, my dear, don't you think?" questioned the countess gently.

"Whatever do you mean, my lady?" Emily questioned politely but guardedly.

"Well, you are obviously well educated. Do you not want to make something more of yourself than being a housemaid for the rest of your life?" the countess questioned kindly.

"There is nothing wrong with a life spent in service," Emily returned with dignity. Indeed, for the first time in her life she was truly proud of her accomplishments and of the hard work she was doing.

"You are right, of course, but maybe you would rather have a bit higher position, such as a lady's companion. I could use a personal companion, now that I am aging, to help me with my various responsibilities. What do you think? Would you like to move to Rosemount with me?"

"I don't know, my lady. I would have to think it over and ask his lordship's permission—he was so kind to give me a position when I so badly needed it. I would not want to leave him in the lurch." Emily tried to explain her hesitation while keeping her fear hidden. "I have not finished with the library either."

"I am sure Philip won't mind, Emily, but you go ahead

and think about it. I will be staying here at Yorkleigh for a while yet, so you have plenty of time to make up your mind."

Their conversation was minimal after that as they prepared the countess for her evening; she and her son had been invited to a soiree at the squire's home.

It was with a sense of relief that Emily saw Lady Clara off. All her duties were done until the countess returned. She could now give free rein to her thoughts about the countess' proposition. She was flattered that Lady Clara would make her such an offer and tempted by the better position.

Companions probably do not have to wear scratchy uniforms, she thought with a bit of vanity. And in some ways she would be safer, free of improper advances from footmen and Lord Philip's friends. It was tiresome to be unprotected. As a companion she would be viewed as a higher class, protected from such advances. However, she'd be exposed to a different form of scrutiny. Her secrets might be more threatened should she accept such a position. As a maid she was nearly invisible to anyone of higher station. Oh, how she wished she could confide in someone and seek counsel on this matter.

While she was at her wishful thinking, she thought wryly, she might as well wish time would move a bit faster. She would be so much safer once she reached one and twenty. But that was almost six months away. The pros and cons of the position with the countess chased themselves around in her mind for a long time, and finally she knew what she had to do. Lady Clara would be going to London when the Season arrived, no doubt. The king was in London. Emily knew that her sovereign could help her with her problems. She just had to stay safe for six more months. Her mind made up, Emily felt much better and briskly set to work, readying the room for the countess' return.

"Excuse me, my lord, do you have a moment? I would like to discuss a matter with you," Emily requested meekly from the doorway of the earl's library.

"Certainly, Emily. What can I help you with?" Philip asked calmly.

"Well, my lord, Lady Clara has invited me to be her companion at her other home at Rosemount. I would like to accept her invitation, but I am so appreciative of the opportunity you have given me here that I do not want to accept without your permission."

Philip felt as though he had been punched in the stomach. His first impulse was to vehemently insist that she not go; she had an obligation to him here at Yorkleigh. But he knew this was completely irrational. *Have I not been spending the last few weeks trying to avoid the girl?* he questioned himself in consternation.

"It is a great opportunity for you, Emily. I am glad for you. I think it will suit you better than doing my dusting." He tried to make light of the situation, but he knew he would miss the bright young woman and the animated discussions they had occasionally enjoyed. But this was for the best for both of them. She would be in a position that suited her far more than housemaid, and he would be rid of her disquieting presence. "Thank you for your gracious consideration of my needs, Emily, but I am sure we will get along just fine if you accept my mother's offer. You may continue in your position here until she returns home, then you will accompany her," Philip concluded imperiously.

"Thank you, my lord. I will tell her. Thank you for your time." With that Emily took herself off, berating herself for the deep well of sadness she felt at the thought of leaving the earl. *You are his maid, Emily; you have no place being interested in a lord. If only we met a year from now . . . But, no, he would only hate me for my subterfuge. It is just silly to be sad to leave here. It will be better with her ladyship,* she argued with herself as she went in search of her ladyship to accept her kind offer.

She felt a curious mixture of nerves and excitement as she anticipated another new development in her life. She marveled that the first nineteen years of her life had been so uneventful, but the past year had been a never-ending tumult of change. She would never complain of boredom again, she thought wryly. If she came out of this safely, she would never again take anything in life for granted.

"I am so pleased you decided to accept my offer, Emily. You will love Rosemount. If you enjoy working in the gardens here, you will be amazed when you see mine. As the name suggests, we specialize in roses. I am quite proud of them."

"I look forward to seeing it very much, my lady," answered Emily. They were sitting together in Lady Clara's chamber discussing the duties Emily could expect to perform when they returned to the countess' main home.

"I hesitate to ask this, not wanting to injure your feelings, but do you have any more suitable clothes, Emily? You will not have need of a uniform once you take up your new role." Being a softhearted woman, Lady Clara was sensitive to other's feelings but could not abide the thought of her companion wearing the drab uniform of a maidservant.

"Well, actually, my lady, this is all I have. Mrs. Simms provided me with it when I arrived here," Emily replied with a shy smile. "Will this not suffice?"

"No, Emily. As my companion you will receive guests and make visits with me. Don't fret," she continued after Emily's gasp of dismay. "A clothing allowance will be included with your wages. Oh, it will be such fun to dress you. My *modiste* will be delighted."

Emily felt a surge of anticipation at the upcoming treat. It would be such a pleasure to have pretty clothes again. After the grime of the asylum, she did not think she would ever be vain again, but it would be nice to dress in something other than scratchy wool. Emily's daydreams of cotton, serge, and silk were interrupted by Lady Clara's gentle question.

"Emily, I have been meaning to ask you, have you heard any of the staff speaking about Lady Maude?"

"No, my lady. Who is Lady Maude?" Emily's curiosity was piqued by the unfamiliar name and the countess' uncharacteristic hesitance over the question.

"She is the Viscount Sedgely's ill-bred daughter," was Lady Clara's cryptic response. "I will tell you more about her another day. I am just glad she has not been here. Things have not yet progressed to that point, thankfully." The countess was obviously troubled about the other woman, but Emily did not press her for details. They continued their discussion about life at Rosemount.

Despite the original plan for Emily to remain a housemaid at Yorkleigh until the countess departed for Rosemount, Lady Clara enjoyed the younger woman's company so much that she cut back Emily's other duties and they spent more time together, getting Emily used to what her situation would be once they journeyed to the countess' primary residence. They developed an enjoyable routine of getting together late each morning when Emily was through with her other chores and Lady Clara was finished with her breakfast and correspondence. Emily would choose a book from the library and read to the countess while she did her stitching.

Emily had a deep love of reading, and she immersed herself in whichever volume they had chosen, becoming completely involved with the characters, making up different voices for each one, and losing all track of time. Many in the household would stop by to enjoy the reading.

Philip was amused to come upon a small group of servants in the hallway outside the salon where his mother was sewing. At the sight of him the assembled servants quickly dispersed sheepishly, and Philip stepped into the room to see what was going on.

The countess smiled up at her son at his approach. "You have just missed the story, Philip," she informed him with regret.

"So I see." He smiled pleasantly toward Emily.

"Are you staying to visit with the countess, my lord?" questioned Emily, standing up and placing the volume on a shelf. "I could go get you some refreshments from the kitchen," she offered.

"Thank you, that would be most pleasant," replied the earl, and Emily left them to some privacy.

Lady Clara and Emily were in the salon doing needle-point when the countess heaved a deep sigh.

"What is it, Lady Clara? Something is obviously troubling you, and I would really like to help you."

"Oh, Emily, I doubt there is anything you can do. I fear my stubborn son is going to make a terrible mistake with his life. I do not mean to sound melodramatic, but I really fear for him. Remember the other day, I asked you about Lady Maude? She is a cold, heartless shrew of a young woman. She is well born, and it is said her dowry is extensive, so you can imagine how sought after she might be on the marriage mart. But despite her popularity, I have seen how she treats the less fortunate. She can be outright cruel, especially to less assured young ladies. Lady Maude is not a diamond, but she is pretty enough, if you can look past her horrid personality. Philip is considering marriage with her. He does not need her dowry and does not even need special alliances; our estates are vast, and he is shrewd about handling his investments. The reason he is interested in her is her bloodline. It is a conceit he learned from his father: perfect bloodlines for his children. Philip's father was proud of how far back he could trace his ancestors and fostered that same pride in Philip. But Philip is taking it much further than his father ever intended."

Lady Clara suspected that this snobbery was the reason

her son reacted so strangely whenever he encountered Emily. Over the weeks of her stay at Yorkleigh she had witnessed Philip's obvious pleasure in Emily's company, then his sudden withdrawal from her whenever he realized he was enjoying her company. The countess suspected that Philip was attracted to her new companion but could not reconcile that attraction with his convictions.

She broke from her thoughts and continued. "Philip's father and I were so happy in our marriage; I want the same thing for my son. I am convinced he will not find that with Lady Maude. But there is nothing I can do. He is a grown man who does not want to listen to his mama. The worst of it is, he wants me to throw a house party with her as the guest of honor so he can spend some time getting to know her and her family before he declares himself. I can barely tolerate the young woman, and her parents are little better. The thought of having her as guest of honor in my own home makes me feel slightly ill. The only good thing in the whole conundrum is the thought that maybe if he spends enough time with her, he will be able to see her for what she really is. I shall need to be shrewd in my selection of the other guests to show her to the least advantage, since I have already agreed to hostess the party."

"That sounds like a wonderful idea, my lady. I can see you have given the matter a lot of thought. It is wise to go along as much as you can. I think men can sometimes do exactly what you don't want them to do just to spite you. You would certainly not want to cause a rift between you and your only son. I will help in any way I can. We shall be devious together." The two women had a chuckle as they put their heads together to plot.

"I think it is high time we go home, Emily. I miss Rose-mount, and we need to set our plans into motion. You need a new wardrobe, and we should get this house party planned and the invitations sent out. How long will you need to pack?"

Emily laughed good-naturedly at the question. "Lady Clara, I do not own anything here at Yorkleigh, so it won't take me any time to pack. But I would be happy to help Smitty pack up your things."

"You are such a dear. It shall be a delight to have you at my home." With that the two women set off in good humor to make the necessary arrangements for their removal to the countess' principal residence.

"You're leaving?" Philip asked in surprise. "Well, Mother, perhaps it is just as well. I have just received a summons from His Majesty the king. He needs my help in some urgent matter. I am to report to the royal presence at the earliest opportunity. I plan to set out at first light. There are no details of what the matter is he needs me to attend to, so I have no idea how long I will be gone. I was going to suggest that you and Emily continue to make your home here, but if you are set to leave soon anyway, that is probably better."

"Yes, my dear, I think we will try to set out tomorrow too. Not at first light, mind you," she added drolly with a slight shudder at the thought.

"By the by, mother. I was thinking, if you are going to have Emily as your companion, we should know her sur-name and be calling her Miss whatever-her-name-is, shouldn't we? I never did learn her full name."

"You are right, dear, as you so often are. I will find out from Emily on the way home. Maybe she will finally confide more of her history to me. It will help us while away the time as we journey. And by the by to you, I have decided to plan this house party you were asking of me quite soon. Where shall I send the details?" Lady Clara was of the mind that once you put your mind to something, you should just go ahead and get it done, particularly if it was going to be unpleasant.

"Oh, thank you, Mother," he replied distractedly. "Send them to the London house. I will likely be there for a while, but if I have returned home, the staff will forward any letters here to Yorkleigh."

"Excellent. Well, we both have preparations to make. Take care, my son. It has been lovely visiting with you. Thank you, too, for sparing Emily for me."

"You are most welcome, Mother. My staff is your staff, as always," he replied in a tighter voice than before. "Safe travels, and I will see you at Rosemount soon."

Chapter Seven

Emily was gazing with rapt attention out the window, barely able to contain her excitement. Lady Clara was watching her in surprise. "Emily, why are you so intrigued with the passing scenery? Surely you must be becoming bored with the landscape; it has not changed much since we left Yorkleigh, and it is not apt to change much in the next few hours as we approach Rosemount. Tell me what you see to interest you so."

"Oh, my lady, I am so sorry. No doubt as your companion I should be making an effort to entertain you." Emily apologized sheepishly and straightened in her seat. "I quite forgot that this would not be nearly as fascinating for you. It's just that I never did much traveling, so the sights intrigue me. You see, I arrived at Yorkleigh in the boot of the earl's carriage, so I didn't see the surrounding countryside," Emily said apologetically, blushing.

"It's quite all right, my dear. I do not need entertainment. It was just surprising to see you so interested in what I consider so familiar. Carry on if you wish."

"No, my lady. If you are sure the scenery shan't change too much, please tell me more about Rosemount."

"Rosemount is a delight, Emily. I am always so happy to return after I have been away. Yorkleigh holds many precious memories for me, but Rosemount really is much more comfortable. The manor is much newer, so it is less drafty and disorganized," she explained with a chuckle. "Yorkleigh was added on to so many times that it occasionally reminds me of a rabbit warren. Rosemount is much better in that respect. You will see for yourself soon enough." The countess paused. "Before we arrive home, however, I was thinking we need to decide what to call you. Since you will officially be my companion, we need to call you something more than Emily in polite society. I will want to introduce you to the staff as well as soon as we arrive. What is your surname, my dear?"

The countess waited politely for Emily to respond. The girl looked suddenly anxious, as if her mind was racing to think of an answer. Had the maid so many names to choose from? she wondered somewhat wryly.

"Spencer, my lady. My name is Emily Spencer," she replied finally.

"That is an excellent name, Emily. I am pleased to make your acquaintance, Miss Spencer." Lady Clara laughed. "I will put you in the rose room. It is quite near my suite, so you won't feel alone. When we arrive home, it will be late, so we will retire directly. I will give you the tour tomorrow, and we can spend some time getting settled. Then we will

start planning this party we shall be throwing for Philip.
Let's try to make it fun for us too, even though we must invite the insufferable female Philip is interested in.

"That's the spirit, my lady! We will make it be the best
house party anyone has been to. Let's pick the jolliest
guests and plan the best entertainment. No one will even
notice that the 'shrew' is there. Actually, my lady, you
might want to invite some other young ladies his lordship
might be interested in. If he is in close confines with this
Lady Maude and has someone else to contrast her with,
perhaps he will see the error of his ways."

"I like the way you think, my girl. That is an excellent
idea. I will give serious thought to whom else we should
include. But for now, do you know any games we could
play to while away the hours?"

Lady Clara was surprised by Emily's enthusiastic response and even more surprised by the number of sophisticated games she was familiar with. They continued their
travels sufficiently amused, passing the time with playing
cards.

"We are just about home, Emily," the countess finally
informed her companion.

"Are we? How the time has flown. You, my lady, are a
tough opponent!" Emily complained good-naturedly. "You
are an expert at cards. We will have to think of which
games we can play during the days of the party. There will
have to be indoor games and things to do outside as well.
Do you have areas on the grounds where we can set up croquet and badminton? If we are having young people, we
shall need such activities. And are there any sights within

an easy ride of Rosemount? If so, we will need to advise those who might be interested to bring appropriate mounts for excursions. And how long will the party last? That will determine how much entertainment we need to provide." Emily was full of ideas, but the countess interrupted.

"Enough, Emily. You are exhausting me just thinking about it all. Let's get a good rest tonight, and we will give it more thought on the morrow after you have seen all that Rosemount has to offer. Then you will know for yourself which of your ideas have merit. Here we are. Prepare to meet your new home."

At that, the coach swayed to a stop in front of the magnificent manor Emily was now to call home. She gazed about with curious eyes as the footman handed her down. It was hard to see very much, as night had fallen during the journey, but she could see the house had at least forty rooms. However, despite its size, it did appear to be quite welcoming, and Emily looked forward to seeing it in the daylight.

"Welcome home, my lady." Rosemount's housekeeper stepped forward along with the butler to greet the mistress.

"Thank you, Mrs. Parks. And Mr. Parks, good evening. How have things been here in my absence?" Lady Clara greeted the couple.

"Quiet, milady. Not too much goes on while you're away. Everyone just waits for your return," laughed Mrs. Parks.

"I would like to introduce Miss Emily Spencer. She has joined our household as my companion. Please make her feel welcome. Come, Emily, meet Mr. and Mrs. Parks.

They have been with us since I joined the family, before the current earl was born."

Emily bobbed a polite curtsy to the Parkses. She knew it was important to be friendly with the housekeeper and butler, especially when they were a team. She found herself holding her breath, waiting to see if they would accept her or not. The pair barely batted an eyelash when told that this young girl dressed in a servant's uniform was to be their mistress' companion.

"Welcome, Miss Spencer. If you need anything, just let me know," welcomed Mrs. Parks warmly. "Spencer, you say? Are you any relation to old Lord Spencer over in Bancroft? My sister's husband's cousin is his housekeeper."

Emily's smile froze on her face. "Not that I am aware of, Mrs. Parks," she answered a bit stiffly, hoping the countess had not noticed.

Lady Clara might have, but she made no comment, and they were ushered in to greet the rest of the servants who had waited up for them. Everyone was further distracted by the bustle of activity produced by bringing in the baggage and getting everyone settled for the night.

Emily was relieved to finally be left alone in her new room. She surveyed her surroundings in delight. *It is a definite step up from servants' quarters,* she thought as she tested out the comfort of the bed and enjoyed the luxury of a spacious chamber. *It will be so nice to have a room to myself again,* she thought with a sigh of contentment. She remembered with delight that Lady Clara had requested one of the footmen to take a message to the dressmaker first thing in the morning. *And it will be so good to have something better to wear,* she thought as she hung up her serviceable frock and put on her nightgown.

Emily felt guilty at the thought, since she knew she should be grateful for what she had in comparison to where she had been just a couple of months previously. She pushed those worries aside as she climbed into the soft bed that had been turned down and warmed by one of the maids. Emily's last thought before sleep finally claimed her was that it was nice not to be a maid anymore. She fell asleep with a smile on her face.

The pleasure Emily felt the next morning as a maid entered the room carrying morning chocolate for her was nearly indescribable. "Oh, thank you so much! That is exactly what I wanted. What is your name?" Emily thought to inquire, remembering her vow to herself not to take anyone for granted.

"I'm Maggie, miss," the maid answered hesitantly.

"I am pleased to make your acquaintance. And I will be very pleased to see you every morning if you bring me chocolate just like this." She smiled at Maggie as she climbed out of the big bed. "I actually do not have much need of you this morning, though, aside from bringing my water if you would be so kind. There will be more to do after I have seen the dressmaker, I am sure."

"Very good, miss," replied the maid politely before she withdrew to get the water for Emily to wash in.

Emily gazed around herself with pleasure. *I am going to be happy here, I think,* she mused with contentment. *Clean, warm, and cozy—what more could a girl ask for?* She smiled as she tugged on her uniform. *Greater variety in clothing,* replied her vanity. *That will be looked after in due time,* thought Emily, determined to be happy with her new lot.

She reminded herself that she just had to stay safe for a few more months, and then she would gain control over her own life. She worried that she was more exposed here than as a maid at Yorkleigh, but this situation suited her better, and Lady Clara would keep her safe. *Besides, no one ever notices the servants,* she thought. *And, really, a companion is just a glorified servant,* she reassured herself. In the meantime Maggie had returned with her steaming water, and Emily quickly washed, then set out to find the countess.

"I have asked Mrs. Parks to join us on our tour. As we look around, she can start making our plans for the house party," Lady Clara informed Emily as they finished their morning meal.

The three women proceeded to poke their noses into every corner of the large manor. Mrs. Parks took notes of all the instructions Lady Clara and Emily had for her.

"We should start airing out the unused bedrooms," Emily mused aloud. "If we start now, it will not be such a burden when we get closer to the arrival date for the guests."

"That's an efficient idea, Miss Spencer," admired Mrs. Parks. "I'll be off now, milady, to see to my other duties. You and Miss Spencer will do all right without me on your tour of the grounds, I'm sure."

"Thank you for your time, Mrs. Parks." Lady Clara graciously excused her.

Lady Clara and Emily exited through the drawing room

out onto the vast, manicured lawn leading gently to the woods, which interspersed the entire estate. The extensive rose gardens were off to the east of the house, the stables off to the west. To the south, on the other side of a copse of trees, were the ruins of the old abbey. Lady Clara pointed out the landmarks as they wandered toward the gardens.

"The lawn area would be perfect for croquet or badminton, wouldn't it?" asked Emily. "And these gardens will give everyone hours of enjoyment. You must have an entire army of gardeners maintaining these beautiful blooms," admired Emily, overtaken by their heady perfume.

"Yes, we do have quite a number of gardeners. You are welcome to assist them whenever the mood strikes you. Now come, my dear, my modiste Juliette will be arriving shortly. In the meantime, you can help me with my correspondence, if you please."

"It will be my pleasure, my lady." With that the two women returned to the salon, where the countess' secretaire was kept, and they spent an enjoyable interlude composing notes to the countess' various friends in the shire, informing them of her return home.

"So we need to set a date for this party, my lady, as well as figure out the exact guest list and what we are going to do with everyone. We can finalize our plans once everyone has replied if they are coming or not." Emily was sitting at the secretaire with a sheaf of paper, a pen, and a small ink bottle at the ready. "How many people are you planning to invite? Shall we plan a ball as the climax of the event? Perhaps invite the gentry from the surrounding area for various activities?"

"Slow down, Emily!" exclaimed Clara with a slight chuckle. "Yes, a ball will be the perfect ending to the house party, and, yes, for that we will invite the gentry from around here. The sons and daughters of my local friends will be very excited to be invited, I am quite sure. I think the event should be at most a week. Some will have commitments and won't be able to come for the entire week but will arrive as the days pass. We will, of course, have the Lady Maude, her brother, and her parents, Lord and Lady Sedgely; Lord and Lady Fitzgerald and their daughter, Julia; Lord Marsden; Lady Waddell and her two daughters, Jane and Ann; and Lord Sutherland. We will start with those invitations first; they will have the farthest to travel. Please write up invitations and see that they are sent out."

Lady Clara paused as she thought of whom else to invite. "I need to give a bit of thought to a few more people. We must speak to the Parkses about hiring some temporary help from the village. Cook will definitely need extra hands in the kitchen. I think you have given sufficient thought to entertainment. Maybe mention in the invitation that if they wish to bring their mounts, they are welcome to. I will make sure there is something suitable for you to ride."

At that Emily interrupted, "Really, my lady? You'll find me a mount? I have not been riding in ever so long. It shall be such a great pleasure."

"Are you an experienced horsewoman, Emily? It will be a pleasure to provide you with a suitable mount, to be sure. Now, where was I? Oh, yes, don't forget to write to Philip telling him the details and the dates so he will be here on time. Let's plan to have people arriving in about three weeks, with the ball exactly four weeks from today. That will give us plenty of time, won't it?"

The Right Honorable Earl of Yorkleigh
The London House

Dear Lord Yorkleigh:

The Lady Clara and I have arrived safely at Rosemount, and all is well with us and the household here. We trust that the same can be said of you and your household. We wish to inform you that the plans for the party are progressing quite well. There will be approximately twenty guests in residence for parts of the week. Your presence is politely requested no later than three weeks from this date.

On another matter, could you please have someone rearrange the shelves of your library containing the works of poetry according to the enclosed list? I have been thinking about how I shelved them while I was there, and I realize that I did it according to my own preference, which, upon reflection, I realize was quite presumptuous. I think the enclosed list contains a much better sequence for shelving. No doubt you would agree.

As well, I have enclosed instructions from your lady mother's head gardener for a better way of grooming the roses. As you know, Rosemount specializes in roses, so could you please pass these instructions on to Henri? I am quite sure he will appreciate them greatly.

We await your attendance upon us here at Rosemount with keen anticipation. We trust your work for His Majesty the king is progressing satisfactorily.

Your humble servant,
Miss Emily Spencer
Rosemount

"Can you believe the little baggage is giving us instructions now, James? And on the proper maintenance of the rose gardens! How do you suppose Henri is going to react?" The earl burst into laughter at the audacity of his former maid.

"Actually, my lord, Henri was quite taken with Miss Emily and will probably be delighted that she remembered him. The library is surely going to seem empty without her when we return to Yorkleigh," replied Mr. Dale wistfully.

"So you have fallen under the little minx's spell as well as Henri, have you, my boy?" queried Philip sardonically. He was secretly delighted by the tone of Miss Spencer's letter. He would have to remember to call her Miss Spencer while he was at Rosemount. It would seem much too familiar to be addressing his mother's paid companion by her Christian name. *It will be a pleasure to see the pretty chit again, though,* he thought.

He would certainly be glad to have this business for the king out of the way. *Progressing satisfactorily,* she had said. *I wish it were,* he thought gloomily. The king had him looking for a needle in a haystack. A peeress of the realm was missing, and somehow it had become his job to find her. Why the king thought he would be able to find the chit, he had no idea.

He would begin his search by speaking to Lord Edwin, the new Viscount Ridley, to see what he had to say for himself. He had the most to gain by the young woman's disappearance, as he was her legal guardian until she came of age. Philip did not believe the story Lord Edwin had related to the king. The king didn't believe it himself, but it would not do to accuse a peer of lying straight to the monarch's face, without irrefutable evidence. The fact that the man seemed shifty was not proof enough, unfortunately.

Of course, Philip reflected, it was a good thing that the king trusted him with a matter that he was taking so seriously. He just hoped he could live up to the king's expectations.

"James, we will need to get more information about Viscount Ridley before we go to meet with him. I want you to find out where he was before he inherited his title, who were his friends and who his enemies. Someone as shifty as Ridley is sure to have some of each. Get whatever help you need. I require this information as quickly as possible. The king wants this matter cleared up."

"It shouldn't be a problem to find out about Ridley. I will get started immediately." James declared, eager to investigate the mystery. "When will you be meeting with him?"

"I am going to his new estate in a couple of days to speak with him in private. The only time I ever met him was when we were in audience with the king. He seemed far too nervous for it to be just awe of the monarch. The king and I both feel he is hiding something, but we need to find out what it is before we make any accusations."

"Certainly, my lord, I will see to it immediately. I know of a few individuals who make it their business to know things. That's where I will start."

"That is excellent, James. I am going to ask around at the clubs to see who knew Ridley before he ascended to the title. We can meet back here late this evening."

"Very good, milord."

With that both men departed on their errands, deep in thoughtful suspicions about this new member of the peerage and what he might or might not know about the missing young lady.

Chapter Eight

Two evenings later the earl sat at his large desk in his library staring despondently into the fire burning in the grate.

"James, I am really having a bad feeling about this. Everywhere we turn, there are allegations about Ridley. Nothing has ever been proven, but the rumors that swirl around him should have made any parent hesitant to declare him guardian to their daughter. What was the marquis thinking when he left his young daughter in his care?" The earl was angry in his frustration over the lack of information about the missing young lady.

"In defense of the deceased marquis, milord, perhaps he did not know what suspicions were attached to Lord Edwin. From what we have learned, the marquis and his wife removed themselves from society many years ago and retired on their principal estate. Would you harbor suspicions over your relations and have them investigated?" asked the secretary reasonably.

"If I was going to leave my children to them, I should like to think I would be responsible enough to ensure beyond any doubt that they would be in good hands," answered Philip heatedly.

"That's reasonable, but we also have found out that both the marquis and marchioness died suddenly in a carriage accident. They no doubt never thought a guardian would ever actually be required for their only child. They were planning to live to see the births of grandchildren who would inherit their wealth and titles, not this distant cousin they knew little about. Naming him as guardian was merely a formality."

"You are no doubt right, James, but let this be a lesson to you to always think of all the possibilities. All rights, let's review what we have found out so far. I drive out to meet the scoundrel tomorrow morning. I have not been able to find anyone who speaks highly of him. Many were unaware of him before he gained the viscountcy, but I met a couple of gentlemen who suspected him of cheating at cards. He has actually been blackballed from several of the hells."

"I too have heard of suspicions of cheating, but it is the missing women in his past that has me the most concerned, milord. In the town where he grew up, there are two peasant families who had beautiful daughters who disappeared after Ridley took an interest in them. Foul play was suspected, but no one could prove anything, and he has remained free. He and his friend, Lord Maximillian Woolfe, are suspected of many things in the village, but they made themselves scarce as soon as Ridley inherited his estate. You will no doubt have to confront the two of them when you go there on the morrow."

"So we are still really no further ahead, are we, James? Everything is merely hearsay and conjecture at this point. However, I think it would be best if you come with me after all. I was planning to go by myself, but Ridley has granted his permission to speak with the servants, and it would likely go more smoothly if there are two of us. Besides, some may be more comfortable talking to you. You seem to have a way with people." The earl laughed in self-mockery.

"You have a way with people too, milord. It's just your title that sometimes gets in the way," returned the younger man calmly.

"Well, James, we had best get a good rest tonight. I want to make an early start tomorrow and get these interviews over with. The longer we take to find the girl, the greater the risk to her safety. As it is, I am beginning to doubt if she is ever going to be found."

"I hope you are wrong, milord. We will see what we can find out tomorrow. Good night."

After James let himself out of the room quietly, Philip leaned back in his chair thoughtfully. Talking about what he would do if he had children to provide for had gotten him thinking. He was intrigued by the ideas running through his head. He really did need to consider setting up his nursery. The countess had recently begun asking after grandchildren. As his mind drifted into thoughts of his future, he was shocked to see Emily's face smiling down at his hypothetical children. He shook his head in dismay;

he really was becoming obsessive about the little maid. She was a striking young woman, but, really, his mother's companion was not a suitable mother for the heir to the earldom of Yorkleigh.

James and Philip rode out not long after the sun rose the next morning. It would take them at least an hour to ride to Ridley's estate, and they were hoping to get as much accomplished that day as possible. They went across country, taking shortcuts the earl was familiar with in order to make faster time. Despite the gravity of their errand, the two men enjoyed the beautiful morning and the view as they passed, but they harbored disquieting thoughts about what they might or might not find out that day.

James was the first to break the silence. "I can't help being surprised that his lordship has given his permission for us to question his staff. How did you convince him?"

Philip laughed ruefully. "I didn't. It was actually the king who commanded Edwin to allow the questioning. The old marquis made his home on the estate much of the time, and Ridley has retained most of the staff, so we realized that some of the servants might know something. They may even know where the girl is or whom she might confide in or turn to for help. It might provide us with some new leads, at least."

"I wonder if they will feel free to speak if they are aware of their new master's past sins. There may be considerable fear to overcome," replied James dubiously.

"That is part of the reason we have started out so early, my boy. I heard Lord Ridley never rises before noon.

With luck we will be able to speak to many of the servants before he even realizes we have arrived."

"Clever plan, my lord," congratulated Mr. Dale as they clattered into the courtyard of their destination. Unfortunately, their plan was soon to be thwarted.

Philip approached the door and was reaching for the knocker when it was opened by a gaunt-looking butler. The butler ushered them into the foyer unsmilingly and waited for them to state their intentions.

"Good morning. I am Philip, Earl of Yorkleigh. The king has sent me here in search of information about Lady Emmaline. The marchioness is missing, and we have been authorized to question the staff. Would you please arrange for us to speak individually with the servants who would have known the previous residents?"

The cadaverous-looking servant just stood there blinking at the earl as if he didn't understand what Philip was asking. Philip tried again.

"Did you know the Marquis of Edenvale?"

"Yes, my lord. I have served here for forty-five years. I knew the marquis and his father before him," the butler answered in a gloomy tone.

"Excellent, then we will start with you. Did you know Lady Emmaline?"

Philip noticed the first real emotions cross the old man's face. It was obvious he knew and was fond of her. But he also appeared sad and afraid.

"Yes, my lord, I knew her," he answered shortly with a sad smile. "She was the sweetest child ever to grace this house."

"Do you know what has become of the young lady?"

Philip questioned gently. He could not help but notice that the butler had used the term *was* in reference to the marchioness. He wondered if the servants knew what had really happened to the gently bred woman.

"No, my lord, that I do not, and that's all I have to say on the matter. I'll let his lordship know you're here, my lord." The old butler began to shuffle away.

Philip tried to stop him. "It's not necessary to disturb Lord Ridley. Mr. Dale and I can speak with the servants without waking his lordship. We do have his permission to ask our questions."

"You may have permission, but I have my orders," replied the butler before continuing on his way.

Philip and James looked at each other in chagrin. Their plan of questioning the servants without the viscount's presence was about to be ruined. They were left standing in the foyer for several minutes before the butler returned.

"Lord Ridley will be with you in a few minutes. If you'll come with me into the salon, a footman will offer you refreshments. Please make yourselves comfortable. My lord will be with you momentarily." With that the old butler bowed himself politely from the room as quickly as he could.

Philip turned to James with a quirked eyebrow. "That was exceedingly strange. The fellow seemed most uncomfortable with our questions, don't you think?"

"Yes, it does seem as though he was afraid of what we were asking. Do you suppose the viscount has instructed his servants not to answer our questions?"

"It would seem so, James. Let's see what he has to say

when he gets himself out of bed. I hate to think that we have wasted our time in coming all this way."

"I wouldn't call it a waste of time, my lord. If we know he has forbidden the servants to speak to us, it proves he has something to hide, don't you think?"

"But we still cannot prove anything, James, can we?"

"No, it seems not," James concluded in dismay.

"Don't worry, James, we will get to the bottom of this eventually. It is just going to take a little longer than we had planned. Let's wait and see what Ridley has to say."

"Sorry to keep you waiting, my lord. I had not expected callers so early," apologized the viscount smoothly as he entered the room.

Philip had to repress a shudder. He wasn't sure if it was his imagination combining with what he had learned about the Lord Ridley, but to his mind the man *looked* as if he was involved in shady dealings. From his greasy hair combed back in an unflattering style to his small, shifty eyes and his clothing that looked as if too much effort went into making him appear a man of means, the new viscount looked like trouble. Ridley reminded one of a weasel eyeing up the henhouse. Again he wondered how the marquis could have left a vulnerable young woman in the care of such a scoundrel.

"We haven't been waiting long," Philip replied politely, hoping he would still be able to speak with the servants who had known the marquis and his family. "We actually did not mean to disturb you at all; we were hoping to speak to some of your servants about your cousin, the marchioness. The king is most dismayed over her continued absence in his court, and he wishes for this matter to be resolved as quickly as possible. I'm sure you understand."

The viscount paled slightly at the mention of the king and the missing marchioness but maintained a calm veneer. He cleared his voice before replying.

"Of course, I fully understand the gravity of the situation. It is such a tragedy that my poor, dear little cousin has gone missing, and it is such a comfort to me that our faithful sovereign has taken an interest in the matter. I truly appreciate your efforts, but I was not aware that you would be coming today. None of the staff will be available to speak with you today, as they are all very busy with various tasks. However, if you would care to make an appointment, I will ensure that they will be prepared to speak with you at a more convenient time. The other problem is that many of the servants who were most familiar with the marquis and his family have dispersed among his various holdings. If you wish, I can have them all gathered in one place, but that could take a considerable amount of time, which I am sure you can appreciate. So, my lord, when would you like to return so that I can have everyone ready to speak with you?" Edwin's smile held a tinge of smugness, as if he was sure he had thwarted the nosy earl and his assistant.

Philip itched to plant Ridley a facer for his obvious lack of cooperation. However, he maintained his equanimity through sheer force of will. The smile he turned on the viscount had an edge of steel to it, and Ridley lost some of his assuredness.

"I am sure the king will be ever so pleased with your willingness to help," Philip said sarcastically. "Do not bother gathering the servants. I am expected at my mother's estate in a week's time. After my visit with her, I will return to speak with whichever of the marquis' servants are still in residence here. Shall we say in two weeks time, if that will not inconvenience your household overly?"

"Oh, yes, two weeks notice should be most adequate. Thank you. Can I offer you gentlemen some refreshments before you go?" With any threat to himself delayed, Edwin seemed more inclined to be generous.

Philip was repulsed at the thought of sharing this man's hospitality. "I do not think so. We need to be going. This has been a waste of our time, and there are many other things we could accomplish this day. We will see you in a fortnight, Ridley."

Philip and James strode from the house briskly, surprised to see that their horses had been left standing outside and had not been provided for. They shook their heads in disgust over such poor, miserly manners, mounted up, and rode to a nearby village with an inn where they could feed their horses and have refreshment themselves while they gave thought to what their next move should be.

After seeing to their horses and being served by the landlord, who had profusely proclaimed his honor at their presence, Philip and James sat down to discuss their options.

"James, I think the best plan would be to go back to the house in London, pack a couple of bags, and set out on a round of as many of the old marquis' holdings as we can manage in the week before we are promised to my mother. The viscount will then not have an opportunity to train all the servants on what they are to say or get rid of any who do not want to cooperate with him. And we will not have wasted two weeks of precious time while the young marchioness is still missing. Maybe we will have found her before we leave for Rosemount."

James shook his head in doubt. "I think it is a sound plan, milord, but I would advise you not to expect to find her any time too soon. By my thinking she either does not want to be found or she has met some foul end, and we may never find out what happened to her."

"Don't be a pessimist, James. I have full confidence in our ability to locate the wench. Now drink up. We should be on our way. If we can make good time, I want to reach the seat of the earldom of Spence, one of the marquis' lesser properties. We could make it there in a couple of hours, find a room at the inn, and speak to the servants on the estate tomorrow morning."

The two men quickly finished their repast, paid the landlord, and got on their way. They had many miles to cover in the next week and not a moment to waste.

Philip and James were nearly numb with fatigue by the time they rolled into the courtyard of the Hatfield Inn late that night. The last few miles had been rough going in the dark, their lanterns casting only a weak glow upon the road ahead. Philip's eyes felt as though they were filled with sand, and he could barely keep them open. Only his keen determination had kept them on the road; he could not bear the thought of having wasted so much time and needed to at least reach a destination where they could ask about the marquis.

It was with profound relief that the two men climbed down from their carriage and entered the inn. They were shown to decent rooms and provided with a light repast before they retired to sleep off the effects of their mad dash around England.

The next morning they were up with the cock crowing, determined to find answers. The landlord was happy to provide directions to the Spence estate after serving them a hearty breakfast. Philip felt refreshed and optimistic as he and James rode out of the inn yard.

They clattered to a halt before the magnificent main building on Spence land. Philip gazed in appreciation at the unique architecture of the old manor house and its well-kept property. The front door of the dwelling was quickly opened by an alert footman, and the dignified butler stepped out to greet them.

When Philip explained the purpose of his visit, the butler ushered him and James into a comfortable front room and sent a footman for refreshments while he explained that, re-grettably, he knew little about the young marchioness.

"I am truly sorry, my lord. The young lady was popular among the servants, but the family really kept to themselves. The only one I can think of that my lady might have confided in is her old nurse. Have you spoken with her?" questioned the worried butler.

"We have not yet had the pleasure, but we fully intend to, sir," Philip answered kindly. "Is there anyone else you could think of, preferably on this estate, with whom we might speak?"

The older man thought the matter over for a moment

before answering doubtfully. "The housekeeper would be your best bet, my lord. She and the old marchioness were quite close, so she might know more about whom the young lady would turn to if she were in trouble. I will bring her here to speak with you, if you will excuse me." The butler bowed himself from the room as a footman came in with small sandwiches and drinks to offer the gentlemen.

The two men were left cooling their heels, waiting for the housekeeper. They heard her coming long before they could see her, and the two men exchanged a glance as they heard the clink of the housekeeper's ringful of keys.

"Terribly sorry to keep you waiting, milord. Hodges tells me you have some questions about the young marchioness?" she questioned briskly as she jingled to a stop in front of Philip. "We are all just heartsore that something has happened to the dear young thing! But we haven't seen hide nor hair of her since before the marquis and his dear wife passed on, so I wouldn't be able to say where the wee thing might be, milord." She paused, deep in melancholy thought, before her face hardened and she continued in a different tone of voice. "Have you spoken to Lord Woolfe? He's a shifty fellow, that one. Came here a couple of weeks ago, sniffing after the young marchioness' belongings. He claimed to be an agent of the young lady's guardian, but he seemed like he was up to no good, if you ask me."

At the mention of Max Woolfe, Philip grew more attentive. He had been disappointed to learn that once again no one in the household had anything constructive to add to their search, but this was a new bit of information.

"Why would Ridley send an agent to Spence?" he wondered aloud.

"Greed," was the housekeeper's succinct opinion. "We sent him on his way. Told him that unless we learned otherwise, our mistress was the Marchioness of Edenvale, and he was to mind his own never-mind. None too happy he was, I can tell you that much, milord. Left here in a bit of a snit, not that any of us minded much. Sinister young man—didn't want to let him around any of the maidservants, that's for certain."

"How long ago did you say he was here?" questioned Philip gently.

"Oh, nigh on a fortnight, I would say, milord. I think he went back to tattle to Ridley that we wouldn't make him comfortable here." The housekeeper didn't seem overly concerned about the viscount's good opinion.

"Thank you so much for your help, ma'am. We should be on our way. We need to find the young lady as soon as possible, as I am sure you can imagine."

The kindly old housekeeper nodded sagely. "You'll find her, milord. You seem to be a good sort of man, even if you're a bit too shiny."

Philip was unsure how to react to that pronouncement, so he merely accepted his hat from the butler and made to leave before the housekeeper interrupted him again. "Milord, we took the liberty of having the cook prepare you a basket. You'll need some sustenance while you search for our wee lady. You bring her back to us safe and sound, milord. We'll be waiting."

As Philip and James swung themselves up into their

carriage, the old butler and housekeeper stood waving them off until they drove down the lane.

"That wasn't terribly informative, but it was a much warmer reception than we received at Ridley, wasn't it, James? How do you suppose Woolfe figures into all of this?"

"I was wondering the same thing myself," James said. "We will have to speak to him at our earliest opportunity."

Philip fell into silence as they continued their travels. They had a fair distance to cover as they headed out toward Edenvale, near Grantham. The two men were hoping to make it as far as possible that day in order to reach the estate and speak to the servants the next day. Their intention was to also visit at the seat of the barony of Westland on their way back toward Rosemount. They were going to be covering many miles in the next few days, and the task was daunting, but Philip kept his disquieting musings to himself as the miles rolled slowly by.

A few hours later he had reached one conclusion. "I am certainly going to have a conversation with His Majesty about the condition of these roads once all this is said and done, James. If it didn't take so long to get from place to place, our search might be not be so arduous. I'm not sure if my nerves can handle much more of this, never mind the state of my wheels," grumbled the earl.

James laughed. "Perhaps you should take your seat in the House of Lords and stir up some politics toward road maintenance."

"Let's not get carried away, James. There's a large gap between complaining and campaigning." The two men laughed good-naturedly and continued their journey, in better humor.

Unfortunately, the next day proved even more fruitless than the one before. The servants at Edenvale were well-meaning but uninformative. The marquis and his family had not spent much time on that estate in the last few years, merely making brief visits to insure all was well there, as he had made Spence his principal residence in recent times. The servants had no idea where the young marchioness would have gone if she needed help, only pointing out what Philip already knew about—the close bond between the young woman and her old nurse.

Again, though, they heard of a visit from the villainous-seeming Lord Maximillian Woolfe. The servants of Edenvale had also put a run to him, not allowing him to poke about the estate, being highly suspicious of his intentions. Philip was growing in determination to question the man at the earliest opportunity as he wondered impotently what involvement he might have in the young lady's disappearance and why Ridley had him riding about the countryside checking on her properties.

By that time, Philip was becoming somewhat dispirited by the endless traveling and fruitless search. The entire thing was beginning to feel like an exercise in futility, and he started to wonder if he should just give up and go home. But he was due at Rosemount in a couple of days, and the last place to look, the holding of the barony of Westland, was not too far out of the way, so he was determined to stop there on the way to the countess' house party.

Since this route had poorer roads and fewer places to change the horses, the men were making much slower progress, and it was with heartfelt relief that they finally reached their destination late the next evening. They settled into the local inn to refresh themselves, with the intention of getting an early start the next morning to speak with the Westland servants and drive on to Rosemount.

Their surprise knew no bounds when they drove up to the gates of Westland and were admitted by a nervous-looking butler who informed them that his lordship would be with them momentarily. Philip and his secretary waited impatiently to see which lordship would be coming to greet them.

"Welcome to Westland, Lord Yorkleigh," rasped the voice of a man unfamiliar to Philip. He was darkly sallow with untrustworthy eyes and greasy hair and skin. He looked as if he had never worked a day in his life and was struggling to control his burgeoning waistline with a poorly concealed girdle. He emitted a slightly unpleasant odor, and Philip looked at him askance.

Then it dawned on Philip quite suddenly who this unknown personage must be. "Lord Woolfe. What a surprise to find you here. Are you endeavoring to help us in our search for the missing Marchioness of Edenvale, Lady Emmaline?"

Something darkly unpleasant shifted in Lord Woolfe's eyes at the mention of Lady Emmaline, but he managed to suppress it before answering Philip's question.

"As her guardian, Lord Ridley has asked me to check on the young lady's properties to ensure that all will be well with them when she returns to her estates," he replied in an effort at reasonableness, which was belied by the evil glint in his eyes.

Woolfe stood regarding his two unwelcome visitors, trying unsuccessfully to mask his malicious antipathy toward them. He had not met the young earl of Yorkleigh before, but he had heard of him by reputation. Despite his penchant for fast living, the young earl was known for his honesty and work ethic, both qualities Lord Woolfe regarded askance. Anyone who worked honestly was likely too slow mentally to do otherwise and was thus beneath his notice. Of course, the earl was acting as agent for the king and must therefore be shown a certain level of respect. With this in mind, Max thought hospitality would be in order.

"Might I offer you gentlemen a light repast before you continue on your way?" His attempt at cordiality fell flat, but Philip remained polite nonetheless.

"Thank you, Woolfe, we could use a drink. We have been on the road for quite a while. We have actually stopped by to speak with some of the servants. His Royal Highness, King George, has ordered that we speak to all the servants who may have been familiar with the marchioness or her parents," explained the earl calmly.

At mention of the king, Woolfe's face paled even more, but he managed to hold his ground. "None of the servants here knows anything, unfortunately. I have already taken the liberty of speaking with them myself."

"Well, that was most kind of you," replied Philip, his voice dripping with sarcasm. "But we would still like to speak with the housekeeper and butler when they have a moment. And while we are waiting for the refreshments you so kindly offered us, perhaps we could ask you a few questions."

Stymied, Max finally sat down, realizing he could not rid himself of the tenacious earl as easily as he had hoped. Philip and James also sat before beginning to probe.

"How do you know the marchioness?"

"I do not know the young woman very well at all. I am an old friend of her guardian, the viscount of Ridley. I had just met the ungrateful little cretin before she ran away," declared Woolfe, realizing he had an opportunity to redirect the search.

"Why would you call her ladyship an 'ungrateful cretin'? Had you performed some service for her for which she failed to show appreciation?" questioned Philip, vastly surprised by this attack on the otherwise well-spoken-of young noblewoman.

"She had a dreadful attitude and gave my dear friend such a hard time." Realizing he could not go too far in this vein, he made another effort at reasonableness. "Of course, in her defense, she had just recently lost her parents and was perhaps misbehaving because of her grief; however, I have never seen the like of the tantrums she would throw when Edwin would not buy her all the things she demanded of him."

"That is quite interesting, Woolfe," replied Philip. "And surprising too. All we have heard of the young woman is how well-liked she is and what a wonderful family the Marquis of Edenvale had."

"Well, of course the servants would speak well of her. They aren't stupid. When she gets back, she could sack the lot of them if they were speaking ill of her in her absence," was Max's smooth answer to Philip's prodding.

James, who had spent the better part of the last month researching the missing young lady and felt that he knew her better than this pompous, viperlike lord, stood up and declared, "You shut your trap! Lady Emmaline is not an ungrateful chit. Everyone from the butler down to the lowliest scullery servant has nothing but good to say. The pastor in every parish sponsored by the marchioness, as well as anyone we could find who ever knew the young woman, sings her praises. Except you. What are you hiding, my lord? If any foul deed has been happened upon her at your hand, we will ensure you get your just desserts."

Philip wanted to applaud his usually even-tempered secretary's heated outburst and managed just barely to maintain his calm veneer as he and James walked from the room.

Woolfe blustered but they paid him no heed. "Where are you going?" Max demanded as Philip headed out the front door. "You cannot just wander around this property!"

"Why not? You do," was Philip's snide reply.

Philip and James strode off in search of the housekeeper. They had a brief, equally fruitless conversation with her. The only new information they were able to glean from the woman was that Lord Woolfe had been in residence for three days and had terrorized the household. There was nothing Philip could do about that, so they had to leave the matter alone.

After leaving Westland Manor they stopped by the manse and spoke with the local cleric. He knew little to add to what scant information they already had, aside

Chapter Nine

Whthe earl was busy investigating, the countess and Emily spent an enjoyable but busy few weeks tending to various responsibilities, overseeing the growth of Emily's wardrobe, and planning for the forthcoming house party. They amused themselves by devising plots to show Philip the foolishness of his pursuit of Lady Maude, congratulating themselves on the wisdom of joining forces.

Emily had not even met the other young woman, but from the countess' description of her and for her own personal reasons, which she refused to fully acknowledge, she was more than happy to scheme with Lady Clara. The time flew by, and before they knew it, they were expecting their guests to begin arriving. Rosemount had been polished, shined, and buffed, and the air was abuzz with excitement. Rosemount hadn't been the site for an entertainment in quite some time, and all the inhabitants, from lowly scrub-boy to the gentry in the surrounding neighborhood, were thrilled at the prospects that lay before them.

The first guests to arrive were the Waddell ladies. They were a pleasant trio, the widowed baroness and her two daughters, Jane and Ann. Lady Waddell was a plump woman with a rosy face that looked as though it would rather smile than frown. She was prepared to enjoy herself fully, and her young daughters took after her in that particular. While Jane and Ann were slightly taller and far slimmer than their mother, the family resemblance was unmistakable, and one only had to look at the mother to know how the daughters would age. Jane had darker curls than her younger sister, while Ann had the look of one who had not quite grown out of her pigtails and short dresses yet. On the whole the three ladies seemed likely to be enjoyable company, and Lady Clara was pleased to see her friend.

The five women settled in the small salon after the Waddells had been shown to their rooms and had left the maids unpacking their trunks. Emily went to fetch the tea trolley. She didn't know any of the people being spoken about, so she found the conversation somewhat insipid.

People should have other things to do than care about who said or did what to whom when, she thought as she was returning to the room. *Although,* she reasoned, *the three ladies do seem pleasant enough, and nothing they said was malicious.* So she determined to try to enjoy the visit.

Emily was carefully guiding the trolley into the room when she almost tripped, shocked at the turn the conversation had taken.

Lady Waddell was speaking. "The Regent is getting concerned—so the rumor goes—about this Lady Emmaline. Apparently she is quite an important personage," the women declared with a flourish. "She is the sole heiress to a vast fortune and multiple titles, which devolve upon the heirs general. Sadly, it seems both her parents recently died, and she was their only child. It was the dearest wish of Lord Hamptonbrook, the Marquis of Edenvale, that his daughter receive all the titles he and his wife possessed, aside from, of course, the more recent one, the Viscountcy of Ridley, which has to go to the nearest male relation. The king wants to officially confer the titles and so on upon her as the parents had wished, but she seems to be missing. Viscount Ridley claims to have no knowledge of her whereabouts, and he does not seem overly concerned, despite being her legal guardian. It is rumored that the viscountcy came with very little in terms of monetary gain, and he is holding the girl's purse strings while she is missing. He does not seem to be searching too hard for the poor girl, so the king has involved himself in the matter." She paused for a moment before turning her blue eyes, bright with excitement, upon Lady Clara.

"Have you even heard of this Lady Emmaline? Did you know the Hamptonbrooks when they were more active in the ton, Lady Clara? It is said that the marquis and his wife had been living quite retired from society for the last many years, so no one even knows where to start looking for their poor, dear orphan. If the girl does not show up, her fortune will line the king's pockets, I'm sure. I do hope the poor girl turns up unharmed."

During this monologue Emily had felt all the blood drain from her face. It was only the tea trolley that kept her from falling down. She felt separated from the events around her and observed distractedly that Lady Waddell was actually able to sound both concerned and thrilled at once. Emily heard Lady Clara making similarly concerned murmurs and managed to pull herself together. She was thankful all the ladies had been so engrossed with the tale that no one had witnessed her loss of composure. She dared not reveal what she knew!

After making suitable comments about the tragic circumstances of the unknown orphan, the younger of Lady Waddell's daughters changed the subject yet again, and the chatter continued to flow. After a couple of pained moments Emily was able to compose herself enough to participate somewhat in the conversation and serve the tea without disgracing herself. Shortly after the tea was poured, the sound of carriage wheels was again heard in the driveway. Lady Clara got up to welcome the newest arrivals.

Lord and Lady Sedgely swept into the drawing room with a distinct air of superiority and with their daughter, Lady Maude, in their wake. Their son, the Honorable Garfield, followed them slowly. He had a twinkle in his eye, as though amused by his family's attitude. Lord and Lady Sedgely oddly resembled each other in a tight-lipped, narrow-eyed kind of way. Their whole family had chestnut brown hair and blue eyes and would have been most attractive if they didn't seem so unpleasant.

Emily found herself scrutinizing Lady Maude, surprised to see that she was not even very pretty—certainly no "diamond of the first water," as the ladies Waddell would say. Emily wondered what Lord Philip was thinking to be interested in this cold-looking woman. As always, though, her sense of fairness came to the fore, and she decided the woman must have redeeming qualities. It was not right to judge by appearances, despite her predisposition to dislike the other woman. She would wait and see how Lady Maude turned out.

While Emily looked on, Lady Clara started to make the introductions but was interrupted by Lady Sedgely, who said in a condescending voice, "Yes, we've met." Emily was shocked by the rudeness as Lord and Lady Sedgely barely greeted the Waddell ladies, and Lady Maude could only muster up an insincere "How do you do?" Only the son, Garfield, stepped forward and was warmly presented to Lady Waddell, Miss Waddell, and Miss Ann. It was obvious the "handsome" fairies were watching over him, as he was the best-looking of the entire family. Of course, his easy smile, particularly in contrast with the rigidity of the rest of his family, might have had something to do with the impression that he was so good-looking.

Emily watched in amusement as the younger ladies blushed and twittered in greeting the young man who bowed gallantly over their hands. She was surprised when he then turned to her and greeted her in the same manner. *Charming fellow, this one is,* Emily thought as she allowed herself the pleasure of enjoying his company briefly. She was abruptly reminded of her place when Lady Maude shrilled, "Garfield, that's the companion, don't you know?"

Garfield winked at Emily as he released her hand and turned to his sister and replied smoothly, "We all need companions, don't we, sister dearest?"

Lady Maude attempted to freeze him with an icy glare, but he deflected her ire with another of his warm smiles before he turned to Lady Clara and complimented, "This is a grand, lovely estate you have here, Lady Clara. It is going to be a pleasure to spend some time enjoying your hospitality. Might I ask if there is any sport to be had in those woods yonder?"

Lady Clara was clearly relieved that at least one member of the family was polite and easygoing. She replied, "Yes, there is game to be found there. My late husband and my son were quite fond of the hunting in these parts. There are a multitude of birds, as well as many stags to be found. You are quite welcome to venture forth and see for yourself while you are here. Lord Philip will be joining us this week, as well as some other young gentlemen who might wish to join you in the hunt."

Then, turning to Lady Sedgely, Lady Clara continued, "Would you care to have a spot of tea to refresh you from your journey, or would you rather be shown to your rooms and get settled first?"

Lady Sedgely must have realized the terrible impression she was making on the mother of the groom she had picked out for her darling daughter, for she seemed to have a change of attitude. "Thank you so much for inviting us, Lady Clara. I do believe it would be best if we retire to our rooms first to freshen up from the travel. You know how it is when you are cooped up in the carriage for hours on end. It is enough to lay one up, isn't it?" she asked rather vaguely.

Emily was relieved. Maybe the trio wasn't as dreadful as they seemed; they were just wearied from traveling. Lady Clara asked Emily to remain with the Waddells to see to their needs while she graciously escorted the Sedgelys to their rooms.

Lady Waddell seemed a bit deflated from the coldness of the greeting she had received from Lady Sedgely and her family, but the girls were obviously excited about meeting the son. Their chatter soon drew Emily out, and she listened as the three ladies told her all they knew about the man.

Jane, Miss Waddell, always the more talkative, revealed, "We had never actually met him before today. He rarely attends fashionable parties, preferring instead to be involved in all manner of sport. It is said he frequents all the gaming hells too," she said conspiratorially.

Turning to her mother, she continued, "But he didn't really look like a rake, did he, Mama? He seemed so nice, and he is really terrible handsome, isn't he? It is so exciting that he is here. All the girls in town are going to be so jealous, aren't they, Ann?"

Miss Ann, being very young and just free from the schoolroom, giggled. Emily shared an amused smile with Lady Waddell, who, despite her penchant for gossip, really did seem to have her head squarely on her shoulders.

More tea was poured, and the women continued comfortably discussing who else would be arriving the next day and what activities the girls wished to enjoy during their stay at Rosemount. The majority of the guests would be arriving late that evening or the next day. After the tea was cleared away and Lady Clara had still not returned to the drawing room, the ladies decided to retire to their rooms to spend some quiet time before they had to dress for supper. They assured Emily they had all they needed and would be fine on their own until they assembled back in the drawing room before the meal.

Emily was pleased to have some time to herself to prepare for what she was suspecting might be an exhausting dinner experience. She was tempted to avoid the meal altogether, but she knew that Lady Clara was counting on her to assist with the hostess duties.

Emily took particular care with her toilette as she prepared for that evening's dinner, not wanting to shame Lady Clara before her guests. She was more nervous than she had ever expected to be for a simple dinner, but she found the Sedgely family terribly intimidating. She was unsure if there was any way they could be made to enjoy themselves.

Emily vehemently wished Lord Philip were here already. He was so much more skilled at this type of thing. Besides, the ones who seemed the hardest to please would be the most happy to see the earl. She was becoming concerned over his absence but didn't want to mention her anxiety to Lady Clara, as she was certain she was also worried. Considering that he had asked his mother to plan this party, one would be excused for expecting him to be at least on time, if not early. Emily consoled herself that someone would have sent word if they truly had cause for concern. Perhaps the matter the king had him working on was proving more time-consuming than he had expected. Maybe he would arrive on the morrow.

In the meantime, Rosemount had guests needing to be appropriately fed and entertained. It was an excellent thing that she and Lady Clara had discussed in such great detail all the implications of the varying ranks of the nobility being assembled for this party. It was obvious the Sedgelys would take offense if they were not given the proper respect. Emily gave her head a shake as she realized she was woolgathering. Taking her wrap to ward off the evening's chill, she went down to join the guests gathering in the drawing room.

The Waddell ladies were again the first to arrive, followed by Lady Clara, Garfield, and Lord Sedgely. The group was kept waiting for Lady Sedgely and Lady Maude, which was not terribly surprising. When the two ladies arrived, Lady Clara briefly met Emily's eyes. It was obvious to Emily that the countess was chagrined over the obvious difficulty they were going to have in keeping these women amused. Emily foresaw a trying few days ahead. Undaunted, she gave an encouraging nod, and Lady Clara squared her shoulders, smiled, and conducted the group into the dining room.

The cook had outdone himself, obviously pleased by this chance to display the full range of his skills. No complaint could be found with the feast spread out before the countess' guests. Lady Clara smiled in satisfaction and gazed in approval at the footmen lined up behind the gathered guests. They were all starched and pressed in their finest uniforms, ready to be of service. Each took his place, and the meal began.

Lady Clara started the conversation by turning to Lady Sedgely and asking about her journey. Lady Sedgely described all the perils of England's roads after a rainstorm and the poor service one received along the way. Lady Clara's smile was just beginning to fray around the edges when Lady Sedgely finally wound down. Emily was pleased to see Lady Jane making polite efforts to engage Lady Maude in conversation, while Lady Ann was speaking shyly with Lord Sedgely. The viscount seemed to be quite taken with the quiet young woman and was making an effort to be kind. Which left Lady Waddell to talk with Garfield.

Emily repressed a smile as the gallant young man tried to look interested in the older woman's conversation. Emily was the odd one out, but she didn't mind. She liked to observe. She was almost lost in thought when her ears focused on what Lady Waddell was discussing. The missing Lady Emmaline again. *Can't the old gossip think of anything else to talk about?* Emily wondered vehemently. Garfield seemed interested now. What was he saying?

"I would love to be involved in the search. Good fun that would be, eh? Too bad no one seems to know where to look for the girl. Why do you suppose she would want to disappear? Doesn't she know what a stir she is causing? Seems she is quite a troublesome wench, wouldn't you say?" The young man seemed to consider everything in life a game, and this was just another example of sport.

Lady Waddell set him straight. "The young lady has not been out in society, and she would not know how things are done."

Emily was shocked that they thought the missing marchioness was just being impolite, inconveniencing the monarch as she was. Hadn't anyone considered foul play? Maybe she was hurt or even dead. No one seemed to be considering the turmoil the young woman might be going through. She decided to give voice to her thoughts.

"Do you think maybe the lady might be more than just on a lark? Perhaps she is hiding from danger or maybe even dead." Silence followed this remark as several pairs of inquiring eyes turned in her direction.

Lady Maude spoke condescendingly. "Peers of the realm do not *hide*. And they do not die without notice. No doubt she will reveal herself shortly." She managed to put Emily in her place and make her feel like an imbecile with seemingly very little effort, leaving Emily to wonder how the monarch's search was going to progress if no one considered that the young woman might have encountered foul play.

Emily agreed that the young woman, no doubt, had not realized that anyone would notice her absence, and the awkward moment was smoothed over.

Lady Clara glanced curiously down the table toward them, but nothing more was said.

The conversation continued to flow around the table, but Emily held herself back from participating. She had no experience with this kind of social occasion, so she would observe more before she again tried to participate. She realized that appearances were much more important to these people than she ever would have expected, and logic did not necessarily play a large part in their reasoning. She should contain her conversational efforts to discussions of the weather, she thought with amusement.

Miss Jane and Lady Maude were now discussing the play that had been all the rage last season and anticipating what they would enjoy seeing when they returned to town. Lady Maude, of course, was not nearly as excited about it all as Miss Jane was, having been "out" for some time now, but she participated politely, if somewhat coldly, in the conversation nonetheless.

It was with relief that Emily watched the last course being cleared away by the footmen and Lady Clara stand to lead the guests to the drawing room for tea. After her *faux pas* the meal had passed more comfortably than she expected, and she started to look forward to the rest of the visit with, if not actual optimism, at least a diminished sense of dread. Everyone was just getting settled and the tea trolley being rolled in when the knocker sounded throughout the house. Emily excused herself and went to welcome the latest arrivals, while Lady Clara remained with the other guests. Emily arrived just as two young bucks were being welcomed into the hallway by the butler, Mr. Parks. She stepped forward, holding out her hand to introduce herself.

"Welcome to Rosemount, my lords. I am Miss Emily Spencer. Lady Clara is occupied with the other guests. You must be Lords Marsden and Sutherland." She dropped them a curtsy as the two young men smiled warmly at her.

They both bowed to her gallantly and introduced themselves.

Lord Anthony Marsden was the epitome of the dandy set. He swept off his hat and made an elegant leg in front of Emily before pronouncing in quite an important tone of voice, "I am Tony, Lord Marsden, tenth viscount of

Elmcrest; and this disreputable oaf is Adolphus, Baron Sutherland, heir apparent to the Earl of Vale. We are pleased to make your acquaintance, Miss Spencer. I don't believe we have had the pleasure of your company in town before, have we? Will you be accompanying the countess this season?"

"Perhaps, my lord," Emily replied vaguely.

Despite his effort to sound important, Tony seemed to be a likeable gentleman. Lord Sutherland was very quiet and had yet to say anything at all. Emily was amused to see them both sneaking glances in the mirror in the hallway, and she graciously offered to take them to their rooms to freshen up before they joined the rest in the drawing room.

Tony jabbed Lord Sutherland with his elbow. "What do you say, Dolph? Should we clean ourselves up a bit before we present ourselves to the countess? Lead the way, Miss Spencer. It's best if we get the lay of the land before we enter the fray."

Emily wasn't completely sure what he meant by this rejoinder, but she smiled graciously and led them toward the wing with the guest chambers to which they'd been assigned.

"Who is here, by the way, Miss Spencer, if we could make so bold as to inquire?" asked Lord Marsden, obviously the more talkative of the pair.

"Lady Waddell and her two daughters arrived early this afternoon, followed by Viscount Sedgely and his family. We are still expecting Baron Fitzgerald, his wife and his daughter, and the Viscountess Eastwick with her son and daughter, as well as Lord Philip. Of course, throughout the week we will no doubt be joined by some of the families in the neighborhood for a few of our activities and dinners."

"A good mixture of company assembled, it seems. What activities have been planned to keep us amused, Miss Spencer?" This finally from Lord Sutherland in a rich baritone. *So he does have a voice,* Emily thought with an inner smile, *and quite a pleasant-sounding one at that. The younger ladies are going to find these two quite interesting.*

Out loud she said, "There has not been anything formally scheduled, my lord, aside from the dance to be held at the end of the week, but we thought the younger set would enjoy badminton or croquet on the grounds, and there are various sights within a short ride. As well, Lord Garfield seems interested in hunting, and the woods around here are teeming with sport. I am sure everyone will be well entertained, whatever his particular interest is." Emily wondered if these two young dandies would want to risk their Hessians by traipsing through the woods and so was somewhat surprised when Lord Sutherland nodded with enthusiasm at the thought of some hunting.

"Here we are, these are your rooms. Please make yourselves comfortable. If you need anything, ring for a footman. When you're ready to join the rest of us in the drawing room, one of the footmen can direct you when you get to the bottom of the stairs. I will bid you adieu for now."

Emily again curtsied and left the young men to themselves. She returned to the drawing room to see of what assistance she could be to Lady Clara. She was pleased to find the atmosphere in the room almost genial. The

Waddell ladies were maintaining a steady stream of conversation that included everyone. They were definitely a good choice to include in this house party; Emily silently congratulated Lady Clara for her shrewdness in judging the characters of their guests.

"Who was that arriving, Miss Spencer?" asked Lady Clara during a lull in the conversation.

"Lords Marsden and Sutherland arrived together. They have been shown to their rooms and will be down shortly after they have tidied themselves up a bit. They rode here, so they were a wee bit windblown," Emily concluded with a smile.

"How gauche," was the comment from Lady Maude.

Emily wasn't sure if the comment referred to her reference to the gentlemen's untidy state or the fact that they would arrive in such a state, so she chose to ignore it altogether.

Meanwhile, she could see the feminine speculation on the faces of all three young ladies, including Lady Maude. *How interesting,* thought Emily, *the lady is not immune to the charms of other men. Maybe the earl's interest in her isn't* a fait accompli, *as Lady Clara thinks.* Emily felt a little thrill in her heart, which she quickly repressed. *What do I care whom the earl might marry? It is none of my business,* she thought fiercely as she turned her attention to the amusement of their guests.

Emily was just about to invite the younger set to join together in some games when the footman announced the young lords. There was a flutter of murmurs as the gentlemen were introduced to those they did not already know and greeted the ones they did. It was apparent they were on genial terms with Lord Garfield when Lord Marsden slapped him on the shoulder and boomed, "Gary, my boy, good to see you. Didn't think you'd show yourself at such an event. Excellent!" he concluded rather vaguely.

Emily decided the young viscount was a cheerful if not too smart fellow and decided he would be best suited to sitting with one of the young Waddell ladies at the next dinner. The interaction of the group changed with the addition of the young gentlemen. The six young people separated themselves from the older ones and sat down at a table that had been set up off to the side.

They were all trying to be terribly sophisticated but failing dismally as they got deeper into the excitement of their game. All, that is, except for Lady Maude, who seemed to be quite put out that the two younger ladies were getting the admiring attention of the young men. Emily was appalled when she saw Maude "accidentally" spill her wine on Miss Ann's dress. Ann was crestfallen and clearly on the verge of tears. Lady Jane was about to take her up to her room to get cleaned up, but Emily stepped in and offered to help, thus earning an icy stare from Lady Maude, who had obviously been hoping to rid herself of both competitors in one stroke.

Slightly subdued, Ann bade everyone good night. It was already late, and by the time she cleaned up, no doubt the others would be thinking of retiring for the night as well. It had been a long day, and the poor young thing's feelings were clearly hurt, besides. Emily tried to console her by reassuring her that she knew just the thing to get the stain out, but poor Ann was inconsolable. "I was about to win," she declared vehemently. "And now I look like a baby who spills things. The gentlemen will never want to spend time with me if they think I'm still a little girl."

"It was not you who spilled the wine, Miss Ann. I am sure it was an accident." Emily tried to be comforting without making any accusations.

"Everyone will think I am too clumsy to be out in society and Mama should have left me in the schoolroom. I am supposed to make my debut officially this Season," she confided. "If I can't prove to mama that I can comport myself like a lady, she will leave me at home, which will be just dreadful."

Emily was not sure how to comfort the young lady. "My dear Miss Ann, you shall have plenty of opportunity to prove what a grown-up young lady you are throughout this week. Everyone will forget all about this little incident. Don't worry about it. Try to get a good sleep tonight, and everything will look much better in the morning."

Emily felt decades older than the young woman despite there being only a couple of years between them. After ringing for the Waddells' maid, she kept the younger woman company as she was helped out of the soiled gown and into her nightclothes. She left the girl tucked up in bed, feeling somewhat more cheerful about the whole event. Emily whisked the soiled gown downstairs to the housekeeper, who had a secret concoction for removing stains from the tablecloths. She hoped it would work on the fabric of this gown as well.

After speaking with Mrs. Parks and being assured the gown would be as good as new by morning, Emily debated about returning to the party. She was too tired to be polite and pretend Lady Maude had not caused the spill that ruined poor Ann's evening. She could not believe no one else had seen what she had done. She had been so convincing in her expression of concern, but she had not been able to hide her disappointment that Lady Jane was not going to be leaving early too. On the other hand, if things were not going well, Emily did not want to leave Lady Clara in the lurch.

She decided she had been running away from problems much too often lately, so she screwed up her courage, squared her shoulders, and marched back to the drawing room. Upon her arrival she was grateful to see that the older members of the party were starting to say their good nights to Lady Clara and gathering their children. It had been a long day for all the travelers, and they were ready for their beds. Lords Marsden and Sutherland were the only ones who looked as if they would've been able to go for a lot longer, but they accepted the end of the evening with good grace, and everyone said good night.

Emily stayed behind with Lady Clara as the rest of the group drifted from the room.

Lady Clara heaved a sigh of relief and exhaustion after the last guest had left. "Well, Emily, what do you think? Not as easy as we had expected, is it?"

"No, my lady, these next few days are going to be a lot more work than I thought. But on the bright side, if milord Philip ever turns up, surely he will not be able to continue in his misguided notion that Lady Maude would make a good countess. She is really quite dreadful, isn't she?" Emily went on to relate what she had seen the young woman do to Ann and how disappointed the younger girl was by the turn of events.

"Oh, poor thing. We will have to see about making it up to her somehow," said Lady Clara.

"I am sure Ann will prove how gracious she can be throughout the week all on her own. She really is quite a sweet young person," answered Emily.

Lady Clara laughed at Emily's proprietary tone. "She can't be that much younger than you, Emily. You sound as if you are her grandmother or some such."

"Maybe not in years, my lady, but our life experiences have greatly diverged, I am sure," she replied with a self-deprecating smile. "But please, you must be exhausted. Let's get you off to bed. Tomorrow is another day, and things are sure to be different with nearly twice as many guests due to arrive. It should be quite interesting to see how things develop." With that the two ladies linked arms and set off to find their own beds for the night.

Chapter Ten

The day dawned bright and cheerful. When Emily opened her curtains, she could see that it was going to be a lovely day, perfect for any of the activities they had considered for the enjoyment of the guests. She rushed through her morning toilette and set out to assist the housekeeper in organizing the staff.

It turned out that the Fitzgeralds had arrived after they had all gone to bed. Upon their arrival, the footman on watch had hastily awoken Mr. Parks to show the guests to their rooms. They would no doubt keep to their rooms much later than the others, who had had a relatively early night. Some of the guests had requested trays be brought to their rooms, but others were gathering in the breakfast room to start their day. The three young lords were already well into their meal, and the three Waddell ladies were just entering the room when Emily arrived.

116

"Oh, Miss Spencer, thank you so much for seeing to my gown." Poor Ann blushed to bring up her disgrace from last evening but was too polite to let Emily's help go unacknowledged. "You were able to work miracles. I was sure it was ruined."

"It was my pleasure, but it really wasn't me. The housekeeper here at Rosemount has a genius for such things. Please, ladies, help yourselves to whatever you would like to break your fast, and sit wherever you want." Emily graciously changed the subject, then turned to greet the gentlemen.

"Good morning, sirs. I trust you all slept well. It would appear it is going to be a wonderful summer day. Maybe we will all be able to spend some time out of doors before the sun gets too hot."

Mr. Garfield replied, "I for one would love to explore the woods, see what kind of wildlife we can find. Maybe if you fellows would like to join me, we could look around a bit before everyone else is up and about, wanting us to entertain them."

"Sounds like an excellent plan, my good man. Lead the way," answered Lord Marsden. He and Lord Sutherland joined Mr. Garfield in bidding the ladies a good morning. "We shall see you ladies a bit later," confirmed Lord Marsden with a gallant bow and a wink.

The young baron, Lord Sutherland, looked somewhat undecided about joining the other gentlemen in the hunt. He had clearly been enjoying the chatter of the young ladies and found them very good company, since he need not put in much conversational effort with them. But the lure of the sport was too strong to resist, and the three gentlemen traipsed from the room with promises to not be gone too long.

Once the gentlemen were out of earshot, the younger Waddell ladies looked at each other and giggled. Emily smiled in amusement.

"This is just so exciting!" exclaimed Miss Jane. "I would never have thought I would be sharing breakfast with three of the most handsome men in all of England. Isn't this just the best visit we've ever had, Mama?"

"Well, my dear, I have to admit, those three gentlemen are very nice and quite handsome. I am glad you girls are having such a good time." Turning to Emily, Lady Waddell continued. "Is it true the Fitzgeralds arrived last night? Lady Fitzgerald must be feeling poorly this morning. Her health is not great at the best of times, let alone after a harrowing travel experience. Have you any idea what detained them? Something dreadful must have happened to make them arrive so late. I do hope all is well."

"Apparently there was some problem with the carriage. They told the butler they were able to spend the time at a very nice inn while it was being repaired. They wanted to arrive yesterday and did not realize they still had so far to go from the village where they had stopped. In the dark, too, they made slower progress. No one was hurt, though, and I am sure after a good night's sleep they'll feel as fit as a fiddle," Emily assured Lady Waddell optimistically.

Lady Waddell countered disbelievingly, "I do not think Lady Fitzgerald has felt 'fit as a fiddle' a day in her life, but I am sure you are right, she will survive. I am glad it wasn't anything too serious."

At that moment Lady Clara breezed into the room,

looking rested and cheerful. "Good morning, everyone," she greeted. "Are we the first to leave our rooms?" she asked in obvious surprise.

Jane laughed and said, "No, my lady, you have already missed the three young gentlemen. They have gone to inspect your forest for wildlife. They said they would return shortly. They just wanted to get 'the lay of the land,' as Lord Marsden would say." All the ladies laughed at her close impersonation of the young man.

Lady Clara filled her plate, and conversation became general as the ladies discussed the weather and what they might do that day. Emily excused herself to go check on the Fitzgerald servants and see what needs the family might have.

She found Belle, the lady's maid for Lady Fitzgerald and her daughter, down in the kitchens getting to know the Rosemount staff. "Good morning. I am Miss Spencer," Emily greeted the young servant. "I wanted to inquire if your mistresses need anything this morning. We weren't able to meet them last night with your late arrival, and I'm not sure how long they'll be sleeping today. Do you know if they've made any special requests?"

"Oh, thank you, miss! My lady sez she don't want to be disturbed 'til she rings. But the miss is up and dressed. She's too shy to come down without her mama," answered Belle.

"Thank you, Belle. I'll go up to her room and meet her. Maybe she'd like to break her fast with the young Waddell ladies."

"Thanks, miss. She'd like that," answered the young maid politely.

Emily smiled at the assembled staff, then left the kitchens to climb up to the guest wing. She knocked quietly on Miss Julia's door. The prettiest young woman Emily had ever seen whisked the door open. She wasn't your typical beauty, but she had large sparkling eyes and shiny black curls with the biggest smile to grace such a tiny face. "Hello," she greeted in a soft, musical voice.

"Good morning. I am Emily Spencer. You must be Miss Julia. Welcome to Rosemount. I am so sorry no one of the family was up to greet you and your family upon your arrival last night."

"That's perfectly fine. We were unavoidably detained. It would have been dreadful if we had kept someone up waiting for us. As it was, the poor old butler was awakened on our account. Mama said it's his duty, but he's an old man, and I felt bad."

"That is very generous of you, Miss Julia. Have you had your breakfast yet? Would you like me to send for something from the kitchen, or would you like to join some of the other guests in the breakfast room?"

"Oh, thank you, miss! I'm actually near to perishing, but I wasn't sure if it would be acceptable to start wandering around by myself. I would like to join the others, if that's all right," requested Julia sweetly.

"Excellent. I will show you the way." The two young women were making their way down the hall as Emily told Julia who else was staying in the big house and which rooms were whose, when they heard a shriek coming from what Emily was sure was Lady Maude's room. Miss Julia turned her large eyes upon Emily in a startled fashion, unsure what the proper behavior was in such a circumstance. Knowing Julia was uncomfortable wandering the big house by herself, Emily hesitated to leave her but knew she must check what was going on behind that door.

With regret she turned to Julia and said, "Please go ahead without me, Miss Fitzgerald. I'll make sure everything is fine here. When you get to the bottom of the stairs, there'll be a footman who can direct you. Lady Clara and the Waddell ladies are there already—they'll make you welcome." Emily dismissed the young woman kindly and turned to the door.

There was now the sound of weeping coming from the room, and Emily hesitated to get involved. But someone needed her help in there, so she knocked lightly on the door, unsure what she'd find on the other side when it opened. Lady Maude herself pulled the door open briskly and stood there quivering in indignation.

"We'll need the services of a couple of servants in here, if you please. I shall be downstairs breaking my fast. I want this mess cleaned up by the time I'm finished," Lady Maude declared haughtily before sweeping regally past Emily and proceeding down the hallway with her nose elevated and her back ramrod straight.

Stunned, Emily watched her walk to the grand staircase before she stepped into the room to see what had taken place. She was shocked to see water and broken glass seemingly everywhere. Strewn about, too, was a mountain of clothing. She helped Lady Maude's quivering maid, Peggy, step gingerly over the broken shards and sent her down to the kitchens for tea after she rang for some maids to help put order to the chaos in the room.

"What could Lord Philip be thinking? Surely Lady Clara is mistaken. There is no way an intelligent man like my lord could be so taken in by this horrendous shrew of a woman." Emily was talking to herself as she helped two of the maids clean up the broken glass in Lady Maude's room. "There must be some mistake."

" 'Tis hard to believe the lady would throw a glass and pitcher at her own maid, ain't it, miss?" asked Maggie innocently.

"Well, Maggie, I would have never believed it before now. However, I have had the misfortune of meeting the lady myself, and I am finding it quite a bit easier to believe," replied Emily, still shocked. "Can the two of you finish up in here? I am going to speak to Peggy and make sure she wasn't injured in the fray. Thank you for helping with the cleanup. I know the two of you already have plenty to do without anything extra like this."

"That's awright, lass. We can handle it from here."

Emily left the two girls and went down to the kitchens in search of Lady Maude's personal maid. "There you are, Peggy. How are you? Did you get hurt at all?"

"Oh, miss, it weren't nothing. I'm used to much worse with that one. I shoulda know'd she was a bit miffy from the ride here yesterday. Never shoulda spilled nothing," answered Peggy good-naturedly.

"Well, if you're sure you're fine, I will go attend to other matters." Emily was surprised at the maid's calmness over what she would've considered a disaster, were she in Peggy's shoes. But seeing that she truly was all right, Emily was happy to leave the kitchen and have a moment of quiet to herself before she went in search of Lady Clara to ensure everything was going smoothly with her.

This is going to be a long week, Emily thought as she checked for flyaway hairs and straightened her gown before plastering on a smile and entering the drawing room, where some of the guests were currently assembled.

Lady Clara was already showing signs of strain, but her face lit up when she saw Emily approaching her. "I was beginning to wonder what had happened to you," she whispered to Emily.

"I'll tell you later. It was quite dreadful, but everything is sorted out now. Has all been proceeding smoothly here?" queried Emily softly.

"Not exactly," was the terse reply.

Emily looked around and took a quick head count. The gentlemen who had already arrived were nowhere to be seen, some of the guests had yet to arrive, and Lord Philip was still not here. Emily was secretly becoming worried about him. Considering that he had asked his mother to arrange this event, Emily had really expected him to be early rather than late. And the ladies currently occupying the drawing room did not look happy. Emily knew she had to do something to create a better atmosphere. With a mental effort she forced herself to wipe all unpleasant feelings from her face and plastered a pleasant smile into place, dredging up a cheerful voice.

"Shall we try some activities? We could go for a walk out of doors; the Rosemount gardens are renowned for their beauty. Or if anyone is up to more vigorous activities, there are various sports to be enjoyed on the grounds."

Lady Jane, Ann, and Julia turned to Emily simultaneously, all three eager and ready to be amused. Miss Julia was the first to respond. "Oh, yes, I have heard so much about the rose gardens here, I would love to see them. I personally don't feel up to anything vigorous after the long journey yesterday. Let's save that for tomorrow." The other girls voiced their agreement and got up to join Emily by the door.

"Wouldn't you like to join us, Lady Maude? It's a beautiful day. We should take advantage of it, don't you think?" Despite her misgivings, Emily tried to be pleasant to the seemingly cold girl. *Surely there must be a heart under all that ice,* she thought. After all, she had seemed almost warm last evening when the young lords were around. Maybe she just didn't like women. Well, that was just tough, Emily continued in her mind. The woman was displaying extremely bad manners, and Emily had been taught that members of the nobility were always polite. *I guess there are a few exceptions to that rule,* she thought wryly. They still awaited Lady Maude's response.

Lady Sedgely finally spoke up. "Go along with the young ladies and get a view of the rose gardens, Maude. A spot of fresh air will clear the cobwebs out of your mind. Run along, girls, and enjoy yourselves. Don't forget your parasol, Maude dear."

It would appear Lady Sedgely was making an effort be pleasant, perhaps to win over Lady Clara. She must have realized the dreadful impression most of her family was making and was trying to counteract that. Unfortunately, her facial muscles appeared unused to forming smiles, and her mind did not seen to run to kindness.

"Yes, Mother," was the cool reply from Lady Maude to her mother.

There was a brief scurry of activity as the young ladies fetched their broad-brimmed hats and parasols before they exited the house. Already it was warming up, and it was obvious they wouldn't be able to stay out in the sun for too long. Jane and Julia had already formed a friendly bond over breakfast, and Ann was closely tagging along with them, which left Emily alone to try to entertain the unfriendly Maude. Emily was not sure if she should mention the incident with the maid and the pitcher.

"Are you quite recovered from the rigors of traveling yesterday?" she inquired politely, striking a neutral balance between ignoring the obvious and being nosy.

"Yes, thank you. I had a wonderful sleep last night and feel quite the thing today," was Maude's surprising reply. It was almost as if the lady had two personalities, thought Emily in bewilderment. "The grounds here are really quite beautiful. Do you tend to them yourself, or is it the responsibility of one of the other servants?" she asked in a deceptively kind voice.

Emily was again shocked at the woman's guile and couldn't think of an appropriate answer to the leading question other than the truth.

"Lady Clara allows me to help the gardener when I have a spare moment. It's very restful for me, working with plants and watching things grow. Have you ever tried your hand at gardening?"

"Oh, no, I never participate in anything menial," was the snidely cool reply. "Have you any idea when Lord Philip is to arrive?" continued Lady Maude petulantly. "I thought he'd be here to welcome us." Maude was clearly not going to put any effort into being pleasant if there were no gentlemen around to appreciate it.

"His lordship had an important matter to see to and was unavoidably detained. Lady Clara is in constant expectation of his arrival at any moment," Emily replied formally. She decided she had had enough of the dubious company of Lady Maude and excused herself. "I am sure you will enjoy viewing the gardens with the other young ladies. No doubt there are matters Lady Clara would have me attend to. Good day."

With that Emily swept away from her and back toward the house, grateful to be rid of the other woman for a while. *I'd rather polish the silver than entertain that one for too long,* she thought. *Being a maid was easier than this.*

Emily found Lady Clara in the small salon with Lady Sedgely, Lady Waddell, and Lady Fitzgerald. Lady Fitzgerald was a birdlike woman with small eyes and a pointy face, but as she spoke it was apparent that she had a heart of gold hidden in her small frame. Despite her apparent frailty, she cast a warm glow upon the group, and Lady Clara was looking much more relaxed than when Emily had last seen her. Even Lady Sedgely appeared at ease as she smiled at something the little woman was saying.

Emily didn't wish to interrupt, so she stood at the door and caught Lady Clara's eye. At Emily's lifted eyebrow, Lady Clara gave a quick shake of her head: all was well, and she didn't require any help at the moment. With relief Emily took herself off to the library to get some needed work done before she went in search of Mrs. Parks to ensure all was progressing well in preparation for that evening's meal.

All the ladies were assembled for tea, and Lords Sedgely and Fitzgerald had joined them. No one was quite sure what the older gentlemen had done with their morning, and the younger gentlemen had not yet returned from the hunt. The younger ladies were disappointed. The older ladies were looking on in amusement as the younger ones perked up at every noise in the hallway, only to be crestfallen when it did not turn out to be the absent young gentlemen. Lady Maude was apparently feeling a bit "miffy," as Peggy would say, and turned her ire stealthily upon Emily.

"So, Miss Spencer, how are you connected to Lady Yorkleigh? Are you a distant relative we haven't heard of before?"

"No, Lady Maude, I am not," Emily replied repressively, hoping this line of questioning would be swiftly cut off. Her hopes were dashed when Lady Maude's inquisition continued.

"Where are you from? Are you some connection of Lord Spencer's from Berkshire?"

"I am not from the Berkshire area, and I doubt if Lord Spencer is any connection of mine," Emily replied politely, unsure how far Maude was going to take her questions. She made a vain attempt to change the subject. "Would you like some more tea, Lady Maude?"

"No, thank you," she replied. She opened her mouth to say more, but Emily interjected.

"Tell us about your part of England, Lady Maude. I have heard it's quite lovely." Emily was proud of herself for so deftly getting out of that awkward interrogation. She could tell that Lady Maude realized what had just happened by the sharpening of that lady's gaze. But there was nothing the other woman could do at that time except answer the question.

Emily soon found herself wishing she hadn't diverted the attention away from herself, as Lady Maude turned her ire upon the sweet Miss Julia. That young lady had never before been the object of unkind banter, so it took her a while to realize what was going on. Lady Maude veiled her cutting words so skillfully that Miss Julia was bewildered and did not have the social experience necessary to deflect them. Emily's heart broke to see the tears welling up in Julia's eyes.

When Maude was finished unsettling Julia, she turned upon Jane and Ann. Her words were couched in such a way that the older guests, caught up in their own conversations, were unaware of what was going on. Emily tried valiantly to intervene, but only the entrance of the three hunters ended Lady Maude's cruelty to the younger ladies. It was as though a magical transformation took place. Suddenly Lady Maude was all smiles as the gentlemen recounted their experiences in the woods. Her smile dimmed a bit when Lord Sutherland went to sit beside Jane and seemed to take particular interest in what she had to say, but Maude carried on genially speaking with the young viscount, Lord Marsden.

Emily began to despair of Lord Philip's ever realizing the truth about the lady, since she seemed to be such an excellent actress. *She should take to the stage,* thought Emily waspishly as she excused herself from the group and went to ensure that supper preparations were progressing well.

Emily had just closed the doors to the drawing room when she saw Lord Philip and Mr. Dale entering the front door. "My Lord Yorkleigh! It is *so* good to see you, my lord!" Emily exclaimed, relief obvious in her tone and manner as she rushed over to greet them. She clasped his hand warmly in welcome, her eyes shining with tears of joy and relief, a wide smile stretching her face.

Philip was surprised by the enthusiasm of her greeting. "Is everything all right here, Emily?" he inquired in concern. "I should say, Miss Spencer?" he corrected himself quickly.

"Oh, yes, everything is fine, my lord." Emily recovered her presence of mind somewhat but could not repress the grin she was casting at the two men. Surely they would save the entire situation now that they'd arrived. "It is just a bit hectic, you know, with all the guests arriving and wanting to be entertained."

"I've brought James with me; I hope that won't throw off your numbers too much. We tried to get here earlier than you demanded, but we were unfortunately detained. Now we quake in our shoes, awaiting the dire consequences of disobeying your edict," Philip teased her.

"Oh, my lord, really," she replied coolly, fully recovering her composure. "Don't tease. We shall be absolutely delighted to have Mr. Dale join our festivities. And you are only a day late, so do not worry. Lady Clara and I hardly noticed and weren't worried at all."

Emily told the barefaced lie with barely a flicker of an eyelash. But Philip caught the telltale flash of pink on her cheeks and merely chuckled at her audacity. "If you're out of rooms, James can share mine," he offered generously.

"No, my lord, there should be a few to spare. We are still awaiting the arrival of the Viscountess Eastwick and her son and daughter as well as a few others, but we've plenty of room as long as George, your valet, can sleep on the cot in your dressing room. Otherwise he'll need to share the servants' quarters."

"That shan't be a problem. Which room shall I put James in? We can show ourselves up. We'll freshen ourselves a bit, then join the company in the drawing room— if that's all right with you," he countered quizzingly, enjoying being able to fluster the normally composed maiden.

Despite her blushing cheeks, Emily lifted her chin in a distinctively proud way. "Mr. Dale can have the green room at the end of the hall in your wing, if you would be so kind as to show him. I was just on my way to confer with the housekeeper. I will mention to her that we shall need an extra plate for dinner. Welcome to Rosemount, by the by. I'll have one of the maids bring you both some water. Adieu." With that Emily swept off to the kitchens.

Both men watched her departure with appreciation. Then Lord Philip chuckled. "She's certainly adjusted well to having some authority in the household, hasn't she, James?"

James agreed with a smile, then said, "She did seem a

bit harried, though, do you not think, my lord? As if we were here to save her from something."

"You're right, James. Maybe the adjustment is taking a bit of effort. Don't forget, as companion to my mother she is assisting as hostess to this event; no doubt it's a bit daunting to someone not high-born. We'll have to see what we can do to ease the burden. Let's go. You'll like the green room—the view is lovely. Miss Spencer must have a soft spot for you, James. Despite its being small, I think it's one of the nicest rooms here at Rosemount. After the week we've been having, spending some time relaxing here at my mother's estate should be just the thing."

Everyone was delighted to welcome Lord Philip, Earl of Yorkleigh. He was respected by members of the ton, and the assembled guests were happy to get reacquainted with the young earl. He wasn't known for going about too much in society, preferring the darker side of life in London than the one frequented by the peers assembled for the countess' house party. Despite his penchant for fast living, though, he had managed to maintain a reputation as a decent fellow who lived up to his title as gentleman. He was known to put in an appearance during the Season, but most of the assembled guests hadn't gotten to know him very well, and all were happy for the opportunity. The young ladies were full of admiration for his handsome looks, vast fortune, and pleasant address, while the young lords admired his reputation at sports. The older lords and ladies had held a deep respect for his father and thus wanted to get to know the heir.

The Sedgelys, of course, felt somewhat proprietary toward the earl, and the viscount was the first to greet him despite Lady Clara's obvious desire to embrace her son. "There you are, my boy," boomed Lord Sedgely overenthusiastically. "We were beginning to wonder if you were going to stand us up!"

Philip was unsure how to politely respond to such a pronouncement, so he chose to ignore it as he turned to greet his mother. He bowed over her hand formally before receiving a warm hug from her. "I apologize for my tardiness, my lady Mother. I was necessarily detained while engaged in an errand for the king."

Lady Clara was just happy to see her son. Much like Emily, she hadn't realized how worried she had been until she was saw him safe and sound. She simply welcomed him warmly, and together they turned to their guests.

Lord Philip included everyone in his explanations for his tardiness and not being there to welcome them when they arrived. "As some of you may have heard, His Majesty has been concerned over the disappearance of the Lady Emmaline. She is a young lady whose parents recently died, and apparently she is quite a substantial heiress and is in the rare position of being able to inherit many old titles that are not entailed automatically on a male heir. With the monarch's permission she may claim several titles that were in both her parents' families for centuries, with the exception of the viscountcy. The new viscount is a distant cousin of the lady's father, and he claims to be unaware of her whereabouts despite being her new guardian."

Many of the ladies in the room were making appropriately shocked and concerned noises while looking at one another with glowing eyes, clearly thrilled to be privy to the latest juicy gossip. Meanwhile, Lady Maude was becoming restless, unhappy to see her supposed suitor so preoccupied with some other female. She suppressed a dainty yawn while looking pointedly at the earl, silently urging him to change the subject to one that she would find entertaining.

Philip had seen the look Maude was sending his way but was unsure of its meaning, so he mentally shrugged and continued his explanation. "I know some of you ladies may find it distressing to think of the poor missing orphan, but the reason I bring this up is because I was wondering if any of you might have known the young lady's parents—the Marquis and Marchioness of Edenvale. They seem to have lived quite retired from society, and we are having trouble ascertaining with whom the young lady might have sought sanctuary. As well, does anyone here know aught about the new Viscount Ridley? He appears to be a shifty fellow and was involved in some shady dealings before he inherited. He's suspiciously unconcerned over his missing ward, but we have yet to prove that anything untoward has happened." Philip paused to let everyone consider it for a moment. Then he continued. "If any of you think of anything over the next few days, please let me know." He then smiled graciously and turned to change the subject and speak more privately with each of his mother's assembled guests.

The room was buzzing with speculation about the whereabouts when Emily returned to the guests. She tried not to draw attention to herself as she busied herself ensuring that everyone was comfortable. She had begun to get used to the speculation and gossip about the missing peeress and the king's search for her, so she was not as flustered as when the subject first came up. However, she couldn't help being uncomfortable during the discussion. She was surprised to see how keenly interested Philip seemed to be in the various ideas put forward by the assembled guests. It would seem everyone had an opinion they were willing to share, and Philip was paying rapt attention as each guest expressed what little information or speculation they had. It all seemed like mere conjecture to Emily.

She had a puzzled frown creasing her brow and was deep in unquiet thoughts when Lady Clara stood up, signaling the time had arrived for everyone to get ready for supper. Adieus were said, and everyone dispersed to prepare. Emily and Philip were the last to leave the room, and Philip detained her quietly. "Might I have a word with you, Miss Spencer?" he queried with a hand on her arm.

"What is it, my lord?" Emily asked.

"I'm concerned about you, Emily; you seem preoccupied and a bit worried. Your welcome when we arrived was much more enthusiastic than one would expect. Is there anything I can do for you? You know it is but for you to command," he told her half-teasingly. Despite his best efforts, he found himself powerfully drawn to the mysterious young woman and really was willing to do much to help her.

"My lord," she began in a lightly reproving tone, "I thank you for your concern, and I'm sorry to cause you any alarm. I am fine, truly."

Philip was unconvinced but did not press the matter. "Please be assured, I will stand your friend, should you require any assistance."

"I appreciate the offer, my lord. Now I must be off to prepare." She left the room hastily, almost running up the stairs, only stopping once the door to her room was firmly closed at her back. She placed a trembling hand to her brow and drew a deep sigh straight from her heart. That organ was in danger of melting from his lordship's kindness.

Now is not the time for silly mooning, Emily reprimanded herself sternly. She gave her head a shake and forced her distracted mind to focus on practicalities, namely, which of her new gowns would be best for this evening's dinner. She made her selection and hurried through her preparations in order to go to Lady Clara before descending to supper.

Chapter Eleven

"**O**h, Lady Clara, you look smashing!" Emily exclaimed, using a term gleaned from the young lordlings that afternoon.

Clara laughed and bobbed a graceful curtsy. "I pass muster, Emily? I confess this is proving a bigger ordeal than I expected. But at least Philip has arrived. That will ease the burden, and with luck our purpose will be accomplished."

"Do you think so, my lady? The Lady Maude seems to have two faces; one she presents to females, and a much nicer one that she shows to the gentlemen. I am beginning to understand how my lord Philip could have been taken in by the little shrew." Emily tried to relate the events of the afternoon, but it was hard to put into words how cutting the young woman could be.

"Don't worry about it, Emily. Philip is an intelligent

man; I am convinced he will not make it to the end of the week without a change of heart with regard to Lady Maude. We just have to keep everyone entertained. I think Maude will cause her own demise, given enough time. Now, let's review how we set the places for dinner. Everyone is here now. I have received word that others have arrived and are quickly preparing for supper, so we will have to shuffle a little to accommodate Mr. Dale." The two women spent a few minutes analyzing their handiwork and pronounced it good. As they descended to the drawing room with their arms linked, neither noticed Lady Maude watching them jealously from her slightly ajar door.

Lady Maude closed the door softly and leaned against it. She could not understand how Lady Clara could be so friendly with the young woman who wasn't much more than a glorified servant. Nobody knew who this Miss Spencer was; why would the countess take such pleasure in the lowly woman? What could be gained from such a relationship? Lady Maude knew that relationships were a means to an end, not a source of pleasure, and it annoyed her to watch Miss Fitzgerald and Miss Waddell getting so chummy too. She took a couple of minutes to think of ways she could break up the girls' little friendship before she left her room to make her way down to the drawing room.

She was most pleased to see she was the best-dressed lady present and threw a triumphant glance at herself in the mirror over the mantel. Lord Philip caught the look and wondered at it fleetingly as he stepped forward to bow gallantly over her gloved hand. Maude preened as he complimented her, and they stood in conversation for a moment.

Lady Eastwick and her son and daughter had arrived late in the afternoon, and most of the assembled guests had not yet greeted them. Introductions were made all around. The young Lord Eastwick was another quiet, handsome young gentleman who seemed as if he would fit in well with the young men already gathered, while his sister seemed to be more serious than the Waddell ladies, despite being of an age with them. Lady Arabella was quietly pretty. Her brown hair, green eyes, and tidy figure were not enough to turn many heads until she really smiled and her whole appearance brightened. Their mother, Lady Eastwick, was an attractive, middle-aged widow with an approachable personality but a deplorably shrill voice. Fortunately, she didn't have too much to say.

Also joining the company was a lively young couple, Lord and Lady Thorpe. They had been married only a few years and had two young children. This was Lady Thorpe's first time being away from her children, and she clearly had conflicted feelings about the matter. While she knew it was considered unfashionable to be so involved in her children's lives, she truly loved and missed them. On the other hand, it had been a couple of years since she had been involved in the social whirl, and she was excited that she and her husband had been included in the party invitations. The Thorpes had each brought a sibling. Lady Thorpe had brought her twin brother, Lord John Brooke; and Lord Thorpe had his younger sister, Miss Alicia Thorpe, accompanying him.

Emily was pleased to make the acquaintance of all the new arrivals. They seemed to be a pleasant bunch who appeared easy to satisfy. Miss Thorpe had come out at the same time as Lady Maude and seemed immune to her tactics. She quickly made friends with the younger girls present and seemed able to deflect some of Maude's malicious darts. Emily realized that there already seemed to be an understanding between Lady Arabella and Lord Brooke, and she suspected it would be entertaining to watch the courtship progressing over the next few days.

The noise level had greatly increased with the addition of so many members to the group, and it took some effort for Parks, the butler, to get everyone's attention before leading them the dining room for the start of the meal.

As they sat down to another one of Cook's masterpieces, Emily could feel Lady Eastwick's sharpened gaze fixed upon her face. "Have we met before, my dear Miss Spencer?" she asked kindly in her rasping voice.

"I do not think I have ever had the pleasure of making your acquaintance," answered Emily politely.

"I am so sure I've seen your face before. You seem so familiar to me. Perhaps it is a family resemblance. Would we have met your parents or another relative?" Lady Eastwick persisted, drawing the attention of the nearby diners.

Emily felt trapped and knew her cheeks were heating as the focus turned upon her. Lord Philip was seated diagonally across from her, and their eyes met as Emily glanced around, wondering urgently what to say to the inquisitive woman. He flicked one eyelid at her almost imperceptibly just before he knocked over his glass of wine. He grabbed the delicate goblet before too much was spilled and stood while one of the footmen quickly mopped up the mess. The incident was quickly over, but it had done the trick; the subject changed, and the focus was removed from Emily and the subject of her parentage.

Lady Clara, at the head of the table, witnessed the entire scene and then saw Philip again meet Emily's eye as they shared a small private smile before turning to the guests at their sides to continue conversing. Lady Maude also saw the exchange and simmered.

In the meantime Emily asked Mr. Dale how his visit in London had gone. He regaled her with some humorous tales from court, leaving out any mention of their fruitless travels in search of the marchioness, not wanting to place a damper on the evening. The rest of the evening progressed without incident.

Farther down the table, Ann's artless chatter was entertaining Lord Eastwick, and Lord Sutherland was becoming more enthralled with Jane. Julia was enjoying the company of her new acquaintance, Lord Garfield. Lady Maude was not so satisfied with her dinner companions. On one side of her was Lord Marsden, who was trying, to no avail, to interest her in a conversation about the morning's hunt, and on her other side was Lord Fitzgerald, who really only wanted to talk about various games of chance.

Philip was disappointed to see that Lady Maude was so obviously bored; he had thought her an easygoing girl. He resolved to further his acquaintance with her before pursuing the courtship. Thus resolved, he continued his conversation with Miss Thorpe, who was on one side of him during the meal.

When the ladies left the gentlemen to their port and collected in the drawing room to prepare a musical entertainment, Lady Maude's claws were again unsheathed. She was disgruntled about her boring supper conversations and felt a need to take it out on someone. It was an anecdotal fact that the Waddell ladies were not the most accomplished musicians in the bunch, and Lady Maude began her attack. "It is well known that you cannot be expected to find an appropriate husband if you can't play well. How can you be a good hostess if you cannot entertain your guests? I can play three different instruments perfectly and have been told that I sing like an angel. Miss Jane, why don't you and your sister play for us when the gentlemen join us?"

Jane blushed scarlet. "Oh, no, Lady Maude, I have heard that you play beautifully. Would you please give us the pleasure of hearing for ourselves?"

The rest of the ladies, most of whom had not heard the beginning of the exchange, added their voices to the request for Lady Maude to play. She accepted with seeming reluctance and riffled through the music sheets to select what she would play. She was just warming up when the gentlemen entered the room. As soon as they were settled, she launched into a beautiful rendition of Chopin's symphony. There was enthusiastic applause when she concluded. She stood, made a graceful curtsy, then turned to the Misses Jane and Ann. "Why don't one of you go next? We would love to hear you play something," she pronounced in cloyingly innocent tones.

Ann looked as if she wanted to burst into tears, and Jane was blushing deep scarlet at the thought of disgracing herself in front of the company. Emily had been one of the few to witness the earlier exchange and knew what was going on. She took a hand, earning herself an icy glare from Lady Maude. "I have heard that the two of you sing a beautiful duet. Why don't I accompany you on the pianoforte while you sing for us? Maybe if you sing something familiar, we can all join in. That will be fun for everyone, don't you think?"

The two young ladies agreed enthusiastically and smiled at Emily in gratitude as she took Maude's place. "Thank you for such a wonderful idea, Lady Maude." Emily couldn't keep herself from goading the girl, earning herself a fierce glare. It took all her control not to laugh with glee as she saw that Philip had noticed the exchange and was watching them with a puzzled look. She tossed him a smile before conferring with the two girls. They selected a lively tune, and the girls proved that the rumor was true. While they could barely play a note, they sang beautifully, almost like the angels Lady Maude had claimed to imitate.

Soon others joined in, and all had a good time. Lady Arabella and Miss Thorpe also took turns practicing their skills at the keyboard, while Lady Thorpe sang a hauntingly beautiful aria, much to everyone's delight.

After that one song Emily had played with Jane and Ann, she had not returned to the pianoforte. She had quietly mingled with the guests, ensuring everyone's comfort. Philip couldn't help but notice how indispensable Emily had become to his mother. He admired her gentle dignity as she made sure each guest had just what he or she needed.

As the evening progressed, Emily could feel Lady Eastwick's gaze following her. Whenever their eyes met, Emily tried to smile at the woman, but it was becoming a strain on her nerves. Philip again noticed the stress she was under, and as everyone was saying their good nights and heading off to bed when the evening drew to a close, he asked Emily to meet him in the library if she had a moment.

Emily waited until everyone had disappeared up the stairs before she knocked softly on the library door. Philip opened it himself and stepped back to allow her to enter. He stood very near after he closed the door, watching her closely. Emily became a little nervous from the scrutiny. "You wanted to see me, my lord?" she questioned.

"Yes, Emily," he answered her softly. "I can see that the others are speculating about you, and it is obviously bothering you. Why do you keep your background such a mystery? It doesn't really matter where you come from. Whatever happened to you in the past is done and gone." As he spoke, he remained near her, and Emily could feel his warm breath on her cheek as he continued in a low tone. "You are safe now here with my mother and me. Do you need our help in some way? You know we would give it to you. My mother is ever so fond of you, as am I."

Emily felt tears welling up in her eyes at his kindness. She could not answer his questions, but she was deeply touched by his concern. She was determined to be strong and look after herself, though his kindness tempted her to lay her burdens at his feet and accept some assistance for a while. She resisted, but she nonetheless felt herself fall a little bit more in love with him and was powerless to stop it.

When he saw her tears, Philip was moved. He reached out and stroked her cheek. "Ah, Emily, don't cry, please. I hate tears. I will do anything, but please don't cry." He leaned over her upturned face and gently pressed his lips to hers. As kisses went it was almost chaste, but Philip was powerfully attracted to Emily, and she had never been kissed before. They both reacted strongly, pulling away from each other. Philip was at a loss for words, the act was so out of character for him. Emily blinked at him with wide eyes and then swept him a deep curtsy, distancing herself from him emotionally, reminding them both of the obvious gulf between them.

"Thank you for wanting to help me, my lord. I realize you caused the distraction at dinner with your wine to get Lady Eastwick to stop questioning me. It was very gallant of you. But I will be fine. I have my own reasons to hold on to my secrets, and I appreciate your respecting that. Everyone will be leaving soon, and things will get back to normal. And thank you for trying to comfort me; I think I am just overwrought from being so busy and a lack of sleep. For that reason I ought to be in bed right now. Good night, my lord." Emily again swept a deep curtsy before stepping to the door.

"Emily, wait." Philip wanted to detain her, but he didn't know what else they could say. Emily turned inquiring eyes upon him, but when he hesitated to say any more, she again said good night and quietly left the room.

Philip remained behind as she closed the door with a

quiet but final-sounding click. He stood staring at the thick door with his fists clenched as feelings of impotence flowed through him. *Why can't I feel this attraction for Lady Maude?* he questioned himself in bewilderment. *She would clearly make a most acceptable countess.* But the thought of her now turned him cold, while all that he felt for his mother's companion ranged from warm to white hot. He shook his head to rid himself of his conflicting emotions as he walked to the brandy decanter to wash them away.

Emily was relieved to gain her chamber without encountering anyone along the way. She sat at the dressing table deep in thought as she took down and brushed out her hair. She knew now that she loved the earl deeply. Unfortunately, according to his mother, he still professed a desire to marry Lady Maude, while she herself was still living a servant's life. And, despite her growing feelings for him, she did not fully trust him. She knew she could not believe everything Edwin had told her, but he had struck fear deep into her heart, and she knew the only one you could truly rely on was yourself. Once she had a plan, maybe then she could turn to Philip. It pained her to know he could kiss her so sweetly without truly having any deep feelings for her.

It was in a very troubled state of mind that Emily slipped into slumber. Her dreams were clouded by images of Lady Eastwick's piercing eyes following her while she watched Lord Philip kissing Lady Maude. Emily awoke the next morning feeling slightly subdued and not at all rested. She picked her most cheerful gown of buttercup yellow to brighten herself up before going to Lady Clara's chamber.

"Good morning, Emily. You're up and about early and looking radiant in your lovely yellow gown. How are you this morning?"

Emily was a firm believer that if you told yourself you were fine, yourself would have to believe it, so she put on a bravely cheerful face, and said, "I'm fine, thank you, Lady Clara. How did you sleep? Will you be going to break your fast downstairs this morning?"

"Oh, Emily, I don't know if I can bear it. I think I will send Smitty down to the kitchen for a tray for me. Would you mind checking on things there for me?"

"It would be my pleasure, my lady," Emily lied graciously. "Do you have a preference as to what activities we should do today?"

"I have asked Cook to pack a picnic lunch for everyone. We could go to the old abbey ruins and see the sights. We older ones can drive over in the buggy with the baskets and footmen, while the younger set can ride. Everyone will be happy to get out of the house, and I know you are eager to be on that horse again."

"Oh, my lady, that sounds like a wonderful scenario."

"Run along and check on the breakfast room, and please pass the message that we will be leaving around the noon hour."

"Yes, my lady. I shall see you then."

By quarter to twelve o'clock all who would be joining in the fun that day had assembled in the front hall. The young ladies wore becoming riding habits with jaunty hats set at rakish angles upon their brows. The older set had caught the excitement as well and were prepared to enjoy themselves. Emily could barely contain her glee at the thought of riding again. It was one of the biggest joys in life in her opinion, and she could hardly wait to get started. In her excitement she again caught Lady Eastwick's sharp gaze trained upon her, but she merely smiled at her before turning her back, busying herself with preparations.

Everyone went out front to wait for the mounts the grooms were leading forward. Emily was already in love with the gentle horse provided for her by Lady Clara. She had not been riding much of late and was happy for the horse's calm nature.

Lady Maude caught Lord Philip taking in the spectacle of a happy Emily in her element, and a green haze floated before her eyes. *How dare that simpleton of an earl pay more attention to the hired help than to me?* she thought contemptuously. *I'll show them both,* she continued viciously as she came up with a plan she thought would be effective.

The group on horseback set out closely clumped at first. They had just begun to spread out when Emily found herself unexpectedly at the front of the pack. She had just turned in the saddle to make sure the younger girls were keeping up when Lady Maude brought her crop down on the rump of Emily's mount. The surprised animal took off like a shot, almost unseating Emily in its fright. Her grip on the reins had been loose, and they were pulled from her hands as the horse stretched out into a gallop. Emily grabbed the mane and regained her balance.

Philip saw the entire byplay and felt his heart lodge in his throat at the danger Emily was in. His anger toward Lady Maude knew no bounds, and he felt an urge to take his crop to her in turn, but he caught himself just in time. The others were crying out in dismay as he urged his high-spirited horse into a gallop to chase after Emily.

By the time he caught up with her, Emily had lost her hat and most of her hairpins, and her glorious blond curls were streaming out behind her. She had regained the reins by the time he pulled up beside her. He was amazed to hear her gleeful laughter ring out as she bent over her horse's neck and urged it to an even faster pace as tears streamed down her cheeks from the wind whipping across her face. They raced neck and neck across the open field, reveling in the joy of being alive. Emily could feel her poor horse tiring, so she pulled back on the reins slightly as they neared the edge of the field. They slowed down to a canter, and Emily's laughter rang out again.

"That was the most exhilarating ride I have enjoyed in years!" she declared triumphantly.

"Have you gone mad?" demanded an outraged Philip now that he realized she was safe. "I was terrified you were going to be injured! Where did you learn to ride like that? If you weren't such an excellent horsewoman, you could have been seriously hurt or even killed. I could ring that woman's neck!" he concluded angrily as he realized who should be the true target of his ire. It crystallized in his heated mind that he would never be able to make Maude his countess, and he was at a loss as to what to do about his tumultuous feelings.

"Lord Philip, I'm all right. No harm done, see? Yes, it was a ridiculously stupid thing for Lady Maude to do, but no harm was done. As it turns out, I am an excellent rider," she concluded laughingly. "So she was foiled. Now let's go back and show the others I am fine. Poor Miss Ann is probably in hysterics by now," Emily surmised accurately.

When she and Philip found the others, it was a scene of chaos as Lord Marsden and Jane were trying with little success to comfort Ann, and Garfield was chastising Lady Maude. The Thorpe family and the rest of the group on horseback had turned their backs on Maude, visibly shunning her for the dangerous thing she had done.

Emily immediately dismounted and took Lady Ann in her arms. Lord Garfield met Lord Philip's eyes valiantly and took responsibility for his sister's vicious actions.

"I sincerely apologize for Maude's stupidity. If you would like, I can escort her back to the house, and we can pack up and be gone from your premises once our parents return."

Maude made a sound of distress but did not contradict her brother. She seemed to realize that this time she had gone too far. Lord Philip could see that even she was shocked by what she had done.

"That will not be necessary, but please keep an eye on her. And keep her away from the other young ladies," was Philip's verdict, despite the disgust he now felt toward the woman.

He turned to see Emily comforting the younger ladies and wiping Ann's cheeks with her own handkerchief. *What an amazing woman,* he thought. He heard her gathering the young women to continue their day as she twisted her hair back into place and returned her hat to its previously jaunty state.

"Come along, ladies. I am perfectly fine. No need to

worry. This little incident shall certainly not ruin our day. Lady Clara's feelings will be deeply hurt if she finds out we aren't enjoying ourselves. My lords, please assist the ladies to mount back up. Let's not waste any more of our precious time on such a beautiful day. If we do not hurry, your parents shall eat the entire picnic without us." At that droll comment, Jane, Ann, and Julia finally broke into laughter, and the crisis passed.

Even Lady Maude was forced to admire Emily's fortitude and good nature. Lord Garfield had already lost his heart to Miss Spencer; he marveled at her strength of character and cheerful spirit. No woman in his life had ever had such a marvelous spirit. Lord Marsden told a witty joke, and the camaraderie returned to most of the little group. Most studiously ignored Lady Maude, and she held herself icily apart from everyone, not even deigning to speak to her brother. They all became determined to enjoy the day.

The day concluded successfully. The picnic had been a delight, and everyone had enjoyed exploring the old ruins. After the picnic, the older guests and Lady Maude returned to the manor to rest before dinner, and the younger crowd rode down to the village to take refreshment at the inn. All returned Rosemount in high spirits.

Over dinner Emily was discomfited by the scrutiny she was again subjected to by some of the guests. Everyone was still curious about the countess' companion, especially after hearing of what she had endured that afternoon.

A subdued Lady Maude remained coldly silent. Her parents had seemed embarrassed when they met up with

Emily in the drawing room before dinner, uncertain whether to apologize for or ignore what had happened. Emily graciously smoothed over the moment by taking Lady Sedgely's hand and asking if they had had a pleasant ride back to the estate. Lady Sedgely squeezed her fingers in reluctant gratitude, made some comment about the weather, and moved on to speak with someone else.

The next day passed pleasantly and uneventfully. The ladies spent the morning in genteel activities such as needlework or letter writing, while the gentlemen returned to the hunt. In the afternoon everyone participated in lawn sports. Dinner went smoothly, and cards, games, and more music enlivened the evening.

Emily was relieved that the end of the week was almost reached. As she sat in her room that night, she reflected on the various relationships that seemed to be developing among the guests. She had chosen to be a spectator as ten of the young guests engaged in a vigorous game of croquet while the elders took a turn in the gardens. James had sacrificed himself to try to entertain the ignored Lady Maude while Lord Philip was busy with estate matters.

Emily had found it fascinating to see the young men and women pairing up. Despite his difference from his haughty family and his respectful attention to her, Lord Garfield couldn't help but be discouraged by her lowly position. The quietly refined Lady Arabella, however, was also to his liking. He seemed to bask in her restful, cheerfully kind warmth. They joined in a friendly competition with Dolph and Jane, who had struck up a mild flirtation. Tony and Julia were on very friendly terms, which left the young Viscount Eastwick to team up with Ann, while

Lord Brooke partnered his brother-in-law's sister and watched jealously as Lady Arabella enjoyed Garfield's company.

Emily smiled as she thought of young Ann practicing her newly developed social skills on the easygoing lord. With a much quieter sister, he seemed to find her artless chatter vastly amusing and responded in kind to her.

It seemed as if most of the young ladies were simply practicing for the upcoming Season, but it looked as though a serious relationship was budding between Jane and Lord Sutherland. Emily had been pleasantly surprised to see the quiet young man engaging in lengthy conversation with the bubbly Miss Waddell. As it turned out, the young baron was actually quite intelligent despite his penchant for sporting activities and his lack of conversational skills. Emily was surprised to find there was truth to the expression that still waters ran deep. There might be a match in the future for the young couple.

Emily reflected on the conversation she had overheard that afternoon. Jane was attempting to draw the young baron out with leading questions. "So what is Sutherland like, my lord? Is it very far from London?"

"Sutherland is a beautiful estate about three hours' ride from London. It's not overly large, since it is not a terribly old title, but the house is really quite comfortable. I have a few excellent tenants that have been with my family for generations, and everything runs quite smoothly."

"Oh, you must be kept so busy," was the admiring reply from Jane.

"Wasn't your father a Baron? His workload would have been quite similar," Adolphus said gently.

Jane had looked uncertain before replying. "My father died many years ago. When he was alive, he had a steward who did much of the work on our estate, and after he died, my mother kept the steward on, and he now does all the work. I am not actually even sure what goes into the running of an estate, so I am ever so impressed that you actually do it yourself."

The baron appeared pleased by her praise but replied modestly. "My father and grandfather set up excellent routines, so Sutherland almost runs itself—unlike the estate I am expected to inherit from my uncle, the Earl of Vale. It is such a drafty old place, I shudder to think of the restorations I will have to make when it comes into my hands. I'm quite fond of my uncle, and he's got several good years left, so I shouldn't worry about it too much, should I?" He then looked seriously at Jane and continued proudly, "I think you would really like Sutherland, Miss Jane. I would like to show it to you someday."

Jane had blushed prettily and murmured an unintelligible reply before the two moved out of Emily's earshot. Emily surmised that an offer for Jane's hand would not be too far in the future if things progressed along the same vein. That would be just as well. If Jane was promised to someone, it would make the upcoming Season easier for Ann.

Emily was happy for all her new friends, who seemed to be having such a good time visiting Rosemount. Emily had a smile on her face that night as she drifted off to sleep.

Chapter Twelve

The day of the big finale dawned brightly. Lady Clara and Emily were congratulating themselves on the uncharacteristically good weather, as though they had conjured it themselves. The two women spent the morning consumed with final preparations for the gala that would be held at Rosemount that evening. Gentry from the surrounding area had been invited, and about fifty-five people were expected for the ball and second supper. A light supper was to be served to the houseguests before the ball.

The house was abuzz with excitement as the staff worked hard to ready the manor for the event. The silver was polished, the windows shined, rugs beaten, and floors waxed. The maids were excited to see everyone in their finery and were proud of their hand in everything. The footmen were busy preparing their own uniforms for the evening. Everything was to be perfect. Lady Clara was most pleased with how it was all coming together. Emily's presence in her home was turning out to be one of the best decisions she had ever made.

The houseguests were left to amuse themselves for a time. Lord Philip took the young gentlemen out riding in the afternoon, as they were getting restless and it kept them out of the way of the servants busily making preparations. The older gentlemen spent a quiet afternoon playing chess, while the ladies tried to enjoy their quiet, genteel pursuits. But to no avail. Most of the young ladies were too excited to sit still, so after taking a turn in the rose gardens, they ran tittering upstairs to begin their personal preparations for the evening. Their gowns had all been shaken out well in advance, but each girl spent painstaking hours on her hairstyle and any other beauty machination she could come up with. Finally the time to assemble for the light, private dinner arrived.

The drawing room was heavy with the perfumes and powders that had been applied so generously just minutes before. Emily could not help her wry smile as she realized that she too was caught up in the magical excitement of the event. Maggie had outdone herself coaxing Emily's curls into the fashionable style. The two girls had pored over the fashion plates to determine how best to arrange Emily's hair for the special event. Lady Clara had lent Emily an intricately stylish black necklace to offset the paleness of her high-waisted white crepe gown. She felt very elegant as she mingled with the gathered company. The first real ball of her life! Who wouldn't be excited?

Emily wondered why they had bothered planning a dinner for the guests, as most were clearly too excited to manage more than a couple of bites. Of course, some of the group would appreciate the sustenance to get them through the evening, she thought with an inner chuckle as she saw resignation upon the faces of Lords Sedgely and Fitzgerald. Doubtless they would prefer a good card game to a ball. She took pity on them and told them she had had a few tables set up in the small salon for those who preferred cards to dancing. She was delighted to see the sparkle return to their eyes.

Many of the other guests had already arrived when the houseguests left the dining room and converged on the ballroom. It was a less formal affair than a London ball, so Lady Clara and Lord Philip had chosen to forego the receiving line in lieu of mingling and speaking with each guest personally. This allowed them to spend a little longer with each one, and they were gracious enough to make everyone feel welcome.

When the band struck up the first song, Lord Philip led his mother out onto the dance floor. Lady Clara felt triumph in her breast as she thought of how the week could have turned out. She had been expecting to see her son leading out the Lady Maude for this special dance, and it was with a sense of profound relief that she realized Philip was not at all disturbed that things hadn't turned out differently. He did appear to be preoccupied, though, so Lady Clara asked him what was disturbing him. He replied that he was thinking about the matter the king had him working on, and he reminded her he would have to leave the next day along with the rest of the guests, as he had to return to his search.

Then, after a moment's hesitation, he asked her, "Mama, what is nobility to you?"

Lady Clara at first wasn't sure what he was getting at until he asked, "Do you think Father was wrong to place such emphasis on good bloodlines?"

The light dawned in Lady Clara's mind, but she contained her excitement and tried to answer his question diplomatically. "I do not think your father was *wrong,* Philip, but you may have misinterpreted things he said. However, this is a rather large topic, and I do believe this song is coming to an end. Let's discuss the matter later, shall we?"

Philip smiled warmly at his mother as he took her into the last turn of the dance. There was a polite murmur of admiration from the crowd before the band struck up the next song and other couples took to the floor.

"I guess I need to do my duty by the other young ladies here, eh, Mama?" Philip laughed as he bowed over his mother's hand before turning to Lady Julia and inviting her to have the next dance with him. Julia blushed and accepted happily.

Emily was delighted when Lord Fitzgerald appeared at her elbow and gallantly requested her hand for the next dance. He said he would "do his duty" before getting lost in the cards. He accompanied this statement with a broad wink, which brought forth a gurgle of laughter from Emily. He turned out to be a graceful partner, and they enjoyed their dance together, after which he went off to play cards. Emily was having a grand time and was thrilled to see that all the guests were enjoying themselves as well.

The young ladies were dazzling in their pastel colors.

The mothers looked on in their deeper-hued gowns as their offspring paired up, then changed partners as each successive dance went by. It was becoming obvious to everyone that Lord Sutherland was courting Lady Jane when he stood glowering from the sidelines whenever she accepted an invitation to dance with any other gentleman. It was clear too that Jane was enjoying every minute of the attention she was receiving.

Emily's own joy was made complete when later in the evening Philip bowed over her hand and requested that she dance the waltz with him. She hesitated before accepting, afraid he would be able to discern her feelings during the intimacy of the dance. He misinterpreted her silence, thinking perhaps she did not know the steps. He had begun to apologize when she smiled cheerfully, took his hand, and accepted the invitation. They danced beautifully together. Many of the other guests stopped and watched as they glided gracefully around the ballroom floor as though dancing upon a cloud. The music and the crowd faded away. The lost themselves in the moment.

Watching them, Lady Maude thought her head would explode from rage. That Philip should seem to enjoy the company of this commoner more than he did hers! Despite her shame a few days prior and her realization that she had stepped over the line, she had expected Philip to continue paying court to her. Watching him enjoy his dance with Emily made her realize he had never seemed that content in her own company. She felt impotent and flounced away from the dance floor, refusing to watch such a spectacle.

Lady Clara, on the other hand, felt her joy was complete.

Lord Philip couldn't still be professing feelings for Lady Maude if he was so obviously enjoying the evening apart from her, she reasoned. The music drew to a close, and the dancers drifted to the sidelines. Philip escorted Emily over to his mother and went in search of drinks for both women.

Lady Clara complimented Emily on her dancing. "Where did you learn the waltz, my dear? You perform it beautifully. You must have had an excellent teacher."

Emily blushed to her roots as she realized her *faux pas*. She grasped for an answer; she had come to love the countess dearly and couldn't bear to tell her more lies. But she dared not reveal her secrets now, least of all in a crowded ballroom. So she told the truth with a quiver in her voice. "My father taught me. He was a wonderful dancer. He and Mama loved to dance together at every opportunity."

Lady Clara didn't pursue the topic further, recognizing that the tears shimmering on Emily's lashes might tumble down and cause a scene. She patted Emily's hand and said, "Well, he did an excellent job of teaching you, my dear. It was pure pleasure watching you dancing with Philip. Ah, there he is with some punch for us. Thank you, Philip. That's kind of you."

Emily soon drifted away to mingle with the guests. She kept an eye out for any ladies without a partner and quickly introduced a gentleman. She was determined there would be no wallflowers at this party. It delighted her to see that all the ladies, even the quiet or plain ones, were enjoying the evening.

In her meandering Emily came upon Lady Thorpe,

who appeared lost in thought. She stopped to engage the lady in conversation. "Are you well, Lady Thorpe? Could I get you a glass of something from the refreshment table?"

"Oh, Miss Spencer, you are so sweet. No, thank you. I'm fine. I was just thinking about how much fun Lord Thorpe is having and missing my children. I feel so very torn. My husband has had such a grand time here at Rosemount that he really wants to go up to London for the Season this year. We have not been since we had our first child."

Emily pondered the subject briefly. Having neither husband nor children gave her very little experience in this particular subject, but she felt the need to help.

"Do you really hate London that much?" she queried gently.

"Oh, no, some of my best memories are of times spent in London, both as a girl with my family and then during my courtship and marriage with Lord Thorpe."

"So why couldn't you go now? Could you not take the children with you, even for a few weeks if not the entire Season?"

Lady Thorpe smiled brilliantly at Emily. "You are a smart girl, aren't you? I never really thought of that possibility." She laughed at her own silliness. "I was just so caught up in missing the children and enjoying Thorpe's amusement that I couldn't see past that to a solution. Of course, the thought of being cooped up in a carriage for three days with the little ones is enough to turn even the fondest mother into a lunatic," said the mother humorously.

"That is why you need two carriages," concluded Emily drolly.

Lady Thorpe was so pleased with the solution to what she had considered a huge problem, she linked arms with Miss Spencer, and they proceeded to the refreshment table for glasses of punch while discussing all the sights to be seen in London and what the children might enjoy. Emily had not yet been to London herself, but she had heard much about it as well as often reading the London papers, so she could add a few details to the conversation.

The rest of the night flew by as the revelry continued. Emily's hand was bespoken for nearly every dance. She was pleasantly surprised to be receiving such gallant attention from the gentlemen despite her lowly position, and she was determined to wring every drop of enjoyment from the evening. She had worked to make everyone comfortable throughout their stay, and evidently they wanted to show her a good time at the ball in return. Emily was passed from gentleman to gentleman with each tune the band struck. She glided around the dance floor with ceaseless energy and still found the time to check on the food and wine supplies. She even delighted the footmen by joining them in a country dance in the hallway after she had checked to see how they were doing. The evening was an unqualified success.

Emily stood just behind the earl and his mother as they waved off the guests not staying for the night. The houseguests were being tucked into their beds by their maids and valets when Emily, Philip, and Lady Clara sat down in the library to toast themselves and the success of their event.

Philip offered, "Mama, I must apologize for begging you to throw this party, but I must also compliment you on how well you carried it off. You made excellent choices on the guest list, and the entire week has been an unequivocal success. I did not realize what difficulties I was asking you to undertake, and I am impressed with how you managed so well. Thank you for doing this for me. It did not have the result I had expected, but that is apparently a good thing." He smiled self-deprecatingly.

Lady Clara was delighted by what he was saying but modestly replied, "I couldn't have done it without Emily."

Emily realized that the mother and son could use a few minutes of privacy, so she excused herself after suppressing a huge yawn. Philip and Clara laughed and bade her good night. Emily left the room and went to confirm that the front door was locked. She had not quite closed the door to the library, and as she passed by on her way to the stairs, she felt her entire world turn upside down.

In the days following as she looked back on that moment, she couldn't believe she hadn't cried out from the pain as she overheard his lordship speaking. "So I'll be off to visit Ridley again tomorrow. We need to get this matter cleared up about his missing cousin." The buzzing in Emily's ears blocked out whatever else he might have said, and she wrapped her tattered composure around herself like a shield as she ascended the grand staircase on the way to her chamber. She realized she had been right not to lay bare her soul to Lord Philip when he had been questioning her about her background. Rage came up into her nostrils as she contemplated what a fool she had nearly been. She had so wanted to confide in him. She was shocked and heartsore that someone she had come to care about so deeply was in league with that devil, Edwin. Emily felt the shards of her broken heart piercing the inside of her chest. She cried herself to sleep that night, unsure if she cared whether or not tomorrow ever came.

Emily glared at the sunshine streaming in through her window the next morning. It was shocking to her that the world did not reflect the tragedy she felt. But it was, she realized, only a personal tragedy. No one would really care, and in fact, no one could even know. She had been right not to trust or confide in anyone, and no one could find out how devastated she was because that would give away too much. So she donned her "happy" clothes, the yellow frock she loved so much, and tried to make herself look as decent as possible, considering how puffy her eyes were. Laying a cool cloth on them for a moment had helped a bit, and, looking in the mirror, Emily was surprised to see that no one could even tell that her heart had been broken the night before.

She went downstairs with a sense of gloom, hoping his lordship had already left so she wouldn't have to face the ordeal of bidding him farewell. Most of the guests were still abed, and Emily was happy to find the breakfast room empty. She did not want any witnesses as she forced herself to swallow a few mouthfuls.

Philip walked into the breakfast room. "Good morning, Emily. You're up awfully early after such a late night." He was delighted to see her, he had thought she would still be sleeping when he departed, and he wouldn't have a chance to say good-bye.

Emily felt the color drain from her face at the sound of his voice and struggled to maintain her composure. She took a deep breath and turned to him. "I am never very successful at sleeping late. Old habits, you know." She laughed self-consciously before turning back to her plate. She prayed he would not endeavor to engage in conversation but would instead bury his nose in his paper or else hurry through his repast. Her prayer was not answered.

"So, are you fully recovered from this ordeal?" Philip asked conversationally.

She almost spilled her coffee before she realized he was talking about the week of entertaining a houseful of company. She smiled wanly at him, popped a bite of toast into her mouth, and just nodded. Surprised at her quietness, Philip figured she was worn out by all the work she had undertaken on his mother's behalf, as well as the scrutiny some of the guests had put her through.

"You needn't make such an effort to impress my mother, Emily—Miss Spencer, I should say. She is terribly fond of you and thinks you are a godsend. You should relax for the next few days."

Emily was unaccountably touched at his thoughtfulness and felt the shards of her broken heart pierce her chest once again. She marveled that he could seem so kind and concerned when she now knew he was a friend of the evil Edwin.

"And I love your mother," she said, choking a bit. "I have not run myself ragged, my lord, if that is what you are implying. It is a great pleasure to serve the countess.

Next to my own mother, she is the best, kindest woman I have ever met."

Philip was impressed by her loyalty to her mistress. Everything he learned about her was impressive, yet he felt such conflicting emotions. He was disappointed to have to leave her for a while, since he so enjoyed her company, but he was conversely glad to get some distance to obtain a sense of objectivity.

Emily could feel his gaze upon her but forced herself to ignore him. She quickly choked down the last of her toast and stood up. "I wish you safe travels, my lord. Perhaps we will meet again." She made to leave but was stopped by Philip's soft but meaningful reply.

"You can be sure we shall, Emily."

Her startled eyes flew to his face before she spun around and ran from the room. She did not stop running until she locked herself in the remotest corner of the attics, where she had discovered a litter of kittens the week prior while the house had been a whirl of cleaning activity.

She wept bitterly for many moments, crying out her grief, mourning for her lost love and wishing her parents were there to guide and comfort her. But one could not remain depressed for long in the company of young animals, and the dear little creatures were able to coax a smile to her face once more. She stayed in the small space until she was able to see, by way of the little window, Philip ride away with Mr. Dale in tow.

She then made her way down to her chamber to wash the tearstains from her face and turn a smile upon the world once more. She was able to go through the motions of helping the guests pack and waving them off with Lady Clara. It had been a tearful parting with the Waddell ladies and Miss Fitzgerald. They all vowed to keep in touch. Emily was happy to have made some friends despite the difference in their stations.

There was an awkward moment when the Sedgelys were taking their leave of the countess. It was painfully obvious they were disappointed with the outcome of the visit. They had been hoping Lord Philip would declare his intentions toward Lady Maude during the house party, but it was abundantly clear that no offer was to be forthcoming. Cloaked in their own sense of worth, they seemed unable to blame their daughter for this eventuality and apparently deemed it was somehow the countess' fault that her son had not come up to scratch. The Sedgelys had stood in the grand entrance en masse, unsure what to say as they took their leave. Lord Garfield saved the situation with his ever-present charm as he stepped forward and bowed before the countess elegantly, kissing her hand with a flourish and making an amusing comment about the great fun he had had under her roof. Always pleasant, Lady Clara accepted his comments with good grace, and the family was able to exit.

Emily had wisely chosen to remain busy helping the Thorpes and Eastwicks with their packing while Lady Clara bade the Sedgely's good-bye. Since the incident between herself and Lady Maude on horseback had probably solidified Philip's resolve not to offer for the woman, Emily did not want the family trying to be polite to her as they made their exit. With her own conflicted emotions involving Philip, she could even find it in her heart to feel a bit sorry for the cold young woman, yet she was also pleased that Maude would not be the next Countess of Yorkleigh.

It had taken half the day for all the guests to finally detest. Emily had nearly run a path in the stairs as she again made herself indispensable to everyone helping with last-minute errands. Lady Arabella could not find her favorite bonnet—Emily discovered it behind the settee in the small salon—while Miss Thorpe had misplaced her parasol in the gazebo in the rose garden. It took quite some time for Emily to find Lord Brooke's missing pair of Hessians, which had been, strangely, left in the pantry. Emily felt she had been running a race without benefit of a horse by the time they waved off the final guests with a sigh of relief.

After everyone was gone, Lady Clara and Emily sat down to a cup of tea to discuss the entire event. Emily tried to enter the conversation with enthusiasm, but it was a strain. All in all she had enjoyed the party. It had been a delight to make so many new friends. But once she sat down to rest, all her sadness over the earl came rushing in to accost her emotions.

The countess could tell that Emily was just tired and finally put an end to the interlude. Emily attacked a weedy patch in the garden to get her difficult emotions under control once more. By suppertime the two women returned to their easy camaraderie and spent an enjoyable evening playing backgammon before retiring early to bed.

Chapter Thirteen

Lord Philip and James rode directly from Rosemount toward the estate of the Viscount of Ridley, determined to get some answers from the shifty lord. Too much time had been lost already. Realizing the hospitality at Ridley would be scant, they decided to stop at the nearby inn in the early afternoon for some refreshment.

The landlord—Jimmy, as he asked them to call him—was delighted to see them again and went out of his way to make them comfortable. Jimmy was a talkative fellow, and Philip was not in the best frame of mind to put up with his chatter after the long ride. He wished only to recuperate a bit. But then his ears caught what Jimmy was blathering about.

"Guess yer here to see Ridley, ain't yez, melord? Lots of goings-on out that way, that's fer sure. They's bin turning off some of the servants without so much as a farthing. That ain't right, let me tell ye. An' that Lord Max, he's a right cool one, he is, making hisself right at home. He's right angry with Ridley for losing the missy, he is. Yes siree. What bizness are you taking up with those two fer, if I may be so bold to ask ye, melord? Ye seem to be a right downy one— why'd you want to go and get messed up with them?" The inquisitive Jimmy seemed quite puzzled by the matter.

"You are quite right, Jimmy. We would rather not have any business with either of those two men. However, we are interested in finding the missing marchioness. You mentioned Ridley has turned off some servants. Would you happen to know what has become of them?"

"Yes siree, I do know. The little missy's old nurse has gone to bide with her sister. She was waiting for them to find the little missy, but now she's gone with a broken heart. None too happy, that's fer sure. Sez it's all his lordship's fault that the little missy is gone."

"Really? Why would she say that?" questioned Philip calmly.

"Don't reckon I know. Jest overwrought, I guess," came Jimmy's uninformative reply.

"Were there any other servants sent away recently?" Philip continued to question the man.

"Sure there was, melord—a groom and a stable boy. Hired 'em on here. Right good workers they are too. Glad to have 'em. Ridley's loss is my gain, don't ye say, melord?" The good-natured landlord grinned.

Philip felt his patience slipping but endeavored not to let it show.

"Might we speak to these two men, Jimmy? They might know something about the missing young lady that would be helpful in our search."

"I don't see why not, melord. They should be out in the courtyard. After you two gents have had your meal, you jest go on out there and talk at 'em all ye want. Makes none of my never-mind," finished the landlord.

"Thank you, my good man," replied the earl. "We'll most likely be returning for the night, so if you could hold a couple of rooms for us, we'd greatly appreciate it."

"That would be me pleasure, melord!" grinned the gleeful Jimmy, clearly anticipating the extra coins he would soon have in his pocket. With that he finally left the two alone to discuss their plans.

"Well, isn't that interesting! Edwin is sending away some of the servants. Is it because he's such a pinchpenny, or did they know something he did not want them to tell us? What do you think, James?"

"From what we have learned of the viscount, it really could be either possibility. He seems such a louse, he could turn away long-time servant without blinking. As the marchioness' guardian he is within his rights, no matter how mean-spirited it is. Or the servants could have found out some of his secrets, and he needed to be rid of them. We can't really be sure until we speak to them ourselves," replied the secretary.

"Indeed. Let us go speak to the former groom and stable boy. Maybe they will know where we can reach the old nurse. After we've spoken to them, we'll ride out and speak with Edwin and what servants remain. With luck we can be finished with this blasted search without any more delay."

"Let's hope you are right, my lord," was James' heartfelt answer.

Unfortunately the groom and stable boy were not much

help. They were unsure why they had been let go from the estate. They also knew very little about where the nurse would have gone except to tell them that the housekeeper at Ridley would probably know where the sister lived. From their conversation, Philip guessed that they probably knew something but that they didn't know what they knew. He needed more information in order to ask the right questions to find the answers he needed from them. It was a frustrating situation to say the least, and Philip's nerves were wearing thin as they rode out to Ridley's estate.

They were expected this time and received a warmer reception than before. The butler quickly ushered them into the library, where Edwin would receive them.

Edwin came out from behind his desk to greet his two visitors. "How good to see you again, Lord Yorkleigh. We've been expecting you today, and any of the servants in residence who knew the young marchioness are prepared to speak with you. I myself took the time to question them, and I have to say that I do not think any of them know anything that will be of any use in the search for Lady Emmaline. Regrettably I think you will find this to be another dead end." Despite his best efforts, he didn't actually sound that regretful, but Philip decided to ignore his insincerity and take him at face value.

"Thank you for making your servants available to us. We would like to get started right away. But before we do, I would like to ask you again, are you sure you have no idea where the young lady is?" Philip tried to be gentle in his asking, but he knew he no doubt sounded quite fierce. He was then surprised by how sincere the viscount's answer sounded.

"I can assure you, my lord, I have absolutely no idea where the lady is. And I have to say that I resent your implication. I have actually been losing sleep over the matter of my missing cousin. I fear we may never find her."

Philip actually believed what Edwin was saying. Even if he had had something to do with the young woman's leaving, he genuinely seemed to be unaware of her whereabouts at this time. He also seemed to be saddened by her loss. *Of course,* thought Philip, *he could be saddened by the loss of her wealth.* If it were determined that she was, in fact, dead, all her holdings were set to revert to the crown, and Edwin was no doubt enjoying having her funds to dip into to line his own pockets while she was missing. Despite his cynicism, he replied more kindly to the viscount.

"We'll do all we can to locate her for you, you can be sure. Now, we would like to speak first with any personal maids the marchioness would have had at her service."

"My lord, the marchioness didn't have a lady's maid, as she had barely left the schoolroom when her parents passed. Her closest servant was her old nurse. The poor woman was so distraught over the disappearance of Lady Emmaline that I had to give her leave to go visit her family." By the conclusion of this little speech, insincerity had again crept into his voice, and Philip knew he was lying.

"Where does the nurse's family live? We shall need to speak with her."

"I don't rightly know where they live, my lord. It's none of my business where the servants go on their time off," replied the viscount haughtily.

Realizing he would get nowhere with Ridley, Philip

sighed and asked to speak with the housekeeper and butler. These two were shown in and questioned. As the afternoon spilled into evening, it became quite clear that the servants were frightened of their new master and would be hard-pressed to reveal anything even if they knew it. None of them had any idea where the young lady would have gone. They only confirmed what Philip already knew: Lady Emmaline was the only child of only children, and her grandparents were long since dead. The closest relative the young woman had was the new viscount, and he was no prize. The marquis and his wife and been content to live retired with their small family and did not socialize much. None of the staff could hazard a guess as to where Emmaline would turn if she needed an escape. When they were questioned about the missing nurse, some of them got uncomfortable and would only admit that she had been very upset when she departed. The only real lead they got was from the housekeeper, who finally admitted that the nurse probably went to stay with her sister's family near Bath.

By the time they had spoken to nearly every member of the staff on the estate and even a couple of the tenants, it was nearly fully dark, and Philip and James decided to call it a day and return to the inn. They fell silent as they rode through the dark, both absorbed in their own thoughts. They clattered into the courtyard and threw their reins to the waiting hands before climbing the stairs into the inn to be greeted by Jimmy.

"Any luck, melord?" he questioned amiably.

"Not much, Jimmy. Could you please serve us a warm meal as quickly as possible? We could use sustenance."

"Didn't show you any 'ospitality, did they, melord?"

"No, Jimmy, they did not, and we are quite famished," Philip answered wearily.

"Comin' right up, melord."

Philip and James were glad for some quiet and a hot meal and tucked right in when Jimmy returned with their supper. They made quick work of the simple fare spread out before them. Both men were exhausted from the long ride and the many hours of questioning and were ready to be shown to their rooms before long. They realized they would not be able to find any new information here and were discouraged by their lack of progress.

"We should head back to London tomorrow and get caught up on our own business for a couple of days before striking out to Bath. It seems the old nurse will be our last chance at finding out what happened to the marchioness," concluded Philip before bidding James a good night.

Several days later the two gentlemen were on the road again, this time in a light carriage, as the journey to Bath would take at least two days. By nightfall of the second day, they reached a hotel Philip was familiar with in the popular town. They questioned the landlord to determine where they might find the old nurse, Mary, and resolved to track her down in the morning.

The next day dawned, and Philip prepared to visit the marchioness' old servant. James was feeling under the weather and would remain at the hotel. It was a pleasant morning, and Philip enjoyed his ride out to the little farm where he had been told he would be able to find Mary. It was a humble home, and several people came out to observe who would be riding up their lane in such a fancy equipage. Philip stepped down and introduced himself, explaining why he was there and apologizing for the disturbance. Several pairs of eyes observed him gravely before a woman with ruddy cheeks and graying hair stepped forward and said, "I'm Mary. I'm who you're looking for, your lordship."

Philip was invited into the kitchen to sit by the fire while Mary's sister offered tea. Philip accepted and gratefully warmed himself after the chill of the morning.

"So you're looking for my wee one are you, milord? You didn't have to work so hard at tracking me down. You should've just asked his lordship, that Edwin, what he did with her. He carted her off in the middle of the night with that evil friend of his; Lord Max." Mary was becoming upset and clenching her fists in her lap. Suddenly she pounded a fist on the table. "I heard them talking about taking my baby to Bedlam. Bedlam, I tell you. How could they take my beautiful, precious, wee one to Bedlam?" She began to weep.

Philip was stunned. "Bedlam! Are you sure? Why would he take her to Bedlam? Was she disturbed?" No one had mentioned that there was anything wrong with the marchioness.

Mary continued to weep but replied to his questions. "There was nothing wrong with the precious girl aside from her refusing to wed that fiend, Lord Maximillian. Edwin had threatened her that if she continued to refuse, he would lock her up. I think the wee bairn didn't truly believe he would follow through on that threat, and so she held out in her refusal. She knew her parents would never have wanted her to marry such a one as he. But one morning I woke up and she was gone, disappeared in the night. I lit into Ridley, let me tell you, screaming like a fishwife I was so distraught, but to no avail. He refused to admit what he had done. He then had me subdued and told me my lady would no longer require my services, that he had made other arrangements for her. He didn't even provide me with the coach fare to leave, just shoved me out the door without even a fare-thee-well." Mary's tears had dried, but she was fairly huffing in her outrage.

Philip was perplexed. "Why didn't you tell anyone?"

"Who's there to tell?" was her practical reply. "Lord Ridley is her guardian, and I had no proof that he had taken her to Bedlam, nor any way of going there to get her out. I had no authority over her; I'm just her old nurse. Even if I had found a way to get to the asylum, they would never have let me in. Haven't you heard the stories about such places? I tremble nightly thinking of the poor sweet lass locked up with all sorts of riffraff. But if you're looking for the young marchioness, you'll no doubt find her in Bedlam. Might I ask you, my lord, why are you looking for her? She has no kin other than the viscount."

Lord Yorkleigh became very grave over this newest development. It was just as well that Ridley was so far away, because at the moment Philip felt quite violent toward the villain. He had definitely heard stories about Bedlam, perhaps worse tales than the nurse knew of. No one should be in there, in his opinion, least of all a gently bred lady of quality. He made an effort to remain calm so as not to frighten the older woman any further while he strove to answer her question.

"His Majesty, the king, has commissioned me to find the

marchioness. It is by his authority that she may inherit all that her parents left to her. As you may know, due to the age of most of the titles, Lady Emmaline is entitled to inherit all the titles and estates. Our sire wishes to fulfill the late marquis' request to have his daughter honored. When His Majesty heard of the marquis' death, he began to inquire about the daughter, and when Ridley did not produce her, the king started a search."

"But what interest do you have in this matter, if you don't mind me being so bold, milord?"

"I have absolutely no vested interest in the outcome of this search, which is why the king has entrusted it to me. My father was a trusted advisor to His Majesty, and in his absence, I was chosen to look into her disappearance."

"Well, it is great news that you and our king are looking for my lassie," declared the nurse. "Just drive over to Bedlam and get her out."

"I have every intention of doing that. Are you prepared to come to her once we've located her? She will no doubt be in need of the comfort of a familiar face after her harrowing ordeal."

"I don't think you'd be able to keep me away, milord," was the instant reply. "I can be ready at a moment's notice."

"Very good. I will send a carriage for you as soon as I've located her. You may also be required to tell His Majesty what you know."

"Speak to the king? Oh, my gracious, I don't know about that, milord," was her flustered answer.

"It may not come to that. Whatever happens, I will send you word. Thank you, Mary. You've been most helpful."

With that Philip took his leave and drove back to the

hotel to collect James and start on the way back toward London.

James was stunned silence when Philip revealed their new destination. After several moments he finally broke that silence.

"Bethlem Royal Hospital. I cannot believe he would stoop so low as to have her locked up in such a place. Better, I think, to murder her than to put her there. Everyone knows what kind of place it is." He broke off in disgust, unable to contemplate the possibility of a gently-bred female being placed in such a situation. "Perhaps he should be hanged for such an action," James continued. "Hanging might be too good for him. *He* should be locked up in Bedlam."

"James, we don't know for sure if he took her there. We only know he threatened to do so. Perhaps the girl ran away to avoid such a fate. Or mayhap he took her elsewhere. We still have very little information to go on. We don't even have a recent likeness of the marchioness to identify her. Let's try to remain calm until we reach Moorfields and see for ourselves. We don't need an accident to complicate an already difficult journey."

Both men subsided into restless silence and they hastened onward toward London, changing the houses frequently to make the fastest time possible. It was impossible to make it to London in one day, no matter how fast they traveled, so they finally broke their journey to seize a bit of sleep and rest the weary horses. Rising at dawn the next day, they hurried on their way once more and clattered up to the cold stone façade of the Bethlem Royal Hospital late that morning.

Philip stared in fascinated disgust at the ghoulish statues gracing the front gate. In the light of day they looked eerie and almost farcical. He shuddered to think what they'd look like by the light of the moon. As he gazed past the iron gates to the granite building beyond, he heard the sounds emanating from within and knew the young lady could not have survived these months if she had truly been left there. But surely Edwin would have been notified of her death, and he seemed truly not to know where she was. This assurance fortified the earl to step through the gates and proceed with his investigation.

Upon their entrance to the courtyard, a great bull of a guard hailed them. He lumbered toward them with a welcoming grin that exposed the few blackened teeth that remained in his mouth. His pockmarked face with its squinty, piglike eyes surrounded by his wild and lanky hair was the stuff of nightmares, and Philip struggled to suppress a shudder as the guard drew up before them. When he spoke, a gust of putrefied air wafted toward Philip, but he managed to keep his face impassive.

"Mornin', guv'nor. Is you here to see the inmates? We charge a fee, ya know."

"Actually, my good man, we are here to collect one of your inmates, not for a viewing. Could you please point us in the direction of the warden or director of this establishment?" Philip inquired politely, although disgusted at the thought of spectators coming to view the residents of the "hospital."

"Well, guv'nor, there's a fee for that too."

"I'm sure there is," replied Philip resignedly as he flipped some coins toward the guard's eagerly waiting hand.

"Warden's through that door over there—can't miss 'im." The guard pointed. "I'll keep an eye out for your carriage, guv'nor," he offered generously.

"That would be most appreciated," answered Philip dryly as he turned toward the door that had been pointed out.

As the two men entered the building, they were assailed by the pungent stench of a multitude of unwashed bodies. James nearly gagged before getting himself under control. By taking short breaths through their mouths, they managed to maintain their composure as they went in search of whoever was in charge of the horrific place.

After a moment another ghoulish-looking brute of a man approached them, wanting to know what business they had there. After they identified themselves, the man's demeanor changed, and he ushered them into his office, trying to appear genial. Philip tried to remain polite, knowing that they would get no information out of this man if he felt threatened in any way. As Philip explained the purpose of their call, the man appeared incredulous.

"Don't have no marchionesses here, milord, I'm sure of that. If you want, you can go check for yourselves, search through the women and see if she's here, but I know for sure she ain't." He was edging toward belligerence, so Philip tried another tack.

"I don't mean to question your establishment, sir. We have been searching for this young woman for a few months now, and this is where our trail has led us. I myself actually doubted that she would be here. Is it possible she was here and died?" Philip asked hesitantly, unsure if he wanted to hear the answer.

His effort at gentleness paid off; the warden appeared more reasonable. "Never been any marchionesses in Bedlam, milord. The Quality looks after their crazies on their own." He paused for a moment in thought. "Haven't had any dead in a while either, 'cept for one old geezer who croaked a couple weeks back. But you said this was a young woman, didn't you?"

Philip felt a powerful mixture of relief and disappointment. Relief that the young noblewoman wasn't enduring such a place, but disappointment that he was at another dead end in his search and had no further leads to go on. He decided to ask one more question before they left.

"Just to be certain, could you think back over the last several months? Have you had any noblemen deliver any patients here?"

The warden sighed deeply in thought. "Let's see. I can only think of one example. Lord Maximilian dropped off a poor, unfortunate girl about five or six months ago. Pretty young thing she was. He said she had gone crackers thinking she was Quality when she was just a housemaid. He paid real good to have her locked up by herself—said she needed 'time to reflect,' whatever that was supposed to mean."

Philip's stomach fairly dropped into his boots. Maximillian Woolfe. He closed his eyes for a moment to absorb his anger, not wanting to stem the flow of information.

James asked the next question. "And is she still here, this pretty little maid?" He couldn't quite keep the scorn from his tone, but the warden didn't seem to notice.

"She was a wily one, she was. She was only here a few weeks before she escaped. Escaped! Can you imagine? We never let 'em get away, and a young wench manages it," he declared in disgust. "Don't know what happened to her after that. We couldn't find her. She's probably dead, she was so cracked in the head, and then wandering around by herself. Escaped at night, you know, on foot. No chance she'd make it very far."

"How hard did you search?" questioned Philip harshly, unable to contain his wrathful disgust at the thought of the young marchioness being confined in such a place.

"We searched hard, let me tell you. Won't get much coin from his lordship if we don't hold on to the wench, will we?" was the shrewd reply. "Why do you care, anyway, about a cracked servant? She was always yammering on, crying for her nurse and offering to pay us if we'd let her go."

"Did it never occur to you that there was something shady about a lord's paying so handsomely for you to keep his maid?" Philip wondered.

"It's not for me to ask questions, milord," was the lofty reply.

There was a moment of silence while Philip thought about what to do next. "Would anyone here have any information about where the girl could have gone?"

"No. Believe me, I did everything I could to find out. I really did not want to tell his lordship we'd lost his servant."

"So you did inform him eventually? What was his reaction?"

"At first he was powerful angry. Threatened to kill us all, which, of course, was an empty threat, as you can see." The huge man grinned, gesturing to his physique. "But after he calmed down, he started to laugh. I think he might be cracked in the head too, come to think of it."

"You're right; I think he is 'cracked in the head' too." Philip shook his head in disgust. Another dead end. But now they truly knew the lengths Edwin and his friend would go to. The old nurse was right; they had taken the young marchioness to Bedlam. The king would have Ridley's head.

Philip and James thanked the man and paid him for his cooperation before trudging back to their carriage despondently. They drove in silence back to the London house. Philip realized it was his duty to inform the king of the results of his search. It was not an interview he was looking forward to. The normally levelheaded monarch was known to have a temper and would be very angry at this development. He might even blame the earl for how long it had taken to get this information.

Sure enough, the audience with the king did not go well the next day. His Majesty was furious that one of his nobles could be so reprehensible. But he kept his anger rightly directed toward Ridley, who by late afternoon had been dragged before the king to explain himself. There truly was no evidence that the girl Bedlam had lost was the missing marchioness, and Edwin denied all knowledge of the incident. What business was it of his if his friend wanted to have one of his servants locked up, he questioned in a reasonable tone. And he explained that the old nurse was grieving and not in her right mind. Who would the king believe, the viscount or the nurse? Despite his anger and mistrust, the king had little choice but to concede that there was no proof of Ridley's misconduct and had to let him go.

After Edwin was dismissed from the room, Philip and his king mulled the matter over in great detail.

"So we're back to where we started," declared Philip in disgust. "The marchioness is missing, and we have no idea where to look for her."

"She is most likely dead, Yorkleigh," was the king's caustic conclusion.

"Your Majesty, with all due respect, I refuse to accept that she's dead. If she managed to escape from Bedlam, she's a resourceful chit and would have found a way to survive," argued Philip.

"You may be right. She would reach her twenty-first birthday about two months from now. If she has not shown herself by a month after that, however, she shall be declared dead and all her holdings and titles will be disposed of as I see fit," decided the king.

"Very well, Your Majesty." Philip had to be satisfied with that. Although he was filled with frustration at his inability to find any trace of the young woman, he was convinced that she was alive somewhere, waiting until Edwin had no hold over her before she revealed herself and claimed her true position. He would have to be satisfied with waiting it out. He had come to take the matter quite personally and was determined to make the acquaintance of the young woman who had lead him on such a chase.

Ridley Manor

Lord Maximillian Woolfe was pacing rhythmically in front of the large oak desk behind which sat the viscount idly sipping from a fine crystal tumbler with an unattractively amused sneer upon his face.

"Why didn't you shut her up in a more permanent manner? It's not like you to be so squeamish," demanded Lord Max with a scornful curl to his lips.

"Before you get on your high horse about which of us did not do an adequate job, I'm not the one who used my own name when I dropped my 'maid' off at Bedlam," countered the viscount sneeringly, as he took another swig of the old marquis' fine port.

"I can't believe the little trollop managed to escape. You have to give her credit for being a sneaky little wench. Such a pity she refused my attentions; it would have been such pleasure to try to tame the wretched shrew," leered Max. "Where do you suppose she went?"

"I have no idea, nor do I give a rat's behind as long as she stays gone. I have been informed that if she does not turn up before one month past her birthday, all her assets shall be absorbed by the Crown. We have to figure out how to liquidate as much of those assets as possible so that they can be 'absorbed' by us instead of crazy old George," pronounced Ridley greedily as he rubbed his hands together in anticipation of taking possession of his cousin's wealth.

"How are we going to manage that with that interfering Earl of Yorkleigh forever under foot, putting his nose into business which is none of his concern?" whined Woolfe plaintively.

"Now who's being squeamish?" demanded Ridley contemptuously. "There's always a way," he reminded his friend as they set to scheming. "We just have to make sure the earl and the king cannot find the alterations we'll make in the books. As the little witch's guardian, I have the right to view the accounts. We need to go back to the other estates and get started right away. We'll start at Westland, since you already proved they're the easiest lot to deal with."

After they had discussed the matter at length, Woolfe pondered contemplatively, "What do you suppose would happen to us if the king ever found out what we're doing?"

With a slight shudder and an evil grin, Ridley replied, "Let's not find out, eh? You have a contact that might be interested in some horseflesh, right? My cousin the marquis always kept a fine stable. Let's start there, then move on to the accounts and rents. The important thing to remember is discretion. We absolutely do not want King George or any of his peons catching wind of what we're doing."

"That's for bloody sure," affirmed Max feelingly as he agreed with the viscount's plan to procure them all the wealth they lusted after. He then had another evil thought. "Maybe we should make sure the nurse can't share her crazy ideas with anyone else. And while we're at it, the warden at the hospital could be taken care of too."

"That would have been a good idea before, but now it would just cause more questions. Better leave well enough alone. It's better to concentrate on the money while we still have some time," concluded Ridley, his greedy scheme uppermost in his mind.

"Fine, let's leave for Westland tomorrow," decided Woolfe as he stopped his pacing and stepped out of the library to set their plans into motion.

Chapter Fourteen

Over the weeks following the house party, while Philip and James were traipsing all over England, the countess and her companion drifted into a comfortable pattern. Emily would assist the countess with her personal correspondence as well as keeping her company throughout the day. They continued to keep in touch with the families who had visited during the house party, with the exception of the Sedgelys, from whom the only word they received was a tersely worded message of thanks soon after they had returned home.

When she was not occupied with Lady Clara, Emily spent time each day in the library, the garden, and the stables. Lady Clara busied herself with visiting the tenants on the estate. Emily accompanied her on many of these visits and ended up adding the tenants to the list of her admirers. The other servants at Rosemount debated the issue as to what it was they liked most about the young woman. Mrs. Parks was the one who finally summed it up: "She's Quality. That's all there is to it. She may have a questionable background, but it's obvious she's genuine Quality." They had all grown fond of her and her gracious, kind ways.

As the days turned into weeks, despite how much she was enjoying life at Rosemount, Emily continued to be troubled by the problems of her past and the feeling that she was living a deception. She was chafing under the fact that she was in hiding. Her parents had always taught her that she needed to confront her problems head-on, not hide from them. She felt impotent, though, in the face of the power wielded by her guardian, and she feared his discovery of her whereabouts while he still had the power to control her. After endless mental struggling and debates within herself, she decided that keeping herself safe until coming of age wasn't an act of cowardice; it would actually be foolhardy to jeopardize her entire future instead of just waiting it out.

She spent many hours contemplating how she would find an audience with the king when the time came to hand her problems over to the sovereign. She realized she would have to get to London somehow. She was determined to be content for the time being, but she couldn't help moments of melancholy as she contemplated the complications in her life.

Despite the fact that Lady Clara was enjoying her stay at Rosemount more than she ever had—she attributed her peacefulness to Emily's presence—she was getting restive once more and decided a change of scenery would be just the thing to put a spring back into her step. She truly enjoyed the company of the young woman who had become her companion, but nothing in life had been the same since her dear husband died, and she grew restless easily. Lady Clara decided she wanted to move again. She was in the small salon working her needlepoint with Emily when she broached the subject that had been on her mind of late as the summer had faded into fall and winter was fast approaching.

"Emily, my dear, I've been thinking," she commenced.

"Not too hard, I hope," teased Emily with a smile.

"No, you imp, I want no disrespect from you! Be serious," chided the countess. "I have been thinking we ought to go up for the Season. It has been delightful here these months with you, but I think I'm getting a bit bored of Rosemount for now. Let's go see the sights of London. There is so much that I would like to show you. And it shall be new once more for me, seeing it through your eyes. You are always so enthusiastic about everything. I think you are bored too. You lapse into these silences and have such a sad look in your eyes at times. What do you say? Maybe we'll even find ourselves a couple of beaux."

Emily turned bright eyes upon the countess. "London! Oh, I would love to see London! How exciting. But I have been enjoying our time here; I have not been bored at all, my lady. Will we get to see some plays, and walk in the parks, and shop in all the stores I have only ever heard about?" She paused a moment to contain her excitement before continuing to put words to her dearest wish. "And see the king?" she whispered reverentially.

The countess laughed, delighted by Emily's enthusiasm,

and agreed to all that Emily suggested. The two women then began to make their plans. The countess called one of the footmen in to take a note 'round to Juliette, the dressmaker.

"We will need some fresh gowns so as not to put ourselves to shame as country bumpkins, you know, my dear."

The women giggled together as they began to make their plans. They looked through the fashion plates Juliette had left the last time she was there, picking styles they thought would be appropriate for the city. Emily didn't know what was fashionable among the ton, but as always her sense of style came to the fore. Lady Clara was so pleased to see the sparkle of interest back in Emily's face; she had begun to worry about her young friend, since she had become so quiet of late. But now the two chattered away happily, thinking of all the entertainments that would be available to them when they reached the capital. Lady Clara realized they should let her friends know they were coming so they would have invitations waiting for them upon their arrival. Emily decided they should tell the Waddells, Eastwicks, and Fitzgeralds that they would be coming too.

"You are going to love London, Emily," the countess declared.

"I think we will be wishing for Rosemount's quiet before too much time spent in London, from the sounds of it," spoke Emily wisely. "But I'm sure we are going to have fun while we exhaust ourselves." After another laugh together, Emily asked some practical questions. "When shall I tell the housekeeper of the London house to expect us? Should we notify his lordship of our intentions?"

"Yes, we should let Philip know what we are up to, I suppose. I will write to him. You can write to Rose in London and tell her to ready the house for us to arrive in about two weeks. If Philip hasn't been there recently, things may need to be aired out and so on. Juliette can prepare us a few gowns here, and then we can visit a London modiste for more later. Two weeks should give us enough time to get ourselves ready, don't you think?"

"Yes, my lady, we are two resourceful women with a plan. We could be ready even sooner if you so wished."

"Let's not rush; we will be exhausted before we even get there. We need to finish off any projects we might have started and so on. Two weeks, it is."

"Excellent, I'll go write to Rose right now," concluded Emily as she suited word to action.

The next two weeks flew by for the ladies, deep in preparations, swamped in various feminine pursuits. Lady Clara arranged for one of the grooms to take Emily's mount up to London for them. All the letters announcing their imminent arrival had been sent, Philip had been informed, and all was in readiness. Before they knew it, the ladies found themselves bundled into the carriage early one morning for the arduous journey to London.

As was the case when they traveled from Yorkleigh to Rosemount, Emily could barely keep her nose off the glass as they commenced their journey. She finally remembered that she was supposed to be the companion and tore herself away from the passing scenery to devote herself to entertaining the countess. They passed several enjoyable hours playing games and reading aloud before Lady Clara nodded off to sleep with the swaying of the carriage. Emily exchanged an amused look with Smitty when the countess began to softly snore, and she again pressed her face to the window in her excitement over the journey. She lost herself in pleasant conjecture of all the amusements they would find in the capital.

She was also consumed with curiosity over the monarch and worry over her own future. How would he receive her when she finally revealed herself? Would he help her with her problems, or would he condemn her for her cowardice and the trouble she had apparently caused? Worry gnawed at her mind and heart.

Her nerves felt slightly frayed from excitement and anxiety when they finally clattered to a stop in front of the magnificent town house belonging to the Earldom of Yorkleigh late that evening. Excitement again came to the fore in her seesawing emotions as the footmen rushed to open the door and let down the stairs. Darkness had already fallen. In the glow of the lanterns she couldn't see all that much but was awed by all that her eyes touched upon in the dim light.

Philip was in residence and was watching from an upper window, unbeknownst to Emily and Clara. He felt his gut tighten in reaction to the joy apparent on Emily's upturned face as she gazed about her in fascination. He could watch her expressive face all day, he realized. He shook his head in resignation as he let the curtain drop and turned away to go greet the countess and her companion.

He hurried from the room and dashed down the stairs before he realized how undignified that was and laughed ruefully at his own foolishness.

Lady Clara was drooping with fatigue from the long trip to town and was leaning a bit heavily on Emily as they ascended into the house. When they reached the top of the stairs, the butler stepped forward and took the countess' outstretched hand.

"Welcome, home, my lady," the butler intoned formally but fervently. A few of the other upper servants had also waited up for their arrival and stepped forward to greet their mistress and be introduced to Miss Spencer. Smitty continued upstairs to the countess' chamber with the bags.

Philip stepped forward to greet them, and both women started with surprise. Lady Clara was delighted to see her son, but Emily was deeply dismayed. She felt the strain of trying to keep her feelings to herself, but in her exhaustion it was difficult. She performed a deep curtsy, which wobbled at the end. Philip laughed at her for her foolishness and ordered her to bed immediately. Lady Clara excused her fatigue, explaining to Philip that it was impossible for Emily to sleep during the journey, since she was always too excited. The ladies bade each other a fond good night, and Emily was gratefully shown to her room while mother and son shared a nightcap.

"What are you doing here, you scamp?" demanded the fond mama. "I thought you were off adventuring, searching for the missing heiress."

"I was. Unfortunately, there is no trace of the poor damsel. Foul play is beginning to be suspected. The viscount is keeping whatever he knows to himself, and the

entire staff is terrified of him. We can't get any information from anyone. One servant came forward despite her
terror of Lord Edwin. She was the lady's old nurse, and
her fondness for her former charge overcame her worry
for herself. She said Edwin had taken the lady to Bedlam.
Upon investigation, though, no trace can be found there of
Lady Emmaline, so either the nurse was mistaken or the
lady disappeared from there." Philip heaved a deep sigh
of disappointment. "It's very disappointing. The lady
would have reached the age of receiving her inheritance
very soon. She would be free of Edwin and safe, if Ridley
truly is the villain in this piece. His Majesty was very fond
of the young lady's father and is disappointed not to be
able to fulfill his wishes. I'm to keep searching, but not
much hope is being held out that we'll find the young
woman, since no trace can be found of her."

Lady Clara clucked her tongue in sympathy before turning the subject. "Philip, my dear, I've been thinking," she
commenced. Philip raised his eyebrows in question. She
continued, "I think we should provide Emily with a dowry."

"What? Whatever for?" demanded the earl in surprise.

"There is clearly more to her than meets the eye," explained the countess. "She is being wasted at Rosemount
as my companion. I have grown so fond of her these past
months and feel this is the best thing for her. I shall surely
miss her, but she will make some lord a grand lady. She
was made to preside over a grand household and raise
babies. I couldn't bear to see her shrivel up into an old
maid alone with me." Lady Clara's tears gathered and
threatened to tumble down her cheeks at the melancholy
thought.

Lord Philip, as always, could not bear the sight of tears but balked at the thought of Emily's being married off. "Let's wait and see, Mama. She is still very young. Why don't you enjoy her company for a few years, and then we will consider marrying her off?"

"Her prospects won't be nearly as good if she has been seen for years as my paid companion. She would only be approached by widowers with a passel of brats that need raising. If we present her as our young friend and go about socializing together, she will have a better chance of finding someone who will care about her," reasoned her ladyship.

"But *we* care about her," insisted Philip belligerently. He realized he was being a bit unreasonable, considering his own conflicted feelings on the matter of Miss Spencer. "Let me think about it," he capitulated.

"Excellent. I know you will do what is right. Now I need to be abed. Sleep well." Lady Clara went off to bed happy that she had planted the idea in his head. Emily wasn't a servant anymore, and Philip needed to realize that she was a candidate for marriage. She almost rubbed her hands together in anticipation of the entertainment ahead.

Chapter Fifteen

The next day dawned brightly. Emily was up and about at her usual time and regretted not finding out what the morning routine was here. She hesitated to awaken Lady Clara, knowing she had stayed up late talking with Lord Philip last night. She wasn't sure if she should go in search of a breakfast room, and she dreaded running into Philip with her nerves still feeling a bit raw. Finally her hunger won out, so she rang for a maid. The maid told her that breakfast was being served in the dining room that morning and that his lordship was already there breaking his fast. Emily was welcome to join him. The maid then informed her that Lady Clara usually had a tray brought to her room while she was in London, since they usually kept such late nights here. Emily thanked the girl politely before closing her door.

She sat at her dressing table and contemplated her reflection. "So what are you going to do, my girl?" she asked her reflection. "Only a total coward would stay here and starve." She smiled at herself bravely before grabbing a wrap and descending the grand staircase. A footman showed her to the dining room. She took a deep breath and entered the room. Lord Philip was still at the table finishing his coffee and reading the morning paper. He stood up politely when Emily entered the room.

"Good morning, Miss Spencer. I trust you slept well. You look much restored this morning."

"Good morning, my lord. Don't you realize it's very bad ton to comment on the fact that a lady wasn't looking quite the thing last night?" she questioned him teasingly.

Lord Philip laughed. "You've obviously fully recovered if you're back to correcting me at every turn."

Emily blushed profusely and turned to the sideboard to survey the morning selections. She didn't have a retort handy, and she dreaded sitting at the table with him. One of the footmen helped her to her seat and poured her a cup of coffee. She thanked him with a smile and tucked into her food. Despite her jangling nerves, she was hungry and was determined not to let his lordship's presence deter her from eating. She could sense his eyes upon her, but she valiantly ignored him until the worst of her hunger was assuaged. She then turned inquiring eyes upon him.

"Did you wish to say something, my lord?" she asked politely.

Philip let out a surprised chuckle before he commented on her healthy appetite. "Most ladies avoid food in an attempt to remain slim. You obviously have other secrets to staying slender, since you are not a stranger to eating."

Emily didn't know if she should be complimented or insulted, so she just smiled serenely and continued eating, much to Philip's chagrin. He had been hoping to engage her in a lively arguement, but she refused to rise to the bait. So he let it go for the time being.

"You and my mother seem to be quite popular. There's already a stack of notes and invitations waiting for the two of you. They are in the library, if you wish to review them."

Emily turned a bright smile upon him. "Truly, my lord? There are notes for me as well?" she questioned eagerly.

Philip was surprised by her enthusiasm but answered mildly, "Yes, Emily, there are notes addressed to Miss Spencer. Others are to both of you or just to Lady Clara."

Emily jumped up, thanked the footman, and excused herself from his lordship in a rush. She then dashed into the hall, only to realize she didn't know where the library was. She asked another footman, and he directed her to the end of the hall, where she quickly stepped into the manly room. She looked around and spotted the pile of letters and invitations on a platter on the desk. She gathered them up and then began to survey the room.

It was an impressive sight, with the ornate furniture and artwork interspersed between shelves of another exquisite collection of books. She knew she could spend countless enjoyable hours here poring over the volumes. She had the bundle of papers clutched to her chest with one hand while the other was lovingly caressing Chapman's translation of Homer's *Iliad* when Lord Philip entered the room and stood watching her. So absorbed was she in her perusal of the shelves that she did not even notice he was there until he spoke. She let out a little squeak and almost dropped her bundle while she blushed rosily.

Philip laughed and repeated what he had said. "You are welcome to make yourself at home in here whenever you would like, Emily. I know how much you enjoyed the library at Yorkleigh."

She was surprised at his kindness. "I would not want to disturb your work, my lord."

"That's all right, Miss Spencer. Besides, I do not spend as much time in this library as I do at home. Please feel free to make use of it at any time."

"Thank you, my lord. Of course, I don't know how much time I will have to be in here, either. The countess and I have ever so many plans. I don't know if there are enough hours in the day," she laughed. "Well, I should take these notes up to her." She excused herself and fled from his disturbing presence.

Emily had such conflicting emotions in her heart. She felt a profound distrust of the earl, knowing he was in association with Edwin, yet she was still powerfully attracted to him. He apparently had many kind qualities, and none could deny his dashing handsomeness. It was a dilemma that she knew would take some time to sort out. She shook her head at her conflicting reasonings as she stood outside Lady Clara's door and knocked softly. She was admitted by Smitty, who was assisting the countess with her toilette.

"My lady, look how many notes have arrived for us!" she exclaimed happily, waving the sheaf of papers in the air triumphantly. "Most are for you, or you and I combined, but there are actually a few for me," she continued wonderingly.

"Well, of course, my dear. You did make some friends during the house party, you know," the countess laughed.

"Yes, I guess I did," Emily realized aloud. She was filled with a renewed sense of zest for life. She had lived a rather solitary existence up until now and was amazed at the opportunities before her. She nearly bounced with delight as the two women began to open the many missives bearing their names.

"But, milady, many of these invitations are for the same dates. What does one do in a situation like this?"

Her question revealed her lack of experience, and the countess laughed before answering patiently, "We either pick one and send our regrets to the others, or we attend multiple gatherings in one evening. Notice, too, that some are for the afternoon, and others are for the evening. We shall be very busy, Emily. You're going to have to get used to town hours and train yourself to sleep later in the morning, since you won't be getting to bed until the wee hours most nights."

Emily was filled with anticipation at the thought. Her cup of excitement ran over with the countess' next words. "Oh, Emily, I almost forgot to tell you, Philip has arranged for us to have a box at the theatre for the Season. So whenever you like, we may go. No doubt he has a schedule of which performances are on which evening, so we can make our plans."

Emily's composure fractured, and she burst into tears, much to the countess' dismay. "Whatever is the matter, Emily? I thought you would be happy."

"Oh, Lady Clara, I am happy. You're being ever so good to me. I just cannot believe I am going to enjoy a

London Season. And my mother isn't here to see it," Emily sobbed.

The countess was at a loss for words. She and Emily had never discussed her personal history in any detail, and she wasn't even sure when Emily's parents had died. It was clear Emily was still mourning her loss, and Lady Clara had not even been aware of it. She patted Emily's shoulder rather awkwardly while the girl pulled herself together.

"I'm sorry, milady, I think I am just overwrought with the journey and all the excitement. Perhaps I will just go to my room and wash my face. I'm fine, really. Please don't worry about me. Maybe you can pick which invitations we shall accept, since I have no idea about such things. I will meet you in the salon in a few minutes." With that Emily gave the countess a wobbly smile and left the room. Lady Clara looked at Smitty and shrugged. What could she do?

Emily escaped to her room, sobbing, her grief seemingly inconsolable. She threw herself onto her bed and wept heavily for some time. She realized she had not truly grieved the loss of her dear parents; things had been too chaotic since their death. Being here in London made it all seem so fresh, since this was what they had wanted to provide for her themselves. They would be so happy to see her here, but they would have wanted to be with her, to watch over her and protect her. Well, she had to protect herself now, with the help of Lady Clara. She went to the looking glass, and it was as though she could see her mother's face. It was a comfort, and she was able to dry her tears and wash the stains from her cheeks. She patted her face dry and felt once again ready to face the world.

She left in search of the countess, determined to wring every ounce of enjoyment from this experience despite the private grief deep in her heart.

Emily found the countess in the small salon at the front of the house going over the invitations they had received as well as the schedule Philip had provided for the theatre where they had a box. Emily dropped a brief curtsy to the countess. "I'm sorry for losing control like that, milady. I think all the excitement had finally gotten to me."

"That is perfectly understandable, my dear. Now look, I have made a plan for us, if you will agree to it. We shall go out shopping this afternoon and visit the modiste to ensure our wardrobe is all that it should be. None of these invitations are for this evening, so what do you say to going to an opera?"

"That sounds fantastic," Emily enthused with a return of her usual spirits.

"Excellent. Tomorrow afternoon we are invited for tea to the Fitzgeralds, and the Waddells are hosting a ball that evening. It gets even busier after that, but let's take each day as it comes. I have made a list of those we need to reply to, with yea or nay after each. Could you please take care of those for us?"

"With pleasure, milady."

"Good. We can leave for shopping in about an hour, then."

After their shopping expedition and a short nap to refresh themselves, the countess and her companion donned their finery and set off for the opera. Lord Philip had declined their invitation to join them, but the two ladies were content with each other's company. They were very excited to see the performance. Emily had never been to the opera, and it had been quite some time since Lady Clara had enjoyed the treat. They were in high spirits as they were assisted down from the carriage by one of the footmen.

Emily took a moment to stare in awe at the ornate edifice before her. There were fashionable lords and ladies climbing the enormous staircase toward the well-lit entrance archways. She allowed her anticipation to mount as she slowly climbed the stairs arm in arm with the countess. They were both fighting the desire to giggle like schoolgirls, so excited were they for the treat that lay before them.

"Whom do you suppose we shall see here, Lady Clara?" asked Emily as an afterthought. She had been so excited for the performance that she had quite forgotten this could be a social occasion as well.

"Oh, we shall see all sorts of people tonight, Emily. I know some of the royal princesses enjoy the opera, so they may be here tonight. And I am quite sure the Eastwicks have procured a box for themselves this Season, so perhaps you shall see your friend Lady Arabella."

They did indeed see many interesting noblemen and women as they made their way to the box. The countess was quite popular and was greeting many people as they made slow progress. They were just getting settled in their seats in time for the performance to begin.

Emily was enraptured. She understood very little, as most of the opera was in Italian, but she did not allow that to mar her enjoyment. She found the entire experience magical. From the beautiful gentry decked out in their fine clothing, to the twinkling of the myriad candles, to the achingly beautiful voice of the buxom opera singer, Emily was entranced by the entire experience, and it was a bit of a blow to come down to earth when there was a pause for intermission. She was quite startled by the rousing applause that accompanied the fall of the curtain, and she turned blinking, slightly out-of-focus eyes upon Lady Clara, who laughed with delight at her owlish appearance.

"I take it you are having a good time, Miss Spencer," she teased.

"This is so much better than I ever could have imagined," enthused Emily before laughing at her own naïve enthusiasm. They were still chuckling together in good humor when there was a light knock on their door.

"Enter," called the countess regally. The effect was somewhat ruined when she accompanied it with another lighthearted chuckle, but both women were delighted to see who entered.

"Lady Arabella!" exclaimed Emily with joy as she rose to greet her friend affectionately. "However did you know where to find us?"

"Well, my dear Miss Spencer, I saw the two of you enter your box just before the program began, and I was trying to discreetly catch your attention throughout, but you were so enthralled with the show that you were oblivious to my efforts," quietly teased the richly dressed young lady.

"Thank you for coming to gain our attention now. How have you been since we last saw you? When did your family arrive in the city?" Emily was so happy to see her friend, she felt she was babbling.

"We arrived almost a fortnight ago and have been busy preparing for the Season. It is always amazing to see all that is required to catch oneself a husband," trilled Lady Arabella drolly as she went on to recount all that had been occupying the Eastwick family since they had departed from Rosemount.

"Sounds as if your mother is trying to run herself into an early grave," commented Lady Clara.

Lady Arabella laughed at the countess' jest before continuing on a serious bent. "Mama rests while I spend a few hours at the foundling hospital, where I have been volunteering," she explained.

"You are spending time at a foundling hospital?" questioned Emily, highly curious.

"Oh, Miss Spencer, you should see these poor orphans. My heart just breaks for their plight. We have such a comfortable life; I feel an obligation to help those less fortunate. Perhaps you would like to come with me one day and see if you might like to help out as well."

Given Emily's background, she was unsure if she wanted to spend any time in a hospital; however, she also felt compassion for other orphans. So, despite her misgivings, she agreed to try it out. The women realized the program was about to recommence, so the girls hurriedly agreed on a time when the countess would not require Emily's assistance and bade each other adieu.

"It was kind of you to agree to spend some time with the orphans," commented Lady Clara. "All of us should be concerned about the plight of others. Although I am surprised Lady Eastwick is allowing her daughter to do so, considering what a stickler she is. You go ahead and give it a try. If it is something you wish to stick with, perhaps I can get involved in some fund-raising."

The two women were happy to set their concerns aside and sit back to enjoy the rest of the opera. Emily was disappointed that it was over much too soon and found she was humming happily as she walked toward the carriage with the countess. The two women unhurriedly made their way home, discussing in minute detail all that they had enjoyed about the opera. Lady Clara was delighted by Emily's enthusiasm for their first official London outing. For, as she said, "One can shop anywhere, but only London has the opera."

Thus began the whirl of activity that would be their lives for the Season. Emily was having a grand time. Every day they were visiting or being visited. At first it was only the ladies Lady Clara was already friends with or the girls Emily had met, but as the days went by, gentlemen began to be added to the list of visitors whenever they were "at home."

There was never a dull moment as the two women went to teas, musicales, poetry readings, shopping—the list went on and on. Emily even found some who were interested in the museum. She enjoyed a fascinating afternoon examining Elgin's marbles, imagining what other civilizations would have been like. Realizing, though, that it was terribly unfashionable to appear to be a bluestocking, Emily kept her keen interest to herself with a great deal of effort. But the artifacts Lord Elgin was shipping back to London were inspiring her to want to do research into the lives of those who had lived in other times. It was awe-inspiring to view objects that could have been touched or used by some of the ancient writers and philosophers of whom she was so fond.

Chapter Sixteen

Most of the friends from the house party had been by to visit soon after the countess and her companion arrived in town. One visit of note was when Miss Jane and Lord Sutherland dropped in with the baron's uncle, the Earl of Vale. It was clear the courting couple had the full approval of the earl as he sat in conversation with Lady Clara and Emily, watching fondly as the young couple sat and cooed to each other.

Lady Clara had known Vale since her own coming-out ball many years previous, and it transported her back to sit and flirt with the still-handsome older man. Emily wondered if she should leave the four alone, since they had all become quite oblivious to her presence. She had never seen the countess appear so girlish as she sat and reminisced with Lord Vale. Lady Clara actually simpered as the old earl bowed low over her hand when he was taking his leave with his nephew and Miss Jane when the pre-scribed time had passed.

"Perhaps we could ride out in the park one fine after-noon next week," invited Vale.

Lady Clara blushed and almost giggled as she answered in the affirmative. Emily hugged her young friend Jane good-bye just before another group of visitors entered to take their place.

After all their guests had dispersed that afternoon, Emily turned smilingly to her countess and declared, "Out with it, my lady. What is the history between you and the hand-some old earl?"

"He is not old," declared Clara emphatically.

Emily burst out laughing. "That was not the point of my question, my lady," she pointed out.

Lady Clara blushed and answered. "Before I married Philip's father, I was torn between him and Vale. The two gentlemen were both interested in me, but Yorkleigh came up to scratch first." Lady Clara gazed off into the distance, reminiscing. "I never really knew if Vale had true inten-tions toward me or not. I could not be sure if he was serious or merely flirting with me. I never regretted my decision to marry my husband, and we were truly happy until his death. But, oh, Emily, it does do the heart good to have a handsome man flirting with one, does it not?"

"You are quite right, my lady. And no wonder he would want to flirt with you." The two women giggled together like girls for a moment before Emily continued. "You know, my lady, the earl never did marry. Maybe he has been keeping the candle burning for you all these years."

"I think you have too many romantic notions in your

head," concluded Clara, although she wore a pleased expression and a faint blush upon her face. "Isn't it time we start our preparations to go out this evening?" she continued, changing the subject.

Despite the countess' nonchalance in the matter, after that afternoon visit the Earl of Vale was often present when the countess and her companion were receiving visitors, and the two aging nobles were often seen taking to the dance floor to certain slower numbers at the balls they attended. Speculation began to mount among the ton whether or not Vale was paying court to the Countess of Yorkleigh.

Emily and Lady Clara were thrilled with the results of their visits to the London modiste. The gowns they had selected were appropriately beautiful. Emily gazed longingly at the richer hues of the gowns for the countess in contrast with the lighter, wispier fabrics deemed appropriate for the younger woman. Lady Clara laughed at Emily's desire for the more dramatic colors.

"Your time will come, my dear. Enjoy being young; it does not last nearly long enough. If you are not so excited about the colors of your gowns, just be glad you can carry off these light shades. Many of the other young ladies look so washed out by the colors that are considered appropriate for those fresh from the schoolroom."

"But, my lady, I am not actually fresh from the schoolroom, am I?" reasoned Emily.

"Maybe not, but appearances matter, Emily. You look quite lovely in that gown; enjoy it. Now let's go. We do not want to be late."

It was still early in the Season, and they had not yet attended any of the grander parties, but Philip began to find it irksome to be constantly tripping over fashionable young ladies and gentlemen who were coming to see Miss Spencer. Besides the young folk coming to see Emily, there was an increasing number of older gentlemen who were beginning to show up to pay their respects to the countess. Philip found that highly disconcerting.

Emily's role as companion began to evolve into that of chaperone. It turned out that Lord Vale's interest in the countess had sparked the idea in other aging potential suitors that the Countess of Yorkleigh might be on the lookout for another husband. Lady Clara was initially delighted by the male attention but then began to find it disturbing. She really doubted if she could ever replace her dear earl and thought it was too late in life to try. She discussed the matter at some length with her companion.

"I see we have another beautiful gift from Lady Thorpe's father," teased Emily.

"Yes," sighed Lady Clara disconsolately.

"My dear lady, you sound quite sad about the matter. You should be in transports. Lord Brookfield is a remarkably handsome old charmer. That fan he sent over for you is quite lovely."

"You are right, Emily. He is handsome and charming and has exquisite taste in gifts. But, unfortunately, thanks to Lord Vale's flirtation with me, I think many of the older gentlemen think I am on the lookout for another husband.

I will admit that the attention was nice at first, but now I am faced with the task of refusing offers for my hand."

Emily laughed with glee at the consternation upon the countess' face. It was vastly amusing to see that the older lady was as confused about her feelings as the young ladies making their debut. She then sobered when she realized that her dear friend was really quite distraught over the situation.

"Is it really so bad, my lady? Have any been terribly persistent? I am sure that Lord Philip would be quite happy to look after the matter for you."

"I don't want to involve my son. Can you imagine how awkward that would be for him? He is still grieving for his father, it seems to me. The reason this is so uncomfortable for me is that the last time I was on the Marriage Mart, everyone had to approach my father first. If I weren't interested in a particular gentleman, my father would deal with him accordingly. It was much simpler that way," declared the countess emphatically.

"Would you like me to make an effort at discouraging the gentlemen?" Emily offered kindly, although not quite knowing how she would carry out such a task.

Her offer had the effect of wiping the melancholy from Lady Clara's demeanor as she giggled girlishly at the thought of Miss Spencer shooing away the persistent suitors. "That is the most generous offer I have received all week." She laughed. "No, Emily, I don't think I shall have to take you up on that offer just yet. I think this is Lord Vale's fault, and he shall have to help me with it."

"You could always become engaged to his lordship for

Chapter Seventeen

Emily was amazed to be the center of attention at times. She was not aware that Lady Clara had put it about that she was a family friend and had a small dowry, but she was considered to be available on the Marriage Mart. Although her success was not brilliant like that of Miss Julia, who was set to inherit quite a considerable amount, Lady Clara was delighted with the attention her young friend Emily was receiving. Emily's hand was spoken for for every dance at the parties they attended, and there was a constant flow of visitors when they were at home in the early afternoons.

Philip was put out to see the bouquets of flowers that were often being delivered for Emily and was annoyed by all the young pups hanging about his front rooms. He knew he was being unreasonable to be so annoyed, but he never got to speak with his mother or Emily himself anymore.

They always slept late, and he had to breakfast alone every day.

One day he realized he had had enough. He bumped into Emily in the hallway as she was approaching the stairs with her nose buried in a bunch of flowers that had just arrived at the door.

"One more poor sot to add to your list of besotted suitors?" he questioned sneeringly.

Emily was surprised at his tone. So was Philip; he realized he sounded almost jealous.

"I do not know what you mean, my lord. Is this not the normal way of the ton during the Season?" she questioned gently.

"Well, you do seem to be surprisingly popular," he replied grudgingly.

"My lord, it makes your mother so happy. Please do not begrudge her the fun."

Philip was surprised by Emily's answer. "Doesn't it make *you* happy, all of this attention?" he queried.

Emily turned wise eyes upon the earl and regarded him with her head slightly cocked. "Everyone likes to be liked," she explained patiently. "But it really does seem to me that it is a bunch of foolishness. For example, the gentleman who sent me this pretty bouquet has probably also sent one to Phoebe Featherington, so one cannot take these things too seriously. The countess is so enjoying the attention I am receiving that I cannot find it in my heart to refuse her this fun. Please do not ruin it for her. She never had a daughter, and her own Season was so long ago."

Philip realized Emily's generous heart was potentially going to get her into trouble, but he was being an ogre for begrudging the two ladies their popularity. He decided he should take a hand in the ladies' socializing and join them at some of the functions they were attending. Lady Clara was delighted to have his escort and was very proud of the picture the three of them portrayed as they attended the fashionable gatherings of the ton. Emily, too, began to forget her trepidation in Philip's company, and they returned to the comfortable banter they had enjoyed previously.

One excursion they all greatly enjoyed was to the newly refurbished Somerset House. Near Waterloo Bridge, the House held exhibits of British painters and sculptors, many of whom were not yet well known. The earl and his mother loved to watch Emily's excitement as she speculated over which artists would gain fame and fortune as they wandered among the various collections. It had become quite fashionable of late to enjoy the arts, and there was a considerable crowd of well-dressed and coifed young lords and ladies vying for a position in front of each piece of art. After wearing themselves out, Philip treated the two women to a refreshing cup of tea at Gunther's before returning them home to prepare for whichever entertainment they were to attend that evening.

After much careful consideration Philip had decided that he was still in search of a wife. Lady Maude had turned out to be unsuitable, but he was not going to let that make him give up. He sat down one afternoon and complied a list of qualities he considered necessary in his future countess. He decided it would be appropriate to ask his mother for her opinion and thus broached the subject with her one afternoon.

"Mother, I have made a list of requirements for my future wife. Would you be so kind as to review my list and make some suggestions of who you think might be appropriate from the girls you have met this Season?"

The countess was somewhat startled by this request. "You have made a list? That seems quite cold, Philip. Don't you think you should look around for someone you feel attracted to enough to want to spend the rest of your life with her?"

"No. Attraction seems too transient. This way I will be able to find someone suitable, and we can grow fond of each other later." Philip knew this was not the way his parents had formed their attachment, but it was common enough in his world. It was high time he found a wife and produced an heir; this was the most practical way of going about it, to his way of thinking.

Lady Clara was at a loss for words. She had not thought Philip had been hurt by Lady Maude, but he really did seem to be affected, if he was trying to be practical in matters of the heart. "Show me your list, and I will try to give the matter some thought."

Philip handed her the piece of paper upon which he had drawn up his lengthy list of "requirements" and waited while his mother took a few minutes to peruse it.

"Well, my son, it seems you have given this a lot of thought. From some of these things you have listed, I think you do not want a very young lady as wife. Level-headed and practical—that rules out at least half of the young women making their debut on the Marriage Mart," Lady Clara declared with a chuckle. She then continued,

"Actually, Philip, this list seems to be a detailed description of our Miss Spencer, don't you think?"

"Miss Spencer?" Philip questioned in disbelief. "But she is your companion. One of the requirements on that list is that she be of good family. We do not even know where Emily is from, let alone what her family history is."

"I will agree with you that Emily has not revealed her history to us, but one needs only to spend some time with her to know she must be from a good family, Philip. She is truly a noblewoman, even if her blood is not as blue as yours."

Philip dismissed his mother's suggestion, firmly determined to ignore his own attraction to Miss Spencer. "You are of no help, Mother. You just think this is a foolish idea. I will find a countess on my own."

After that, Philip joined them at all the parties the countess and her companion went to every evening. Lady Clara and Emily watched in some amusement as he joined in the marriage hunt. It soon became an *on dit* about town that the Earl of Yorkleigh was searching for a wife. All the matchmaking mamas who had given up on him years ago were suddenly introducing him to every young debutante not on the shelf. The countess could not help wondering why her son was so mule-headed that he couldn't see the obvious—that he need not look any farther than his own guest room. She knew he would be frustrated by his search for the appropriate bride, since it was obvious that he already had feelings for Miss Spencer. But she wisely held her own counsel and sat back to enjoy the spectacle he made of himself. Despite her love for and pride in her only child, she realized it would do him good to learn a little humility, and this experience was sure to provide that.

Lord Philip danced and chatted with many young ladies every night, and each day he took a different young woman for a ride in the park in his phaeton. He found the experience entirely insipid and dismissed each miss from his list of potential mates. He could not believe how alike they all were. The conversations were all the same:

"Wasn't the party at Lord and Lady What's-Their-Name such fun last night?"

"Isn't the weather quite lovely today?"

"Have you been to see the play being presented?"

It seemed that none of them had an independent thought, and if he tried to delve further into the workings of their minds, they would turn wide eyes upon him and ask innocently, "Whatever do you mean, my lord?" None of the young wenches ever asked him anything meaningful, and while he was sure they had all been raised with the necessary skills to run a household, he strongly doubted if any of them would be able to engage his interest. He was hard pressed to remember their names, so alike were the girls he saw every day. The thought of spending the rest of his life with any of these young women made him realize what a boring existence it would be.

The only young woman whose company he enjoyed was Miss Spencer, and that would just not do. Maybe his mother was right; perhaps he needed an older bride. He cast about in his mind, thinking of the spinsters or widows in his acquaintance, but they too did not seem to meet his standards. Maybe it was futile; he was beginning to doubt he would find a satisfactory match. He broached the subject with his secretary late one afternoon, as they were finishing up their work for the day.

"James, can I pour you a drink? I would like to ask you something."

"Maybe I shouldn't have a drink—this sounds serious," joked James as he accepted the crystal goblet being handed to him.

"It is serious, but you will probably need the fortification," laughed Philip as he downed some of the strong liquid. "I've been thinking you should choose my bride for me."

James nearly choked on his drink. After his coughing fit, he turned watery eyes toward the earl, looking at him as if he had run mad. "Why would I choose the next countess? I think that would most decidedly be your job, my lord."

"I can see why you would think so, James, but I am quite fed up with trying to choose for myself. All these young ladies are so much the same. They are all varying degrees of pretty and can dance gracefully and no doubt could stitch a houseful of beautiful cushions, but each one is tedious. You know me best; you could make a good, appropriate choice.

"That seems a rather cold way to choose a wife, my lord. Why don't you wait until next Season if none of this year's ladies are to your liking?"

"I thought of that, James, but I am not getting any younger, and I think next year the girls will be even sillier when I am one year older and they are one year younger."

James nodded at this reasoning. "I can see what you are

saying, but I just cannot see how I can be the one to pick your wife. If you do not feel that you can wait any longer to hold out for your heart to be engaged, then ask your mother to pick. She would be in a much better position to make an appropriate choice. And if you do not make a love match, your mother will probably spend more time with your wife than you do, so she actually has a vested interest in your choice," concluded James in an attempt to lighten the situation.

"You make an excellent point, James. Unfortunately, I already asked my mother for some suggestions, and the only woman she could think of was Miss Spencer."

"Well, Miss Spencer is a fine woman. You could definitely do much worse, my lord. And you seem to enjoy her company, so what is the problem?" questioned James reasonable.

"You too, James?" exclaimed Philip in consternation. "Why does everyone think I should marry my mother's companion?" questioned the earl pompously.

James merely looked at the earl with a raised eyebrow, wondering why his usually kind, intelligent employer was acting so out of character.

Philip looked back at James despairingly. "Yes, James, I am being a simpleton. Never mind, I will figure this dilemma out for myself. Maybe I should broach the subject with my mother again." With that he dismissed James for the evening and settled back to think. He decided he should let the matter rest for a while. There really was no urgency to the matter of his marriage. He had waited this long; he could wait a bit longer.

Chapter Eighteen

One sunny day Philip, remembering Emily's love of riding, invited her to take a ride in the park with him on an afternoon that had a surprisingly light list of engagements for the ladies of the house.

"I would love to go riding with you, my lord. Let me run up and change. I will be with you in ten minutes," Emily called out as she ran up the stairs.

Philip sent a footman to the mews to saddle up their mounts and bring them around. He was surprised to see Emily ready in less than ten minutes. He complimented her on her promptness.

"I have been so wishing to go riding, my lord. I didn't want to keep you waiting and thus risk having you change your mind," she explained with an impish grin.

Philip laughed in delight as he handed her up into her saddle. They rode away from the house in comfortable silence, pleased with each other's company and enjoying the afternoon more than any in recent memory.

"Are you having a good time here in London?" Philip asked conversationally, breaking the comfortable silence between them.

"I'm having the best time!" declared Emily emphatically. "Everyone has been so nice, and Lady Clara is the best friend I could ever have. There is certainly never a dull moment here in London, that's for sure. One would have to be a complete simpleton not to enjoy oneself."

"I hear we are to attend the ball to mark the come-out of the oldest daughter of the Duke of York tomorrow evening. That should be quite a squeeze," commented Philip.

"Yes, apparently so. I still don't quite understand why it's considered a success when you can pack your house full of twice as many people as you should. It isn't the most comfortable experience to be in such a crowd. But my lady assures me it's quite the thing, and one must be seen at all the most fashionable gatherings. And I'm sure she would say I must not admit to not enjoying myself immensely at such a gathering," she concluded with a roll of her eyes.

Philip laughed, enjoying her company and realizing they both felt quite the same about such things. He marveled that they always seemed to see eye to eye on various matters. He was having a good time chatting with Emily when he realized that an older woman was staring at them and beckoning.

Emily looked at him questioningly. "Do you know that woman waving to us?"

"Yes, that is old Lady Merrivale. She was my grandmother's dearest friend, and she's a huge gossip. I am sure she is wondering about you. Let's get this over with, shall we?"

Emily turned her horse toward the older woman's carriage, smiling at the lady. Lady Merrivale's sharp gaze focused on Emily's face as Philip performed the introductions.

"Miss Spencer, you say," barked the old lady loudly, being slightly deaf in one ear. "You look awfully familiar. I just can't place where I have seen your face before. Must have known your parents, or maybe even your grandparents. But I don't know any Spencers. Are you sure that's your name?" she demanded somewhat rudely, so clearly she did believe she knew everyone.

Emily blushed and stammered out an acceptable answer. She was quite flustered and berating herself for so carelessly forgetting that in London she would be even more likely to have her identity discovered before it was safe. She did not quite know what to say and was relieved when Philip was able to excuse them after a few moments of polite conversation.

"My apologies, Emily. Lady Merrivale prides herself on always being in the know. She keeps track of all the comings and goings of the members of the ton. You must have one of those faces that people think they recognize. Remember Lady Fitzgerald at Rosemount being so convinced she knew you from somewhere as well?"

"I certainly remember that, my lord," Emily answered stiffly.

"Don't let it bother you, Emily. They are just old women with nothing else to occupy their time. They will turn their

mind to something else once they realize you are not whoever they think you are," Philip consoled.

"I'm sure you are right," Emily replied politely, as she
thought with terror of what would happen if they did place
where they'd seen her face before. On her mother.

Philip was sorry to see the clouds of doubt in Emily's
eyes and longed to comfort her. She was such a sweet thing,
he thought with deep affection. He wished they could go
for a gallop, but it was approaching the fashionable time to
be in the park, and the place was beginning to get crowded.
He knew the crowds would be especially bothersome to
Emily now, so he decided to quit the park and show her
some scenery outside of London.

"Come on, Emily, let's go for a ride. You don't have to
be home for a couple more hours, right?"

"That's right. What did you have in mind?"

"Just follow me. I'll show you." And he took off at a canter, quickly leaving the fashionable park behind.

Once they left the crowd behind, Emily brought her
mount abreast of Philip's, and they were able to converse
as they rode out into the countryside. Emily shook off her
disquieting thoughts and told Philip all about the sights
she had been enjoying thus far in London. She asked him
his opinion of some of the people she had met, and he
laughed at her impersonations of some of the more ridicu-
lous members of the *beau monde*.

They carried on companionably before Philip brought
them to a halt on the brow of a small hill. Emily's breath
caught in her throat at the beauty of the scenery. Tears
sprang to her eyes as she turned to Philip and said, "It looks
just like home!"

Philip racked his brain for what part of Yorkleigh or Rosemount she would consider similar to this, until he realized she meant her own home, wherever that was. He meant to console her when he reached over and took her hand and therefore was not prepared for the sizzle that jolted through him at the contact. She squeezed his hand in return as she gazed about her at the breathtaking vista, then turned shimmering eyes up to his face. "Thank you for bringing me here, my lord. This is just what I needed."

He whispered, "Please, call me Philip," as he leaned over and gently kissed her upturned face. Again they both felt the jolt of awareness they had experienced during their first kiss. Emily's eyes drifted shut as Philip kissed her more ardently. He knew she lacked experience and did not want to scare her with his enthusiasm. Not yet prepared to declare himself, after a moment he broke the contact and raised his head.

He almost lost what little control remained to him when Emily's eyes drifted back open and he saw the look of wonder in them. Her every emotion lay bare for him to see, and he knew she felt the same as he did. In that moment he gave up the struggle he had been fighting for weeks, maybe even months. Her background did not matter anymore; he accepted that he loved her. But then she blushed rosily, blinked rapidly, and managed to wipe her thoughts from her face.

She cast about in her mind for something suitable to say but came up blank, so she just gazed straight ahead and cleared her throat. There was an excruciating moment of silence before she finally said, "Well, I suppose we ought to be getting back. Lady Clara will be wondering what has become of me." With that she wheeled her mount around and started back the way they had come.

Philip watched her go in consternation. Did the chit expect him to apologize, he asked himself in incredulity. He realized she was getting away and spurred his horse after her. They continued back to the town house at a brisk pace in silence, both lost in their own chaotic thoughts. Emily was berating herself for being so foolish as to fall in love with someone she could not trust with her heart. Philip was wondering how his mother was going to take the news that he wanted to marry her companion. He was surprised at his own equanimity at considering marrying so below himself in station when he had been so resistant to the idea for so long. They were both deeply relieved when they arrived in the mews behind the house.

Emily jumped down without assistance, threw the reins to the waiting groom, and dashed to the house without a backward glance. She didn't stop running until she was in her room with the door locked. She knew she was being foolish, but she was at a loss what to do. She was half afraid he was going to follow her, and she was half afraid he wouldn't. She was unsure which would be worse. She wanted to sit down and cry out her frustration, but she refused to give in to such weakness. Instead she threw off her riding habit in exchange for a proper afternoon gown and ran down to the salon, where Lady Clara was at home to guests.

When she entered the room, Emily felt many eyes upon her. She curtsied to the room in general before going to join Lady Clara on the settee. The countess could tell there was something amiss with her young friend but knew this was not the time or place to ask what was wrong. She confined herself to giving Emily's hand a squeeze while continuing her conversation with Lady Waddell.

Emily looked around the room to see who was there. She was relieved not to see Lady Merrivale. She had half expected the old harridan to be here, spreading doubts about her identity. Emily took a deep breath to steady her nerves before smiling at the young gentleman trying to catch her eye. Her thoughts were too scattered to recall his name, but he didn't seem to notice; he was more interested in telling her how wonderful he was. She suppressed a grimace while trying to look interested. She calculated in her mind the exact amount of time she had to listen to him so as to carefully balance not being rude with not leading him to have expectations. She was beginning to realize how foolish all this was and why her parents had chosen to leave it behind. When the prescribed amount of time had passed, she excused herself and went to join Miss Fitzgerald, who was sitting in the window seat, for the moment alone.

Julia was such a dear girl, and Emily was pleased to maintain the friendship. Both girls readily slipped into the effortless conversation that was their trademark, and Emily again felt at ease. She determined to put the interlude with Philip from her mind and sort it all out later. Their private conversation, though, was soon joined by others and became more general. When Philip entered the room, it was to see Emily at the center of a circle of young people, happily chatting and laughing joyously. He felt old and excluded for the first time in his life; but then Emily must have felt him looking at her, for she smiled briefly at him in acknowledgment, and all was right with his world again. Lady Clara had caught the exchange of looks and smiled delightedly.

That evening they were invited to a dinner and poetry reading at the Eastwicks'. Emily was looking forward to it with keen anticipation. She enjoyed the company of the literary philosophers with whom Lady Eastwick associated. One was guaranteed to be highly entertained with that group, since many were high-strung and temperamental. Emily enjoyed the good-natured banter and spirit of competition the artists shared. She wished she could participate in some other way than just as a spectator, but it was not to be, and it would be enjoyable nonetheless.

She dressed with great care, anticipating the evening spent in Lord Philip's company. Her nerves had settled after a short nap, and she realized she had been foolish to run away after that kiss. She really needed to face things head-on; she would try to speak to him at the first opportunity. It would be awkward, no doubt, but she couldn't have it hanging over them. Of course, since he was the gentleman, perhaps she should leave it to him to broach the subject. Maybe she would ask one of the philosophers that night, she thought to herself with a chuckle as she went to meet Lady Clara. It would be sure to spark a lively debate among the forward-thinking group.

Lady Arabella welcomed them warmly as her mother was already tied up with other guests when they arrived. Lady Clara went off to join a cluster of her friends while Emily and Arabella walked to a private alcove to enjoy a quiet conversation.

"I have not seen you about these last days at the parties. Is everything allright with you and your family?" questioned Emily in concern for her friend. "You actually look quite happy, so I should say there can't be anything too wrong."

"You are right, I am deliriously happy. John, I mean, my Lord Brooke, has asked permission to pay his addresses to me, and I have accepted. We are to be married this coming summer." The usually quiet young woman nearly squealed in her excitement.

Emily was happy for her friend but felt a momentary sense of envy darken her mood. This was the second betrothal of a close friend. Just the day before Jane had informed her that the details were all worked out, and she would be marrying her baron at the earliest opportunity. Emily felt lonely, considering her own uncertain future. She then realized that she was being a wee bit selfish and determined to be glad for Arabella. Emily smiled encouragingly and allowed Arabella to fill her ears with all the details of how he had proposed and what plans they had already made for their life together. She then carried on singing the praises of her fiancé for several moments. After rattling on for some time, Lady Arabella stopped midsentence and slapped a hand over her mouth.

"I am so sorry, Miss Spencer! Here I am yammering on like a ninny. Your barely even know my John, so you must be bored to tears."

Emily protested. "No, no, Lady Arabella, I truly am happy for you. I like hearing all about it."

"Well, I'm done talking about it for now, but I cannot promise I shall stay silent on the matter for the entire evening," she declared in good humor. "However, I have missed you; tell me what is new with you. I have been so caught up in my private business that it is as though I have been sequestered. Tell me all of the goings-on about town."

With that the two girls launched into a delightful

conversation about all and sundry until the entertainment began. After that they mingled with the other guests and did not have a chance to speak again for the rest of the evening. Lord Brooke had arrived, and Lady Arabella was very much occupied.

Lord Philip had observed the interaction between Emily and her friend. He considered all he had gleaned from his time spent with many of the young ladies of his society, and he realized that Emily was unique among the young women. He could see that she was genuinely happy for her friend as she learned of her betrothal. He had seen a darker emotion flit across her face, but he knew she really enjoyed the company of the other young lady and was glad for her happiness. As he stood there mulling the matter over in his mind, he realized that, although he was sure that he and Emily agreed on many subjects, there were so many things he did not know about her. They only discussed subjects of interest to *him* when they conversed. He truly had no idea what Emily wanted from life. She was obviously hiding her past; maybe she wanted her life to remain the way it was as his mother's companion. He reflected on how she had run away after that kiss; she was obviously frightened of her own feelings.

He resolved to hold off declaring his intentions until such time as she felt more comfortable around him and he really knew what she wanted. He did not want her to marry him out of a sense of obligation. He marveled at the change in himself; he was already thinking of her feelings over his own. He really was turning into a moon calf like everyone else who got struck by love, he thought in self-mockery, as he went to procure her a glass of punch.

Chapter Nineteen

The next day the countess and Emily slept late and had a quiet afternoon in anticipation of the grand ball they were to attend that evening. Preparations started early, as they wanted to look their very best for what was expected to be one of the biggest events of the Season. It wasn't every day a duke's daughter was presented to Society, and everyone wanted to join in the festivities. Lady Clara lent Emily the use of Smitty to set and style her hair for a truly glamorous look. Emily and the countess then spent the late afternoon giggling and gossiping together as they prepared for the evening to come.

At one point Lord Philip happened by the door to his mother's room and heard the peals of laughter emitting from within. He shook his head in amusement, happy to see his mother so joyous and youthful-sounding. It had been a long time since he had seen her so happy, and he

231

was glad for the change, knowing it was Emily's presence that had brought it about. He was determined to find out that night how his mother felt about her companion joining the family on a more permanent basis. He did not think she would mind, since he had a feeling that was what she had been hinting at for weeks now. But at that moment he decided he would leave the ladies to their feminine enjoyment of the day—enough time for serious considerations later.

All the preparations were worth the effort as the countess and her young companion descended the grand staircase together to meet the earl as he waited for them. He was full of admiration for the beauty before him. The countess was looking radiant in her gracefully aging beauty. The family rubies glistened around her neck and were reflected in the deep burgundy hues of her gown. Emily, youthful beauty personified, was dressed in a gown of deceptive simplicity with a necklace of pearls encircling her slender neck.

"I shall be the envy of every man at the ball when I enter with the two of you on my arms," complimented the earl gallantly as he helped them on with their wraps and escorted them to the waiting carriage.

In the carriage, as Emily belatedly recalled that at such a large gathering ones such as Lady Merrivale would be in attendance and might renew the speculation about her, her anticipation was dampened by trepidation. She hesitated to voice her concerns to her companions, but they must have sensed her disquietude, since they both applied themselves to allaying her fears. She was soon distracted by Lord Philip's witty repartee and Lady Clara's jests, and before long they were deposited in front of the imposing edifice that was the London residence of the Duke of York. Emily, with a supreme effort of will, managed to keep her chin from dropping in awe. Although she had seen the huge but graceful building before, it truly sparkled this evening. The glow of the lanterns cast an extra special luminousness to the evening as myriad candles shone through every window to light up the entire street. It was clear that no expense had been spared for this special evening.

As the three stood waiting in the reception line, Emily's fears threatened to resurface, but she put a brave face on for the sake of her friends. They soon came to the front of the line, and introductions were performed. Emily took an instant liking to the young lady being introduced to Society, and the two girls struck up a brief conversation. Others were waiting, and they had to move on, but the girls promised to meet again later in the evening.

As they descended the grand staircase into the massive ballroom, there was a momentary hush as the last notes the band was playing drew to a close. It seemed like a magical moment that would be burned into Emily's memory forever as she looked out into the crowds gathered to wish the duke's daughter well as she made her official bow to society. Emily realized this moment epitomized all that the Season offered. Thousands of candles twinkled above the fashionable heads, sparkling off the myriad of jewels and gems arraying the noble guests. There was a heady combination of perfumes from the elegant floral arrangements placed strategically about the room and the soaps and sprays used by the beautiful people squeezing into the cramped quarters. As the Earl and Countess of Yorkleigh began to descend the staircase with their companion, familiar faces became visible among the throngs of people. Emily could see that all her friends were present, and she had many people she wished to speak with before the end of the ball.

After that the evening flew by in a pleasurable blur for Emily. There was never a moment to herself as she was whirled through every dance with a different partner for each one. As soon as they had reached the bottom of the ornate staircase, the talkative Lord Marsden had grabbed Emily's hand and swung her into a vigorous dance. As that song ended, Lord Garfield bowed over her hand and whirled her through the turns of a county song, only to pass her over to Lord Sutherland. Emily enjoyed the respite, as it was a slower number and Lord Sutherland a restful partner. She quietly asked him about the plans he and Miss Jane Waddell were making. He stammered out an answer before handing her over to Lord Brooke, who was really longing to be with Emily's dear friend Lady Arabella but due to appearances could not be in her pocket the entire evening. Emily took that knowledge in stride and was happy to join Lord Brooke and Arabella after the dance was over as they refreshed themselves with a sip of punch. After a few moments the enamoured young couple again took to the floor, leaving Emily to chat with Lord Brooke's sister, Lady Thorpe. Emily was happy to see her, as they had not yet met up during the rounds of the Season.

"We have only recently arrived in town, Miss Spencer," Lady Thorpe responded when Emily commented that she had not yet seen the couple at the other fashionable gatherings.

"Oh, welcome to London, then," Emily said with a grin.

Lady Thorpe smiled back enthusiastically. "We had such fun at Rosemount that my husband really wanted to come up for the Season. We took your suggestion and traveled up with most of our household." Lady Thorpe laughed as she related the cavalcade they had made up as they clattered into the city with their multiple carriages and outriders. "The children and their nurse and governess had one carriage, Lord Thorpe and I had another, and our personal servants were bringing up the rear with all the trunks and baggage. We must have been quite a sight."

Emily laughed good-naturedly along with her aristocratic friend before the lady continued. "You were right, Miss Spencer, we are having a grand time. I can spend time with the children during the day and then go out in the evening with my husband. The children are a bit young to really appreciate most of the sights of London, but they are still caught up in the excitement of the change."

The two women chatted pleasantly for a few more minutes. Before another gentleman arrived to claim her hand for the next number, Emily promised to come by to meet the children one day that week.

Her pleasure was marred only briefly when she came face to face with Lady Merrivale, and her deepest dreads were fulfilled as the old woman said not unpleasantly, "I haven't figured it out, but I will!"

The young gentleman Emily was with turned to her questioningly. "What was that all about?" Emily was successful in hiding her distress. She just shrugged her shoulders and said disarmingly, "The poor dear thinks I look familiar, but she can't place whom I remind her of. It seems to be driving her to distraction." Emily even managed to muster up an unconcerned laugh, and the incident was allowed to pass, although there were times throughout the remainder of the evening that she could feel the lady's gaze following her. Emily was determined not to let her fears mar her enjoyment of the evening, but it was disquieting despite her best efforts.

Her joy reached new heights as Philip appeared to claim her for the waltz before leading her in to supper. He took her into his arms, and it felt like coming home. They progressed down the dance floor in the now-familiar steps, both lost in the beauty of the moment. No words were needed as they each sensed the other's need to simply savor the experience. When the music drew to a close, it was almost painful to come back to earth. They were happy it was the supper song, and they went in to dine, striking up a conversation about all and sundry.

They were never at a loss for things to say to each other, and this was no exception as they filled their plates and looked around for somewhere to sit. They were surprised to see a pleasant-looking Lady Maude beckoning them to join her and a gentleman they did not know.

"My lord, Miss Spencer, let me make you known to Sir Humphries. He's temporarily in town from his estate in Yorkshire." Lady Maude actually had a genuine smile upon her face and seemed truly happy to see them as they approached.

Philip and Emily exchanged surprised looks. Well-versed in the social niceties, Philip stepped forward with an outstretched hand. "Good to meet you, Sir Humphries." Emily was almost shocked by the transformation of Lady Maude and was curious to know what had taken place.

"Please, join us for a repast," invited Sir Humphries pleasantly.

Although they each secretly wished to spend the time privately together, they accepted the unexpected request with good grace. They spent an enjoyable interlude conversing with Maude and her friend before slipping back to the dance floor as the band struck up another waltz.

Philip reluctantly returned Emily to his mother at the end of that song, only to have her hand claimed by yet another suitor. Emily was laughing and breathless when she again returned to Lady Clara and was surprised when Lord Philip claimed her hand for an unprecedented third dance.

"My lord, people will talk," Emily cautioned.

"Let them," was Philip's reply as he swept her into the rhythm of the dance. He had had enough of standing on the sidelines, watching jealously while she whirled about the dance floor in the arms of other men. He might not be prepared to declare himself just yet, but he was determined that enough was enough for that evening.

Emily didn't put forth any further protest, as she could not find it in herself to mind, although she did notice a few curious stares from the gossips who kept track of such things as well as some jealous glares from other women who had had their eye on the handsome earl. Emily decided she didn't care, at least for this one evening. Every girl should get a magical evening at least once in her young life, she thought, and this seemed like the perfect one to be hers. She might actually dance a hole right through her pretty slippers, she mused in amazement. She had always thought that was just an expression.

"What has you smiling so mysteriously, Miss Spencer?" Philip asked teasingly.

Emily laughed joyously and shook her head. "I'm just having a good time, my lord."

"I'm glad, Emily," he replied gently as he looked tenderly into her eyes.

The gracefulness of their steps drew many eyes as they swayed together in harmony. Lady Merrivale's eyes were sharp upon them again in open speculation. Philip and Emily were too caught up in their own bliss to notice the old busybody approaching Lady Eastwick, who was also watching them closely with a look of concentration upon her face.

"Lady Eastwick," barked Lady Merrivale, "I see you are watching Yorkleigh dancing with that girl too. I know I have seen her face before, and I just cannot quite put my finger on where. Have you been able to ferret it out?"

"No, Mildred, I have not. I feel as I know her from somewhere, but I am sure I never met her before the house party we attended last summer at Rosemount. She is so young; I don't know how I could have met her before."

Lady Merrivale continued gazing at the couple while musing aloud. "Do you think she is some relation to Yorkleigh? No, that is not possible. If she was a relative, they wouldn't be so tight-lipped about her history. Perhaps she was born on the wrong side of the blanket, and she resembles one of her parents." Her face brightened perceptibly at that idea. "That has to be it, Eastwick. Think back about twenty years—were there any scandals of that sort?"

Lady Eastwick laughed good-naturedly. "My dear Lady Merrivale, there are always scandals of that sort. That will not help us narrow it down much. But you are right to think back twenty years, which would be about the time she was born. That was just a couple of years after I married my viscount," reminisced the viscountess mistily. "I shall think on it some more. Perhaps you should come for tea tomorrow, my lady, and we can mull it over at length."

"I shall do that. It is driving me mad, trying to determine how I know this chit," grumbled Lady Merrivale, more determined than ever to unravel the mystery.

Blissfully unaware of the speculation of the two notorious gossips, Emily sighed happily as Philip escorted her back to the countess. She was glad to have a moment to sit down and rest her feet while the earl went to fetch the two ladies glasses of the now-tepid punch.

"You seem to be having a good time, my dear," commented the countess.

"I am having a glorious time, Lady Clara. I hope you have been too. I'm sorry to have left you to your own devices for so long. I hope you have been well occupied," Emily replied contritely. "Although, wasn't that the Earl of Vale I just saw walking away as I was approaching?" Emily questioned teasingly.

"I, too, have been having a grand time," replied Clara uninformatively. "Don't you worry about me, my dear. While I may not be able to dance the night away as you seem to be doing, I am holding my own. You are not the only one who has collected some beaux," declared the countess with a shyly proud smile. "Although, I do think it shall be time to take our leave shortly."

"That's fine; I think I am pretty much danced out anyway. I never would have thought I would say that, but it's true," Emily said with a smile. Taking the countess' hand warmly into her own, Emily continued, "Have I thanked you lately for all you have done for me, my lady? I truly do appreciate it."

"No thanks necessary, Emily. It is truly mutual. It makes me feel young to watch you enjoying the Season." The two women shared a warm, companionable silence watching the mingling crowds as they awaited the earl's return. Then the three of them slowly extricated themselves from the thinning crowds and made their way to the waiting carriage.

By the time the trio arrived home, Emily was wilting with fatigue. She quickly said her good nights and made her way up to her chamber. She could barely stay upright long enough to disrobe and put her things away. She had considered leaving her clothes until the next day, but her time as a maid had trained her well; her conscience would not allow her to leave her gown in a heap. She was already sleeping by the time her head hit the pillow with a smile upon her face as she relived the evening in her dreams.

Meanwhile, Lord Philip asked the countess to join him for a nightcap in the library before retiring. Lady Clara was delighted to comply. It was so rare these days that she had the opportunity to share a *tête à tête* with her son, she was not going to pass up the occasion, despite the lateness of the hour.

Philip kindled the fire in the grate of the library hearth

to ward off the chill in the air while his mother took a seat in one of the comfortable wing chairs that flanked it. He then poured them each a drink.

Lady Clara was intrigued. "What is it, Philip?" she questioned gently. "You seem almost nervous to talk to me. What could possibly be on your mind that you would be shy about discussing with me?"

Philip took a deep breath before plunging right into the matter at hand. "I have developed very deep feelings for your companion, Miss Spencer, and I would like to know if you would oppose the match," he said in a rush.

Lady Clara blinked at her son for a moment before letting out a trill of delighted laughter. "Why would I ever oppose the match, my dear? Miss Spencer is one of the dearest girls I have ever met. I will miss her as my companion, but I'm sure she will make a delightful daughter. I have actually been hoping you were headed in that direction. I have seen the two of you exchanging looks over the past few weeks and have been holding my breath waiting for you to realize how you feel. I have often despaired of your ever finding someone you cared about as your father and I cared for each other. It would make me very happy to support a match between you and Emily."

Philip laughed with relief before dropping into the chair across from the countess. "Really, Mama, you wouldn't mind? What do you think my father would have to say on the matter? Father was always going on about good blood."

"It is true, you and your father have been sticklers about 'good bloodlines,' as you put it. But I think your father's greatest concern was to be sure there was no insanity running in the family," she continued with a little chuckle.

"The thing is, Philip, your father's deepest wish was for you to have a happy future and continue the line of Yorkleigh. And when one looks at Emily, it's evident she comes from good breeding. We don't know her true story, but it is clear there is much she has not told us. Perhaps once she's married, she will feel safe enough to confide in us. In the meantime, you must follow your heart. Make Emily your countess. It will make us all happy."

"You won't mind being the dowager?" Philip questioned teasingly.

"Not if you make me a grandmother as soon as possible," answered the soon-to-be dowager countess with aplomb as she finished her drink and set the glass on the sideboard. "Now, my son, you have made me very happy, but I must rest. It has been a long day. By the way, have you told Emily how you feel?"

"Not yet. I have been waiting for the right moment," he answered a bit sheepishly. "And I am thinking Miss Spencer may need more time."

"Well, don't wait too long. Someone else might snatch her up if you're not careful," she teased as she kissed him gently on the forehead as she had when he was a boy.

Philip watched his mother fondly as she gracefully left the room; he then lost himself in thought as he contemplated his suddenly rosy-looking future.

Chapter Twenty

The next morning everyone slept late, and it was nearly noon when Emily made her way to the breakfast room. She had debated about the propriety of eating breakfast so late, but she really wanted her morning coffee, so she made her way downstairs, wincing with certain steps, laughing at herself for such foolishness. When she finally made it to the breakfast room, Philip was just finishing up his own meal and demanded to know what was so funny.

"I'm just laughing at myself, milord. It was really quite foolish to dance so long and energetically last night and then have to limp around today," Emily explained a bit shamefacedly.

"It's nothing to be embarrassed about, Miss Spencer. You should be delighted that you were so painfully popular," Philip replied with a teasing laugh. "Besides, most of the young ladies in London are probably enjoying a similar fate today, so don't be too hard on yourself."

"That's not really any consolation, Lord Philip. It just shows that we're an entire town full of silly people," Emily concluded with an impish smile.

Philip returned her grin, happily considering that he'd have her sweet face to look at every morning for the rest of his life. He watched her as she daintily picked at her toast and sipped her coffee. He realized he was acting like a lovestruck youth and shook his head in disgust with himself. He abruptly stood up to take his leave. He had had every intention of giving her some time for them to get to know each other, but he could not wait any longer.

"Miss Spencer, when you can spare me a moment, might I have a word with you in the library?"

Emily was surprised at his sudden formality but managed to maintain her calm demeanor as she replied, "I'll be with you momentarily, my lord." He made a polite bow and smartly left the room.

Emily caught the inquiring eye of the footman and simply shrugged at him with a grin. He was as surprised as she by the earl's suddenly serious mien. Well, she wasn't worried; he was probably either grumpy from the late night or had something weighing on his mind. Perhaps the matter he was working on for the king hadn't been resolved yet, she thought to herself. With a mental shrug, she finished her toast and coffee quickly and went to knock lightly on the library door.

"Come in," Philip commanded from within.

"You wanted to see me, my lord? Is now a good time?"

Emily asked hesitantly, seeing him sitting at his desk with a quill in hand.

"Yes, yes, come in, come in, now is wonderful," he almost babbled, standing up and approaching her with an outstretched hand. Emily took his offered hand and allowed him to draw her forward to the warmth of the fireplace. Sensing his nervousness, she began to feel uneasy, wondering what could possibly cause the usually calm earl to seem so jumpy.

Lord Philip had Emily sit by the fire before he began to pace in front of her. She watched him go back and forth before her for a moment longer until she could bear it no more. "My lord, what is it? Is something wrong with the countess? You are making me dreadfully nervous. Please, tell me what has happened. What did you want to talk to me about?"

Philip realized he was being foolish and dropped to his knee beside Emily's chair, grasping her hand as he contritely answered her, "No, no, nothing is wrong. I'm sorry to scare you. I'm just nervous about what I have to say. I've never done this before, you know, so I don't know just how to begin."

At that uninformative remark, Emily had had enough. "If you don't tell me what's going on right now, Lord Philip, I think I'm going to have to box your ears," she threatened mock-menacingly.

It was exactly the right thing to say, for it made Philip laugh and got him past his nerves. "Ah, Miss Spencer, you're such a dainty little thing, aren't you?" he teased. He took a steadying breath, grasped her hand, and commenced.

"Miss Spencer, ever since I've known you, I've greatly enjoyed your company. We agree on most subjects and debate admirably those we don't agree upon. I find I don't want to spend the rest of my life without you in it. I've grown to love you most deeply, Emily. Will you do me the honor of becoming my countess?"

Throughout his declaration Emily's eyes had grown huge as her face paled. She was shocked by his proposal and blurted out the first thing that came to her mind. "But you think of me as a maid. Isn't it beneath your dignity to marry the hired help?" she asked.

"No, I don't Emily, I promise. I think you are Emily Spencer, the owner of my heart," he declared sincerely. "I realize in the past I've seemed to be hung up on rank and position. I know that's why I fought my attraction to you for so long. But I've realized how foolish that is. Say yes, Emily. Say you'll marry me."

Emily felt tears threatening to fall as she realized how deeply she wanted to say yes. But she was terrified. She had heard him talking to his mother—he was friends with her guardian and as such she couldn't trust him. But she loved him so much despite all that! What was a girl to do?

Philip was surprised to see tears spilling from her eyes. "Why are you crying? I hope these are happy tears," he joked nervously. She was trying to frame a reply when there was a sharp knock on the door, and a footman burst into the room.

"Not now! Can you not see we're occupied?" demanded Philip curtly.

The footman blushed but stood his ground. "I am deeply sorry, my lord, but it's urgent. The king has sent a messenger; you're to come quickly. He said it's about the Lady Emmaline and Lord Edwin."

Philip cursed foully, causing Emily to blush rosily before he apologized profusely. He dismissed the footman with the words, "I'll be there in a minute. Have the messenger wait."

He turned to Emily and said, "I'm so sorry, Emily. This is such rotten timing. I must go see to His Majesty. There must be some new development."

Emily was intrigued, momentarily forgetting why she was in the library in the first place. She had a sense that her future was hanging in the balance. "Who are Lady Emmaline and Lord Edwin?" she questioned him carefully while watching him searchingly.

"It's this matter I've been looking into for the king. Lady Emmaline is the missing marchioness everyone was discussing during the house party, remember? And Lord Edwin is her louse of a guardian. That is to say, he was her guardian. During the search we've discovered he is wholly unworthy of that position, and the king has taken it upon himself to be the lady's guardian. It's all for naught, though, since we cannot find a trace of the lady in question."

Philip heaved a deep sigh of frustration before he took Emily's hands again, drawing her to him. He cupped her cheek and looked deeply into her eyes, noting the confusion swimming there but misinterpreting the source. He lightly brushed her lips with his own and said, "I'm so sorry to have to leave you like this; you haven't even given me an answer yet." He laughed ruefully. "Now you will have some time to think about it. I will be back as soon as I can." He then swept her into his arms for a deeper embrace before setting her back on her feet and striding briskly from the room.

Emily stood there in stunned silence, needing to re-assess all she thought she knew and debating what her next course of action should be. Clearly the earl had to be told the truth about her past before she could accept his proposal. She needed to gain access to the king, she thought fiercely. She stood in the middle of the library debating the issue with herself for long moments before she snapped her fingers with a decisive nod and strode from the room in search of the countess.

Lady Clara was still in her chamber, propped up in bed with a tray, gazing off into space, when Emily tapped on the door and stepped into the room.

"I was just thinking about you," she said with a smile.

"Lady Clara, I need your help. Lord Philip has asked me to be his countess. I hope that's acceptable to you." She started, realizing the countess did not know the truth about her history and might not take well to the idea of a lowborn daughter-in-law.

"Of course, my dear, I'm delighted to have you in the family. You're one of the few young women I won't mind becoming the dowager for. But you seemed rather urgent when you stepped in her. What's the matter?"

"I need to see the king and clear up a few matters before I can accept your son's proposal. And I must tell you a few things." Emily embarked on her tale while the countess listened in silence with widening eyes. "So I need to see the king right away," she concluded. "Can you help me do that?"

Lady Clara remained silent for a few heartbeats. She shouldn't have been so surprised, given all she knew about Emily, but she was startled to realize who had been acting as her companion over the last few months. She gave a decisive nod. "Yes, my dear, I can help you. You must change. Let's go to your room and see what's appropriate. Speed is of the essence."

They proceeded to Emily's room, decided on the appropriate gown and jewelry, dressed Emily's hair carefully, grabbed a wrap, and called for the carriage.

"Won't you come with me, my lady? I don't know if I can bear to go through this on my own."

"No, Emily, I cannot come. But you won't be alone; Philip should be with His Majesty."

"Will they be quite angry, do you suppose?" Emily questioned nervously.

"His Majesty will be delighted, I'm sure. Philip, on the other hand, may be a bit put out that you didn't confide in him, but I have no doubt he will be fair-minded enough to allow you to explain yourself. It'll be fine. I've sent a groom ahead requesting the audience, so you should be permitted access to the royal presence. Don't worry, and don't forget to smile—the king has a soft spot for beautiful young women," the countess said kindly while squeezing her hand in farewell.

Emily felt her anxiety rising the closer they got to the palace. She had not been formally presented to the king and his queen, and here she was, seeking an audience. *Had she run mad?* she questioned herself fiercely. Knowing there was a chance Edwin would be there tripled the butterflies swarming in her belly. Knowing Philip would be there helped to quell them slightly, but he too would no doubt be shocked by her presence. What a mess it all was, she thought rather desperately as the carriage pulled to a halt in front of the imposing edifice that was St. James Palace.

Elsewhere in the city, the Ladies Eastwick and Merrivale were sipping tea and riffling through their old memories of all the young lords and ladies they remembered from two decades previous. They were enjoying rehashing all the old gossip they remembered from days gone by. They were giggling to remember all the high jinks noble society got up to before they grew up to be staid and responsible parents and grandparents.

Lady Eastwick hooted with laughter as they remembered one incident involving a young lord who grew up to be Speaker in the House of Lords. "Do you think he ever remembers the time he got drunk and threw up on Lady Bryant? She is the Duchess of Islington now."

"Probably haunts his nightmares," giggled Lady Merrivale as she took another sip of tea.

Lady Eastwick recalled another story. "Oh, I remember the last season before my children were born. I was still going to some of the parties, even though I was in an interesting way, wanting to put off the inevitable as long as possible. Remember, there was that gorgeous young woman—what was her name?—all the young men were hot on her trail. She was a diamond of the first water, with wealth and a title thrown in for good measure. And she was so sweet. Baroness Westland! That was her name. There was such a buzz about her before she married." Lady

Eastwick was smiling in pleasant remembrance, until she remembered more details of her story.

At the same moment both ladies realized what they had been trying to figure out.

"Why, that conniving little sneak!" declared Lady Merrivale admiringly. "By Jove, we have figured it out! We must tell the king immediately!" she declared with glee as the two women stood up excitedly and rang for a footman to have the carriage brought around. This was too good to be delayed. They rushed from the house, delighted with their discovery and anticipating the popularity they would enjoy when it became known that they had solved the puzzle.

Chapter Twenty-one

Emily was grateful to see the countess' groom waiting for her to help her down from the carriage and show her the way. The gown she and the countess had considered appropriate was not at all comfortable nor easy to maneuver, and she needed considerable assistance. Once she had extricated herself from the carriage and shaken out her folds, they began the arduous task of gaining access to the monarch. The butterflies in Emily's stomach made her question the wisdom of eating. Of course, she thought, it would not do to have one's stomach growl while in audience with the king. That thought made her smile and helped quell some of her anxiety.

There were, in Emily's opinion, an inordinate amount of people from whom she needed to gain permission to finally find herself before the ornate doors leading to the room in which His Majesty was granting audience that day. She had already been informed by somebody or other that Lord Philip was present with His Majesty. They would not be expecting her, but this had to be done.

Emily stood before the Lord Chamberlain and drew a steadying breath. She thought of all she had been through in the past months and the changes it had wrought in her. She had gone from a naïve young girl safe in the loving embrace of her small family to a bewildered orphan upon the sudden death of both her dear parents. She knew she had been infused with all the good they could each give her, and they would be smiling in approval if they could see her now. Despite the choices they had made for themselves, they would want her to take her rightful place in Society and would applaud her decision to approach King George.

The Lord Chamberlain stood at the door, looking down his nose at her in a superior manner, demanding to know her name and title in order to announce her to the nobles gathered on the other side of that door. Emily told him. He barely acknowledged his surprise, although Emily would have sworn she saw his eyes widen slightly despite his iron impassivity. She smiled serenely at him. He didn't look quite so supercilious as he threw open the door and announced:

"Lady Emmaline, Marchioness of Edenvale, Countess of Spence, Baroness of Westland."

The previous din in the king's audience chamber died a sudden death upon that announcement. Emily felt the full force of all eyes upon her as she entered the room. She could see the sun streaming in through a large window and was bemused that the weather did not accurately portray the turmoil she was experiencing. If it did, there would be a storm, she thought in momentary distraction. Through sheer force of will she kept a serene, gracious smile upon her face as she bowed her head and dipped into the deep, courtly curtsy she had been taught since childhood. This was the world she had been raised to enter one day. She was proud of herself that she did not wobble or in any other way disgrace herself or her noble heritage as she came up from the low stance and stepped toward the throne.

Edwin—or the new Viscount of Ridley, as she needed to now remember him, she thought with loathing—was there, growing paler by the moment as she drew nearer. He was trying to intimidate her with a fierce glare, but she could see the fear in his eyes, and she felt a moment of triumph before her own nerves nudged that aside as she considered all the explaining she had to now do.

In an attempt to cover his own perfidy, Edwin went on the attack. "Emmaline, you ungrateful child, where have you been? Considerable effort has been put into finding you," he declared with venom dripping from his tones, not bothering to follow the proper protocol before the king.

Emily, on the other hand, knew she could not speak in his presence. She could not address Edwin's comments before being acknowledged by her king, so she made a valiant effort to ignore her cousin's effort at undermining her confidence. But it did have the effect of adding to her fear. Emily could hear the whispers swirling around the room as she stopped before the throne and descended into another deep curtsy. She remained in that submissive position until granted permission to rise.

"Rise, my child, and tell us what you have to say for

yourself. Is it true what my lord chamberlain just announced? Are you truly the Lady Emmaline we have been searching for so diligently?" the king asked somewhat incredulously but not unkindly. He raised his monocle to better view the proceedings.

His Majesty certainly would not expect to have the missing heiress show up on her own when he had had his officials searching for her Emily realized, so he was understandably dubious about her claim. Of course, one look at Lord Edwin would confirm that something was amiss with that gentleman. The sight of her here visibly shook him.

Emily nodded. "Yes, Your Highness, I am Lady Emmaline," she confirmed with pride. She noticed an older person cowering in the background and turned incredulous eyes upon her. "Whatever are you doing here, Mary?" she asked.

Mary dashed forward and wrapped Emily in a warm, mothering embrace, her tears flowing unheeded down her ruddy cheeks. "Oh, milady, I am *so* glad to see you! I been tryin' to tell these gents how his lordship sent you away an' all, but seems nobody really was believin' me. Now's you're here, I guess they'll have to believe me, eh?" Mary's tumultuous emotions had a disastrous effect upon her diction, which forced a smile to Emily's lips.

Up until this point Emily had avoided looking at Philip, afraid to see if he was angry with her. Now she had no choice and turned to him for direction in the matter. She raised questioning eyes to his face, and her knees nearly buckled from relief to see that he merely looked confused rather than repulsed by her claims. He seemed genuinely surprised by the maid's assertions that this was the Lady Emmaline for whom he'd been searching so diligently.

"Mary," Philip interrupted questioningly, "are you saying you know this young lady? Is this truly the Lady Emmaline His Majesty has been searching for?" He was slightly incredulous at the thought that the object of his search had been under his nose all along. And there had been clues along the way that he had foolishly ignored, he realized.

"Yes, milord, this is my lady—Lady Emily is how we call her at home. I've been trying to tell you that milord Edwin had milady locked up somewhere." Realizing she was no longer in danger from Lord Edwin, the old nurse had adopted a somewhat belligerent tone of voice.

"Mary, mind your manners," cautioned Emily in a warning tone. "How do you come to be here?" she questioned in warmer accents.

Mary took a deep, calming breath before launching into her tale. She was less distraught but kept a firm hold on Emily's hand; her fond heart could not bear to lose sight of her wee one again. "The new viscount sent me away after he got rid of you, my lady. I had nowhere to turn and didn't know how to help you." She began to weep again.

"Don't worry, Mary, there was nothing you could have done."

"So I went to stay with me sister up north, until his lordship, the earl, came to ask me about you. I told him all I knew, but when that was of no use, I realized I had to come and tell his majesty meself."

Philip turned to Emily, starting to become slightly agitated that he had had the missing heiress under his roof all along and she had kept herself hidden from him. "Emily, I mean Lady Emmaline," he began.

"Emily is fine, if you would not mind. It was what my

parents called me, unless I was in trouble," she contributed impishly, unable to repress her ready sense of humor despite the gravity of the current situation.

"Lady Emily," Philip recommenced, "why have you kept your true identity a secret?" Before she could answer, Philip turned to the king. Your Majesty, this is the young lady I was telling you about earlier, the woman who has been companion to my mother. As it turns out, she has an interesting tale for us, it would seem."

The king was beginning to look amused by the goings-on before him, realizing that a slip of a girl had led the much too serious Lord Philip on a merry chase. As the king sat back to enjoy the byplay that was to unfold before him, he gestured discreetly to one of his guards to keep a restraining hand on Lord Edwin, who was trying in vain to slink away. He then turned to Emily.

"Let us say for the moment that you are the Lady Emmaline that we have been searching for. Where have you been? This maidservant was just trying to accuse your guardian here, Lord Edwin, of having you locked up somewhere. Is this true? And is there a reasonable explanation for Lord Edwin's actions?" the king demanded.

Emily hesitated to answer, afraid Philip would be repulsed that she had been confined in the asylum. But she could not avoid the truth and faced up to her monarch. "Yes, Your Highness, Mary is correct. My dear father had trusted that his distant cousin, Lord Edwin, would be happy with the inheritance he received and would fulfill my father's wishes as my guardian. Unfortunately, Lord Edwin was disappointed by the size of his estate and the income it generated. He coveted all that was to become mine upon my marriage or my twenty-first birthday. He had made an arrangement with a friend of his—I only ever knew him as Lord Max—that I marry Max, and then he and Max would divide my wealth between them. I refused, knowing my parents would never have consented to such a match. I would have gladly given Edwin all my money if he would have just left me alone. Unfortunately, a lot of my inheritance is entailed and cannot be broken up, it must be inherited, not given away. I did everything I could to reason with him, but instead of accepting my offers and arguments he had me committed to the insane asylum, Bethlem Royal Hospital."

The king turned incredulous eyes upon Edwin, who was now cowering under the heavy hand of the guard. "You had this young creature thrown into Bedlam?" he demanded disbelievingly.

Edwin saw he might have a chance of dissuading the king from severely punishing him. "The girl is mistaken. It wasn't me. She was very confused." He stumbled to a stop at the fierce expression on the king's face.

"Actually, Your Highness, he is right," Emily said. "It was not he who actually took me to the asylum. My cousin Edwin drugged me and then had his friend Max take me there. I guess they decided that if they could not force me into marriage, they would gain control over my parents' wealth by getting rid of me. None of us realized that anyone would even notice. I apologize for putting you to the trouble of searching for me, Your Majesty and your lordship."

"None of this is your fault, my dear child," answered King George kindly.

Philip turned to Emily, and he could see the strain she

was suffering having to relive the experience through the recounting. He questioned her gently. "How long were you in this place, and how did you escape?"

Emily looked him in the eye and replied truthfully, "I'm not actually sure how long I was there, my lord. I was very frightened at first, but we were kept drugged a good bit of the time, which took the edge off the fear. It was only when one of my doses was missed that I came to a realization of what was going on around me. After that I was able to avoid swallowing most of the drugs they forced upon us. Once I had recovered some of my strength, I waited for an opportunity to escape. One night, one of the other so-called patients tried to escape and was caught. While everyone was celebrating her capture, I was able to run. The guards thought we were all drugged and that no one would be brave enough to try after what had happened to Collette. That was the night I hid in the boot of your carriage, my-lord, and you know the rest from there."

Emily had managed to keep her composure through-out the tale. Mary wasn't so successful and was weeping openly and loudly over the terrible ordeal her young mis-tress had been put through. Emily tried to comfort her, bringing a soft smile to Philip's stern face that she would be able to comfort others when she herself so obviously needed consolation. He knew there were, no doubt, many details Emily had chosen to leave out of the recounting, and he didn't press her. In time he hoped she would feel able to unburden herself to him. He still wondered why she hadn't told him when she knew he was searching for the missing heiress, and he asked her as much.

"But my lord, I didn't know. At Rosemount, when you

told the others, I was too busy with all the guests to pay much heed. And when I overheard you telling the countess that you were going to see the viscount, I suspected that you were in league with Edwin. I'm so sorry, Lord Philip, and you too, Your Majesty, for all the trouble I've put you through." By the end of this speech Emily was holding on to her control by her fingernails, and Philip could see she was near her limit; he didn't press her for more. The king seemed to sense this as well. He turned to Edwin.

"You have disgraced yourself and the house of Ridley. You are not fit to fill this position. You shall be sent to the Colonies to repent of your sins; you are not welcome on English soil. All the property and entails attached to the viscountcy shall pass to Lord Philip, Earl of Yorkleigh, for his fine service in this matter."

Edwin sputtered a vehemently angry protest in defiance of the guards holding him on each side. He let fly with every obscene word and thought he could muster as he released his vitriol on his cousin, the earl, the king, and the old nurse. As he was being hauled from the room, he concluded his diatribe with a final utterance against Mary.

"I should have let Max kill you when we had a chance, you stupid old cow!" he bellowed as he was dragged away from the royal presence chamber.

Philip, for radically different reasons, also made protest at the transfer of Ridley to himself, not wanting to profit from the ordeal his poor Emily had been put through. But the king paid him as little heed as he had Edwin and proceeded with his pronouncements.

"Lord Maximillian Woolfe is to be found and brought

before me to be dealt with as he deserves. He may join Edwin in the Colonies, since they seem so fond of each other."

After making this announcement in a harsh voice, the king softened his approach and turned to Emily and Philip.

"As for you, Lady Emmaline, your father was a dear friend of ours and loyal to his country. He would be proud of the courage you have displayed, and we shall see that his wishes are carried out over the dispensation of his property and titles. We are now your guardian until such time as you wed, and you shall receive all that your father had to pass down to you and your offspring."

The king now turned teasing. "On the matter of your marriage, Lord Philip was telling us that he had made you a proposal but had not as yet received an answer. We would be pleased with that outcome, as, we're sure, would be your parents."

Now Philip really did object. "Your Majesty, I can make my own proposals, thank you."

Emily had nothing to say and flushed scarlet.

The king took mercy on them and excused them, matters here more or less satisfactorily concluded.

There was a commotion at the door as Ladies Eastwick and Merrivale bustled in, full of their news. Before they could approach the throne, they saw that Emily and Philip were already there. They were highly disappointed to realize they were late with their discovery as they overheard the buzz in the room solving the mystery of the missing marchioness. The news would be all over town within hours, and no one would realize how very clever they had been to figure it out.

Emily and Philip bowed themselves out of the audience

chamber while other supplicants took their place before the monarch.

Philip guided Emily to a private library within the palace. There was a table with a decanter and glasses. He sat her in a comfortable chair and pressed a glass into her hand. She seemed to be almost in shock over the sudden turn of events, and Philip worried for her health. "Are you feeling quite the thing, Emily? Should I fetch a doctor?" he questioned gently.

Emily looked at him with tears threatening to spill over. "I can't believe I can be me again. It has been so awful to keep so many secrets from you and the countess. You have been so good to me, and I didn't trust you. I'm so sorry, Lord Philip." She stumbled to a stop as the tears tumbled down her pale cheeks.

"Ah, Em, not tears. You know I hate tears." And he gathered her into his arms for a comforting embrace. The embrace soon intensified, and Philip, realizing where things were headed, pulled back slightly, still holding Emily in his arms.

"So, my lady. I had thought I would be elevating you to a nice position in society, and here it turns out you will be marrying down the social scale. You will marry me, won't you?" he questioned her with some concern; she still hadn't actually accepted his proposal.

She whooped with laughter, throwing her arms around his neck. Then she shyly gave him her answer. "If you will still have me, my lord." They sealed the bargain with another kiss.

attraction. But, she reasoned, he was her sovereign, and he had tried to save her from Edwin. It wasn't his fault that she had managed to save herself.

She reflected on all the changes that had come about so suddenly. Edwin had been dispatched to the Colonies immediately after that first audience with the king, and Maximillian Woolfe had followed shortly after. The viscountcy of Ridley had been assigned to Philip, and all of the holdings and titles that had belonged to Emily's parents had come into her possession upon her birthday a few days before the wedding. A team of solicitors had been engaged to review all that Edwin had done and ensure everything was in order as Emily took over the responsibilities as marchioness. Emily and Philip realized they would be constantly on the move, needing to oversee all their vast properties. But they both looked forward to making Yorkleigh their home. Eventually the other properties would be assigned to their children, should they be so blessed.

Lady Emmaline, as most were now calling her, shook her head, realizing she was woolgathering outside the magnificent cathedral. While she was anxiously looking forward to becoming Philip's countess, she was dreading stepping through the massive doors into the cavernous, vaultlike edifice where the ceremony would take place. Emily had been the center of everyone's attention ever since she announced her identity that day at St. James' Palace. All those who had previously considered the Countess of Yorkleigh's paid companion to be beneath their notice were eager to make her acquaintance as the Marchioness of Edenvale, and Emily deplored the toadying to which she was subjected. While she had enjoyed much of the Season as the unknown

Miss Spencer, she now longed for the quiet of the country and doubted if she would want to return to London any time soon.

That suited Philip quite well, for he had barely had a moment alone with his bride-to-be after she had accepted his proposal. He now stood in front of the gathered throng, waiting with the bishop for his bride to walk down the aisle. He was so proud of her. He felt as though he had aged a decade as the full story of her past had been revealed in pieces over the past few weeks. She had endured seemingly insurmountable obstacles put up by her cousin trying to steal her wealth. Then she had truly saved herself. While the part of him that wanted to be a knight in shining armor for his lady was slightly disappointed, he loved her all the more for the strength she kept hidden in the folds of her sweet, sensitive personality. He could barely contain himself, waiting to take her as his own.

Knowing how much Emily was dreading the attention of this lavish wedding, Philip was not completely convinced that she would actually show up. She was skilled at disappearance, as he knew quite well. Philip was determined that he would search to the ends of the earth for as long as it took if she did not show up that day. But then he remembered that, even more than she hated the attention, she would hate to be a coward. He knew in his heart of hearts that his brave bride would show up there that day.

Suddenly there was a hush, and the wedding march was struck. There was a collective gasp as the congregated throng took in the magnificence of the marchioness' wedding attire. Her jewel-encrusted gown sparkled in the candlelight with each step she took.

Emily needed a steadying breath to maintain her

composure as she felt myriad eyes upon her. But then her gaze roved over the masses, and she was able to distinguish specific faces.

The Fitzgeralds were sitting together with Lady Merrivale, who was smiling cherubically at Emily as though it were her own powers of deduction that had saved her from Edwin's coils. Emily smiled warmly at both ladies, knowing in her heart that they really did wish the best for her. Her gaze then moved on to see the Waddells sitting with Lords Vale and Sutherland. All three women were weeping copiously, which made Emily want to giggle. The Thorpes had managed to make it as well, even though Lady Thorpe was beginning to show that she was again in an interesting condition. Emily was so glad to see how happy they looked. The biggest surprise was Lady Maude sitting with the elegant gentleman from the ball a few weeks back, looking quite pleased for the earl and marchioness without a sour look anywhere upon her face. Emily reminded herself distractedly to look into that curious situation as soon as they returned from their wedding trip. She then saw her dear friend Lady Clara near the front of the crowd, looking at her with loving affection as she valiantly fought the tears threatening to stream down her own cheeks.

Seeing how many dear ones really were happy for her joy fortified her spirits to face the long walk up the aisle. Then she gazed past the assembled crowds into Philip's loving eyes, and everything else melted away. Emily raised her chin proudly and floated gracefully toward her groom, warmed by the heated promise she saw as he gazed upon her with all his pent-up love shining in his eyes. She was going home to Philip, and that was all that mattered to her now.